MW00877956

Taking a Risk, Part Two

R.I.S.C. Series

Anna Blakely

Elizabeth -
Love & happiness
are always worth taking
a risk :)

Anna Blakely

Taking a Risk, Part Two
R.I.S.C. Series

First Edition

Copyright © 2018 Anna Blakely

All rights reserved.
All cover art and logo Copyright © 2018
Publisher: Anna Blakely
Cover by Lori Jackson Design
Content Editing by Trenda London
Copy Editing by Tracy Roelle

All rights reserved. No part of this book may be reproduces in any form or by any electronic or mechanical means, including information storage and retrieval systems—except in the case of brief quotations embodied in critical articles or reviews—without permission in writing from the author.

This book is a work of fiction. The names, characters, and places portrayed in this book are entirely products of the author's imagination or used fictitiously. Any resemblance to actual events, locales, or persons, living or dead, is entirely coincidental and not intended by the author.

The unauthorized reproduction or distribution of this copyrighted work is illegal. Criminal copyright infringement, including infringement without monetary gain, is investigated by the FBI and is punishable by up to five years in federal prison and a fine of $250,000.00.

If you find any books being sold or shared illegally, please contact the author at anna@annablakelycom.

Dedication

This book is dedicated to the men and women who serve, or have served in the military, EMS, fire, and/or law enforcement.

You are the true heroes.

Prologue

"What the fuck are we waiting for?" Marcus asked him impatiently. "Let's just take her now and get this shit over with."

He wanted to snap the man's neck like a twig. "It is not the time."

"The fuck you mean, it's not time? The bitch is alone, man. There's no one around. It's the *perfect* time. Besides"— the shorter, African-American man hugged himself closer— "I'm freezin' my ass off out here."

He wanted to kill him, but couldn't. Not yet. There was still much to do, and though he hated to admit it, he needed both Marcus's and Carlos's help.

He hadn't had any trouble from Carlos, which was why he'd entrusted him to wait in the car as a lookout of sorts. Of course, Carlos was so desperate to please him, the guy would probably suck his dick if asked.

Marcus, on the other hand, had been a pain in the ass since the day fate had joined them.

The man had a mouth that never stopped. His constant questions and second-guessing made him want to put a bullet through the idiot's brain.

That time would come. For now, he'd settle for making

sure Marcus understood how things worked in his world.

He moved fast, not giving Marcus time to react. His fingers wrapped around the imbecile's throat, and he began to squeeze.

"W-what...the...?" Marcus could barely get the words out as he tried to fight back.

"We will take her when, and only when, *I* say it is time."

The fool still tried to argue, so he tightened his grip even more. This time, he completely cut off Marcus's oxygen supply. "I told you before, *I* am in charge. Do you understand?"

Marcus's face turned an ugly shade of purple, and his eyes were beginning to bulge. Unable to speak, the man's lips finally moved, mouthing his silent agreement.

"Good." He released his hold roughly.

Stumbling, the idiot coughed. "Jesus, man...take it easy. I was just...askin'."

"Your job is not to ask questions. Your job is to do what I say, when I say it. Is that clear?"

Marcus rubbed his hand over the red marks on his neck. The other man wisely answered, "Yeah. Sure." He coughed again. "What the fuck ever, man."

He turned back toward the house and looked through the trees. The front door opened, and his heart rate increased as he watched with anticipation.

Dressed for work, the woman stepped outside with so much haste, she almost stepped on his little surprise. Even though they were hidden in the thicket at the edge of her property, he could still hear the scream she let out when she saw it.

He smiled, enjoying the fear he knew she was feeling. Felt himself go hard as he watched her slowly bend down to study the very personal gift he'd left for her more closely. He wondered if she would even realize its significance. If she didn't yet, she would.

Olivia Bradshaw was smart and clearly resourceful. He had no doubt the bitch would figure out just how important his little surprise was. The only question was, what would she do about it when she did?

Visibly upset, she quickly went back inside. To call the police? Possibly, but he wasn't worried. He and Marcus had prepared for such an occasion.

Soon, she came back out onto the porch with something long and metal in her hand. After taking a picture of his gift, she slid her phone into her scrubs pocket. Then, using the pincher end of the tool, she poked his surprise a few times.

He nearly laughed out loud when she used that same end to pick up his gift and walk it over to the field on the west side of her driveway.

She threw it into the weeds, nearly dropping the tool in the process. Satisfaction rolled through him when he saw her whole body shiver.

The bitch took the tool back into her house, and then nearly ran to her car. Her head swiveled as she moved, scanning the area for anyone who might be there. She couldn't see him, of course.

He continued to stare at the tiny, white house, even after she was gone. He'd been in it several times, now. Knew the place inside and out.

It was ridiculous how easily he'd been able to break in. Her only form of security was a deadbolt and a shotgun by the back door.

He'd found the gun the first time he'd been inside. For a moment, he'd considered removing its shells, but in the end decided to leave them. Give her a fighting chance.

The thought made him smile. She'd have no chance. Not this time.

When he finally did make his move, Olivia Bradshaw would pay for what she'd done to him...with her life.

Chapter 1

Olivia parked her Honda Civic in the gravel driveway. She turned off the ignition and, with an exaggerated sigh, let her head fall back against the headrest.

Closing her eyes, she allowed herself a moment of peace before re-opening one eye to look down at her watch.

Seven forty-five a.m. She grimaced before getting out of her car, not wanting to stay out in the open alone for too long. Just in case.

Yawning, Olivia put her hand over her mouth. She barely noticed the slight chill in the air as she walked up the small sidewalk, wishing she hadn't covered the night shift. Again.

She'd been doing that a lot the past few weeks…covering for nurses who couldn't make it in for one reason or another.

Olivia was pretty sure everyone thought she was just trying to prove herself since having come 'back from the dead'. The truth was, she needed to stay busy.

The hospital here wasn't as non-stop as Dallas Regional—where she used to work—but the minor injuries and illnesses seen in the ER here were enough to provide the distraction she desperately needed.

So, for the past month and a half, Olivia had signed up for every available shift she could. It helped...or, at least it used to.

She'd moved to Northern Falls six weeks ago. It was a small city located half an hour northwest of the Dallas-Fort Worth area.

Its population of nearly 6,000 made it a tiny spec compared to DFW's three million. It was exactly what Olivia had been looking for.

Northern Falls was quiet. Peaceful. After the chaos that had become her life, Olivia felt she had no choice but to leave the city for somewhere smaller and more secluded.

Now, that same seclusion she craved just a few short weeks ago was becoming yet another source of heightened anxiety.

As she made her way to the quaint porch, Olivia studied the small house she'd rented. It was the only one around for miles.

Before, she thought she'd never want to leave the city. After barely surviving what Olivia now referred to as "The Volunteer Mission from Hell", that changed.

Everything changed...after.

Her life was like that now, clearly divided into two halves—Before and After. God, how she longed to go back to Before.

Before she'd ever stepped foot in Madagascar. Before her new friends had been ruthlessly murdered right in front her. Before some idiot had decided to fixate on her.

Before Jake. An invisible weight fell on her heart as his name entered her mind.

For years, Jake had been her best friend. For one magical night, he'd been so much more.

Then, the big jerk left without so much as a word. Two freaking months ago.

Olivia quickly shut the door on those thoughts. At least, she tried to.

Even on mornings like this, when she was so bone-tired she could barely make it up her porch's four steps, thoughts of Jake somehow managed to push their way through.

She'd tried everything to keep from thinking about him, including nearly working herself to death. Some days it worked, but lately, even the double-shifts weren't enough.

No matter what, Jake always seemed to be there. Drifting around in the back of her mind.

Olivia would be in the middle of completing a patient's chart or stocking a room's cart with various medical supplies, and she'd find herself wondering where he was and what he was doing.

Day after day, no matter what she did to avoid it, the same questions would roll through her mind.

Was he ok? Had he been hurt on the job? Was he ever coming back? If he did come back, would he even bother to come see her?

Then, she'd start to worry he *would* show up, which created a whole new set of questions.

What the hell would she say to him? Would he still want to be her lover, or would they go back to being just friends?

Could they even be friends after the way he'd left her? Did she even *want* to be his friend anymore?

It began to consume her. So much so, Olivia hadn't been able to resist contacting Homeland Security Agent Jason Ryker—Jake's handler and one of the agents who'd questioned her about her abduction—more than once to try to find out what she could.

Olivia had only recently learned that Jake left his Delta Special Forces team—and the Army altogether—a few years ago to start R.I.S.C., an elite, private security company.

The acronym, which stands for Rescue, Intel, Security, and Capture, pretty much sums what Jake and the other members of R.I.S.C.'s Alpha Team do.

While running for their lives in the Venezuelan jungle, Jake explained his team often worked with Homeland Security, and sometimes even the FBI and CIA.

R.I.S.C. sometimes took on private citizens as clients, depending on the people involved and the situation.

Thanks to the very limited amount of information Jason had been willing to share with her so far, Olivia knew Jake and his team were on some big, important job. Supposedly, they had been since their questioning that first day back had ended.

Not every job R.I.S.C. took on was dangerous, but from what Olivia understood, most were. This explained why, even though she was beyond ticked at the man, she was still worried about him.

The last two times Olivia spoke with Agent Ryker, he'd assured her that he'd been in contact with Jake, and that he was fine. Each time he told her that, she'd had the same, roller-coaster reaction.

She felt immediate relief in knowing that, at least for the time being, Jake was safe. Then, just as quickly as her relief hit, the anger and pain would start to slide in.

When this part of the cycle came, Olivia's mind would conjure up all sorts of mean-spirited—and very colorful—things to say to her good buddy, Jake. Words that would make a sailor blush.

Because the obvious question was, if Jake really was okay,

then why hadn't he contacted her? He'd obviously spoken to Homeland, so why hadn't he called *her*?

The night they spent together aside, he was her best friend. He should have at least found the time in the last two months to pick up a damn phone and let her know he was okay.

Olivia would then start to think that maybe it was a *good* thing he hadn't called. Jake was always so intuitive. The minute he heard her voice, he'd know something was wrong.

He'd worry. Probably catch the next flight home from wherever he was and swoop in to try and save the day. Olivia didn't want that. She just wanted…him.

Yawning again, she didn't even bother to cover her mouth, this time. Okay, so she wanted Jake *and* a good night's sleep. It had been far too long since she'd had either one.

After returning from South America, Olivia had started to dream about her late brother again. The dreams were different each time, but they were always terrifying.

She'd see her brother, Mikey, in the midst of various training exercises. The dreams would then cut-scene and change.

Mikey would be hurt and, despite knowing what needed to be done to save him, she'd just stand there, watching helplessly as he suffered and died.

Olivia and her father had never been given the exact cause of Mikey's death. The only information the Army had shared with them was that her brother had died during a training accident. Which probably explained the multitude of ways her mind had imagined him dying in her dreams.

Lately, however, the nightmares had started changing mid-way. Instead of Mikey dying, it would be Jake.

As if that wasn't enough, her dreams would morph, *again.*

She'd find herself back in the jungle with Jake and, like before, they'd be running for their lives.

No matter how the dreams played out, Jake always ended up dead, and Olivia was always awakened by her own screams.

Both physically and emotionally exhausted, Olivia knew she couldn't keep going like this. Something had to give, and *soon*.

As for Jake, Olivia was also starting to realize that if he truly wanted to be with her, he would have found a way to call or text. Plain and simple.

With that in mind, she unlocked her door, stepped inside, and closed it before securing the two deadbolts, and entering her alarm system's code.

She was starting to get used to this new routine. She hated it, but after everything that had happened, Olivia wasn't taking any chances.

Removing her Glock 43 from her purse—something she never thought she'd carry on a regular basis—she headed down the narrow hallway to her bedroom at the back of the house.

Her eyes did a quick sweep as she moved, making sure nothing was out of place. A habit she couldn't seem to break. Thankfully, everything appeared as it had when she'd left for work yesterday morning.

Breathing easier, Olivia placed the gun in her nightstand drawer and began getting some things together. She'd just pulled a clean pair of panties and a short pajama set from her dresser drawers when the doorbell rang.

Although it had been over a week since her break-in, adrenaline immediately began pumping through her system. Suddenly, she was very much awake.

Common sense told her if whoever was on the other side of the door wanted to hurt her, they probably wouldn't have bothered ringing the bell.

Even so, it was pretty early for someone to just drop by. And, with the way her life had been going lately, Olivia wasn't about to risk everything on another person's common sense.

Grabbing her gun again, she walked back into the hallway and toward her front door.

She drew in a deep, calming breath before lifting up on the balls of her feet and looking through the tiny peephole. In that same instant, every ounce of air she'd just put into her lungs came rushing out with a loud *whoosh*.

Dropping back to down her heels, Olivia didn't move. She just stood there like an idiot, staring at her door and wondering what she should do.

Open it? Ignore it? The choices bounced back and forth through her mind like a ping-pong ball.

The doorbell's second ring snapped her out of it and she shook her head in disgust. Why was she hiding like a guilty person? *She'd* done nothing wrong. *He* was the asshat who'd left without saying a word. *He* was the one who should feel badly. Not her.

With new determination, Olivia quickly tucked her gun into the waistband of her scrub pants. Resting it against the small of her back, she pulled the hem of her shirt down to cover it.

The fitted scrub top hugged the contour of her waist, but the back was loose enough to keep the gun hidden. She hoped.

Entering her security code with more force than necessary, Olivia then unlocked the deadbolts. With one more deep breath, she lifted her chin and opened the door.

Jake looked as sexy as ever as he stood there, shoving his hands into his jeans pockets. He'd cleaned up since the last time she'd seen him. His dark brown hair was fixed in that messy, yet amazingly sexy way some guys did theirs, and his scruff of a beard had been neatly trimmed.

His heather gray, long sleeve shirt stretched tightly across his sculpted chest, shoulders, and biceps, but went loose at his narrow waist.

Olivia couldn't stop her eyes as they began wandering down to his perfectly worn jeans, or keep from remembering exactly what he looked like beneath it all.

Just the sight of him sent a shot of arousal through her body, dousing the flames of the oh-so-terrifying wrath she'd intended to pummel him with just seconds before. *Well, crap.*

"Hey, Liv."

Her eyes snapped back up to his. God, just hearing his low, alluring voice again made her insides clench. Then, he gave her that slow, crooked smile and her heart melted a little more.

"H-hi," she stuttered.

Yep. It was official. She was pathetic.

They both just stood there, staring. Each lost in their own thoughts and memories. In reality, it was probably less than a minute, but it felt like an eternity before Jake tilted his head slightly and widened his smile.

His entire face lit up, and those strikingly gorgeous eyes twinkled. Actually. Freaking. *Twinkled.*

"Aren't you going to invite me in?"

For months, Olivia had been dreaming of seeing him again. Time and again, she'd gone over what she would say to him if he ever decided to reappear in her life.

She'd visualized every possible scenario, from jumping his

bones to punching his gorgeous face and telling him to go to hell.

Now that he was actually here, all she managed to do was fumble out the words, "Uh, yeah. Of course. Sorry."

Mentally chastising herself, she moved to the side to give him enough room to pass by. As he did, his familiar scent assaulted her. It was a mixture of woodsy soap and pure male heat.

More than that, though, it was simply...Jake. He had a tantalizing fragrance all his own.

Olivia's mind betrayed her, replaying the memories she'd tried so hard to avoid. Him naked. On top of her. *Inside* of her. Jake grunting out her name as he...

"Thanks."

She blinked again. Had he just said something? She shook her head as she closed the door, automatically going through her routine with the locks and alarm again.

As her brain finally decided to come back to the land of the living, Olivia started wondering why Jake was finally here, surprised to find she was both excited and afraid of the possibilities.

****

Jake felt as nervous as a whore in church. He'd heard Olivia moving around inside after he'd rang the doorbell that first time. Knew the precise moment when she'd looked through the peephole, and exactly how long she'd stood there afterward.

When he finally saw her for the first time in months, it was all he could do not to grab her and pull her into his arms. Knowing that would go over about as well as a fart in a spacesuit, he'd purposely stuffed his hands into his jeans pockets to keep from doing just that.

Now, he found himself awkwardly waiting as Olivia locked the door and punched in her alarm code. The telltale bulge under her shirt was not lost on him, and a fist reached inside his chest and grabbed hold of his heart when he saw it.

She most likely was suffering from PTSD. Completely understandable, given everything she'd been through. Still, Jake couldn't stand the thought of her being so scared she felt the need to carry in her own home.

He'd seen several men fight that unforgiving bitch of a battle after returning home, and it was a hell like no other. Nausea rolled through his gut knowing she could have been struggling with that same internal torture while he'd left her all alone.

A new wave of hatred against the men who had taken his woman and tried to sell her rushed over him. His only consolation was the knowledge that they were all either dead or behind bars. And those who were behind bars would never, *ever* see daylight again.

Even so, Jake's protective streak prevented him from remaining quiet. Because, fuck yeah, he still thought of her as his.

"Everything okay?"

Olivia turned to face him, a fake-as-shit smile plastered on her face. "Everything's fine."

Damn. She was lying, which meant everything was definitely *not* fucking fine.

That fist squeezed his heart again, and Jake was grateful she couldn't see his fingernails digging into his palms. He tried to lock it down. She didn't need him going all caveman on her, now, after all this time.

"I tried calling before stopping by, but the recording said your number was disconnected."

She broke eye contact. "Oh, yeah. Sorry."

That was it. No explanation. Nothing. *Don't think so, sweetheart.*

"Why did you change it?"

While continuing to avoid his eyes, she licked her lips. An adorable little habit she had when she was nervous.

"There, uh, were a lot of reporters calling for interviews. After." She shrugged casually. "I got tired of it, so I changed my number."

It was a plausible explanation, but Jake's gut was telling him there was more to it. He narrowed his eyes slightly, really taking her in.

She'd gained some weight since he'd found her in that God-forsaken jungle, and the renewed curves looked good on her. *Really* fucking good.

That aside, she was too pale, and the shadows under her eyes worried him. Jake wondered when she'd last had a full night's sleep. He also noticed Olivia was skittish as hell.

Stepping closer, Jake pulled his hands from his jeans and rested them low on his hips. Trying his best not to come off too gruff, Jake willed himself to speak calmly.

"What's going on, Liv?"

Finally making eye contact again, she looked much too innocently when she answered, "Nothing." She started to pass by him to head toward the quaint kitchen on her right. "Would you like something to drink? I can make us some coffee or tea or—"

He gently grabbed ahold of her wrist, stopping both her movement and her words. He heard her tiny gasp, and knew from the pulse pounding against his fingertips that she was just as affected by that simple touch as he was.

Good. We'll come back to that later, sweetheart.

Speaking more sternly this time, Jake asked, "Are. You. Okay?"

****

The worry on Jake's face was touching, but Olivia needed more than his worry or pity. *Much* more. And that was the crux of the problem, wasn't it?

She would always want more than he was willing to give. That pesky little fact proven by his noticeable absence these past two months. Remembering this, Olivia jerked her arm away.

"I told you. I'm fine."

Doing her best to keep her irritation at bay, Olivia walked into the kitchen to get them both something to drink. She pulled two mugs off the pegs of the black, wooden stand by her stove and set them on the counter.

When she turned around to ask if he wanted tea or coffee, she found Jake standing right in front of her.

Her breath caught in her throat. Mere inches were now all that separated their bodies. The man was so freaking stealthy, she hadn't even heard him walk over to her. *I've got to learn how he does that.*

Olivia's mind short-circuited, her thoughts coming in quick fragments. *He's close. So close. Too close.*

She could feel his warm breath on her face. Smelled the intoxicating mixture of soap and his natural scent.

Olivia remembered his touch. His taste. And it was all too much.

Suffering from sensory overload, she wanted to tell him to

back up and give her some space. She wanted to yell and ask him where he's been for the past two months.

A part of her even wanted to scream at the top of her lungs for him to get the hell out of her house and never come back.

She'd been doing just fine on her own, and didn't need him showing up here unannounced with his perfect body and freaking crooked smiles.

Just being in the same room as him was messing with her head. So, yep. She wanted him gone.

Then, why aren't you telling him to leave?

"Is that really what you want to do, Liv?" Jake's deep voice interrupted her thoughts. He glanced at the mugs behind her. "Drink tea and exchange pleasantries?"

Opening her mouth, Olivia tried to tell him what she *really* wanted was for him to go, but nothing came out.

What was wrong with her? Was she really so weak for the man that she'd actually lost her ability to speak?

Apparently, because as Jake leaned toward her with pure determination in his eyes, her vocal chords froze. When his gaze fell onto her mouth, her breaths began to come in short, shallow spurts.

Olivia licked her lips—something she seemed to do a lot around him—and when those blue eyes rose up to hers once more, she realized the very last thing in the world she wanted was for him to leave.

She wanted him to take her in his arms and kiss her the way she'd dreamed about for months. Wanted to know he'd missed her every bit as much as she'd missed him.

Soon, that want became a ferocious need.

She suddenly needed Jake's lips on hers more than her next breath. The ache between her legs grew exponentially, and despite her earlier thoughts, Olivia couldn't stop her body's natural reaction to this man.

He hasn't even touched you yet, and you're melting into a puddle. Get a grip, Bradshaw!

Except, she couldn't. This was Jake, and when it came to him, all traces of logic and common sense flew right out the flippin' window. Along with her self-control.

Her entire body ached for him, now, every muscle screaming for his touch. The only thing she could do now was stand there and wait for those sensual lips to find hers.

Jake leaned in and began to wrap his arms around her. Rather than fight a losing battle, Olivia closed the gap between them.

Her breasts brushed against his hard chest, and she felt ridiculously triumphant when his fingers pressed into the flesh at her shoulder blades in reaction.

Reaching up, Olivia clasped her hands behind his neck. When she lifted to her tiptoes, both of Jake's hands began to slide lower.

She closed her eyes. Her lips neared his as his fingers continued their torturous decent. Slowly, they moved even lower until finally, blessedly, he made a move to grab her...*gun?*

Before Olivia could react, Jake had the weapon freed from her pants, and had broken out of her grasp. He stepped back, putting some distance between them.

Her eyes flew open. He was just standing there, with her gun at his side.

Olivia couldn't keep up with the sudden onslaught of emotions. She was confused. Disappointed. Mortified and...*pissed.*

Raising an arrogant brow, he said, "Care to explain yourself?"

Both stunned and furious—mainly at herself for falling for the almost-kiss tactic—she blurted out, "What are you…give that back to me!"

Like two children playing keep-away, Jake held the gun above his head and out of her reach. To no avail, Olivia jumped, trying to snatch it from his hand.

"Not until you tell me what's going on."

His voice was stern, and she could tell he was starting to get angry. *Well, isn't that just too damned bad?*

"Nothing's going on," she stopped jumping and glared at him. "I'm a single woman, who lives alone. And, I have all the necessary paperwork for the gun."

His expression told her he wasn't buying it.

Getting more frustrated by the second, Olivia said, "I have every right to protect myself, Jake. For crying out loud, lots of women carry guns."

She reached for it again, but he continued to hold it away from her with very little effort.

"Sure they do," Jake agreed. "But I'm willing to bet most don't feel the need to have their guns in their hands before answering their fucking doors."

He took a breath, his eyes searching hers as he continued pushing for the truth. "Give me a break, Liv. You've moved, added new locks and a high-end security system, changed your phone number, and now *this*?" Jake tilted his head toward the gun.

Olivia watched as he emptied the bullet from the chamber, released the magazine, and had her gun completely dismantled and on the table behind him…all in a matter of seconds.

She definitely should *not* be turned on by that, but holy moly, that was hot.

"I think someone's bothering you, and I want to know who it is."

Jake was glaring at her, now, his hands low on his hips. He looked so…

Dominating.

The word forced its way into her thoughts and, damn, if she wasn't even more turned on than before. *What the hell is wrong with you?*

It was a sickness. It had to be. She was certifiably, mentally ill.

At least that would explain how, even though she wanted to beat the crap out of him for treating her like his best friend's kid sister again, Olivia also wanted to strip him naked and take him right there on the cold, linoleum floor.

Her panties got wet just thinking about it. *Yep, you are one sick puppy, Bradshaw.*

Reining it all in—barely—Olivia shook her head and cleared her throat. "No one's—"

"Damn it, Olivia! For *once* in your life will you stop being so fucking stubborn and tell me what's going on!"

She jumped. Didn't mean to. Not with him. As mad as he was, Jake would never, *ever* hurt her. Not physically, anyway. *Tell that to your heart.*

Of course, he noticed. "Shit, Liv." His voice lowered. "I'm sorry. I didn't mean to yell. It's just that…damn it, you *know* I can help you."

Olivia opened her mouth to deny it again, but the look on his face told her he wasn't going to let it go. He'd keep pushing and pushing until she finally gave in.

God, the man could be insufferable, and as usual, Olivia

had zero resistance when it came to him. She bit her bottom lip and tried not to let him see how scared she really was.

"I'm handling it."

Instantly, the lines on Jake's forehead smoothed, and his expression hardened. "Handling what?"

"It's nothing you need to worry about, Jake. Really. It's—"

"You do realize, I make one phone call to Derek, and in less than two minutes I'll have any and all complaints or police reports you've ever filed."

Olivia actually felt her jaw drop. Flustered, she said "Derek can't hack into the NFPD's computer system. That's…illegal!"

That damn eyebrow rose again, and he looked as though she'd just made the most ridiculous statement in the history of the world. Which, she had.

Of course, super-secret black ops types wouldn't care about a silly thing like illegally hacking into Nowhere, USA's police database. Especially not a guy like Derek West.

A literal computer genius and member of R.I.S.C.'s Alpha Team, the former SEAL was much too good at what he did to get caught.

Not that Derek needed to hack the department's computers now, anyway. Olivia had just confirmed Jake's suspicions herself. She *had* filed a police report since moving here. Three, to be precise.

Shit, shit shit.

Jake turned away, quickly reassembling her gun before handing it back to her, butt-first. Praying he didn't notice how the gun shook in her hand, Olivia took it and sat it on the counter behind her, next to their still-empty coffee cups.

"I don't want to call D," Jake's soothing voice rumbled. "I'd much rather hear it from you." He took a step closer.

"You're obviously scared of something, Liv." He reached up and caressed her cheek. His eyes pleaded with her as he whispered, "Talk to me, sweetheart."

Ah, man. Sweetheart? *Really?* With that one endearment and his heartfelt plea, the final thread of Olivia's resolve disintegrated.

She became putty in his hands. Strong, callused hands that were currently touching her with loving caresses.

Hadn't she known all along this would happen? Olivia silently cursed herself because when Jake looked at her like he was now, she knew she'd give him any damn thing he asked for.

"It's nothing big, Jake. Some…things have happened since I've been back." She quickly added, "But, I'm fine. *Really*."

The muscle in his jaw flexed, and his brows furrowed. He let his hand fall to his side, and she immediately longed for it back.

"What sort of things?"

Olivia was too damn tired to keep up the pretense anymore. The man was like a freaking dog with a bone. He wouldn't give up until she'd spilled every single detail, so it was pointless to waste more energy arguing.

She blew out a steady breath. "Look, Jake. I've just come off my third double shift in ten days. If we're going to have this conversation, then I really do need that coffee."

His brow crinkled in the middle. For a moment, he genuinely looked as though he felt badly for keeping her awake. Not bad enough, apparently, because his only response was, "Better make a full pot."

Chapter 2

After waiting in painfully awkward silence for the coffee pot to fill, Olivia and Jake sat at opposite ends of her oval-shaped oak table.

Olivia inhaled deeply, the smell of freshly-roasted coffee beans somewhat soothing as she tried to decide where to start. Her life had become such a train wreck lately, it was hard to choose.

As if reading her thoughts, Jake said, "Why don't you start with why you left Dallas."

She wrapped her fingers around the porcelain mug, absorbing its heat. "What I said about the reporters was true. After you left…"

She paused, literally biting her tongue to keep from ripping into him about the *way* he'd left. She cleared her throat and tried again.

"After the Homeland agents were done questioning me about what happened in Madagascar and then…after, I was placed under their protection for a few days. As soon as I could, I went back to my apartment, except it wasn't *my* apartment anymore."

Her eyes rose to find his, and she gave him a sad smile. "Turns out when your landlord thinks you're dead, he doesn't tend to keep your place waiting for you."

Jake didn't smile back like she'd hoped, so she kept going. "But, he had another unit available with the exact same setup as mine. Thankfully, he'd boxed all my stuff up and put it in storage." When Jake looked at her questioningly, she explained, "He said he thought maybe a family member or a"—she broke eye contact again—"uh, boyfriend or someone would eventually come by for it."

"That was nice of him."

She nodded and stared at the dark, steaming liquid in her cup. "Yeah. Of course, there was no one to get it, so it was just there, waiting for me to pick it up and start over."

Olivia looked across the table at him, but he glanced away. Her little dig had hit its mark. *Good.*

A few seconds of silence crept by before Olivia went on. "Anyway, he helped me move my stuff into the new apartment, and I went back to work at Dallas Regional. It was almost like I'd never left."

"Except you had."

She glanced up again, surprised to find understanding in his eyes. "Yeah. I had. And I was reminded of it every time I turned around. I couldn't work on a patient without either them or their friends or family members recognizing me. Even the staff at the hospital that I'd worked with for years couldn't help themselves. I was constantly bombarded with questions, and when they weren't actually asking me about what happened, I'd find them staring at me."

Olivia knew they didn't mean to, but everyone there made her feel like a freak show. "All I wanted to do was take care of my patients," she mumbled more to herself than Jake. Then, she added, "The few girlfriends I occasionally hung out with were even worse. They constantly treated me like they were waiting for me to break or something, you know?"

Jake nodded with sympathy. "So, you moved."

"Not at first. I thought it would die down. I mean, it had only been a week at that point, so I figured they'd all lose interest. Then, the reporters found out I was still living in the city and had returned to the same hospital I'd worked at before. They started hounding me. I couldn't leave my apartment or the ER without a camera or microphone being shoved into my face."

Olivia took a sip of coffee, mainly to give herself a second to regroup. "People started leaving me stuff, too. I got hundreds of letters in the mail, most wishing me well and offering prayers. I'd come home from work and find flowers, stuffed animals, and other gifts by my door."

She looked across the table at Jake. "I know the gestures were meant to be nice, but it creeped me out. Knowing all those strangers, knew where I lived. Apparently, Jason's idea to release my public statement the way we did hadn't work as well as he'd thought it would."

"*Jason?*" Jake asked as if he'd never heard the name before.

Confused, Olivia said, "Jason Ryker. The guy you work for, or with, or whatever." Olivia moved one of her hands in the air as she explained.

All of a sudden, Jake almost looked angry, though she didn't understand why.

"I know who he is," Jake grumbled. "I just didn't realize the two of you were on a first-name basis."

Interesting. If she didn't know any better, Olivia would think Jake was jealous. That was impossible, though. He'd actually have to *want* her in order to be jealous of another man.

She shrugged, "He helped me out. After." She looked around at where she now called home. "He was actually the one who found this place for me."

Jake rested his elbows on the table, his fingers intertwined in front of him. "Ryker found you a *house?*"

Olivia understood his skepticism. She'd called the Homeland agent merely looking for advice. Instead, the guy had stepped up in a pretty surprising way.

"The reporters calling and following me, the letters and gifts…it became overwhelming. I wanted to leave, but I wasn't sure where to go. I figured the guy worked for Homeland, so he'd be able to suggest someplace quiet. Safe." Although, Olivia understood now that safety was just an illusion.

She took a sip of coffee and backtracked a bit. "After my statement was released, I asked him to take me to see you, but he said you'd already left."

A flash of pain crossed Jake's eyes. "Liv, I—"

Not ready to hear whatever excuses he wanted to throw at her, she talked over him. "Two agents took me from the building where we were questioned that day. They drove me to an apartment they called a 'safe house'. It's where my statement was recorded, and where they kept me for the few days after. My last day there, Jason handed me his card. Said to call him if I needed anything while you were away. So, I did."

She chuckled at the memory. "I was only looking for his advice, but in just a few short days he'd found this place and secured a job for me in the ER at Northern Falls Memorial. He even arranged for a moving company to bring all my stuff here, and paid the guys extra to set up the furniture so I wouldn't have to."

Jake's face was deadpan. "Ryker did all that. For you."

Olivia shrugged it off. "Trust me, I was just as surprised as you are. I think maybe he felt guilty for putting me through the ringer the way he did that day. Whatever the reason, I'm grateful." She glanced around her little home. "I like it here."

Jake looked like he wanted to say more about his agent friend. Instead, he asked, "And the reporters? Did they follow you here?"

Olivia shook her head. "None have come by so far. And the letters stopped. I didn't fill out a forwarding address with the post office. That was Jason's idea. He even went so far as to have every hospital employee, including the CEO, sign non-disclosure agreements to prevent any of them from sharing the fact that I work there with anyone."

Jake's brows went up at that. "And did it work?"

"Seems like it. The people there have left me alone as far as any of that goes, and I haven't gotten even one request for a statement or interview from anyone."

Olivia took another drink. "The people here...they're different. I know we're only an hour away from the city, but this really is a tight-knit community. They care about each other, but at the same time, they seem to be focused on their own lives rather than getting into everyone else's business. At first, I got a few stares, or the old, 'Hey, aren't you the girl who' bit, but *nothing* compared to what it was like in the city. These people live their lives and let me live mine."

Jake's gaze became more focused. Narrowed. "So what aren't you telling me?"

"Jake, really. I'm—"

He leaned forward even further. "Swear to God, Olivia. If you say you're fine one more time, I'm going to put you over my knee and spank that sweet ass of yours."

Heat instantly flashed through her system, and that familiar ache began building low in her abdomen. Her insides involuntarily clenched, and Olivia shifted in her chair to find some relief. Unfortunately, there was really only one thing—one man—who could give it to her.

She'd never understood the appeal to the whole, dom-submissive thing she'd read about. But, the picture Jake's words drew in her mind's eye was one of the most erotic things she'd ever imagined. If she wasn't mistaken, the look Jake was giving her right now meant he was thinking the same thing.

Unfortunately, he blinked and, just like that, the heat was gone. Now, he was just looking at her expectantly, waiting for her to share the rest.

Olivia shifted in her seat again. "I started—"

Her voice cracked like a boy going through puberty, and she could actually feel a blush crawling up her neck. She cleared her throat and tried again.

"Before I came here, I started getting these phone calls. No heavy breathing or anything like that. Just silence and then they'd hang up."

"They never spoke?"

Olivia shook her head. "Never. I changed my number, and they stopped. Then, one night, I got to my apartment, and there was a man waiting for me by my door."

Worry spread across Jake's face. "Did he hurt you? Did you call the police?"

"No, he didn't hurt me. Yes, I called the police. He said he just wanted my autograph. When I politely turned him down, he got a little pushy and refused to leave. But, that's *all* he did. When the police got there, they recognized him."

"Name," Jake practically growled.

"I'll tell you, but you really need to chill. This is old news, and the guy has already been taken care of. Okay?"

Olivia knew Jake wanted to say more, but he only nodded.

"His name is Norman Rogers. The poor man is mentally ill, but he's homeless, so he couldn't get the care and medicine he needed. As a result, he's been in and out of jail for most of his adult life. Just petty things, like trespassing, loitering, that sort of thing. Nothing violent. And before you ask, no, he's not in jail, now."

Jake started to speak, but she cut him off. "I made a few phone calls to my contacts at Dallas Regional and was able to get him admitted into the psych ward that night. After that, Norman was transferred to a *secure* mental health facility."

Olivia was relieved to see some of the tension leave Jake's shoulders. "It's a non-profit place that specializes in patients like Norman. Ones who would otherwise be put back on the streets or stay in jail. Norman has no family, so the doctors there were able to get a judge to sign off on his admittance. He won't be allowed to leave there without the court's permission, and that will only happen after getting consistent medication and therapy for several months. Possibly years."

Jake took a minute to process that information. "Okay. You said that was all *before* you moved here. So what's happened since then?"

She didn't even bother to lie. "Three weeks ago, I was on a break at work. My cell phone rang. It was an unknown number. I answered it, but no one was there. At the time, I didn't really think much of it. Then, that night, it happened again. I started keeping a log."

She saw a muscle in his jaw bulge. "How many calls, Liv?"

Olivia bit her bottom lip, praying he didn't freak out. "In two days' time, I had forty-eight hang-ups. One every hour."

Surprisingly, Jake's only reaction was to take a deep breath in through his nose and let it out slowly. Then, he asked, "Did the caller ever say anything those times?"

"No. After that, I went to the police."

He gave a slight nod of approval. "What did they say?"

"What I expected. That they're a small department and aren't equipped with the staff or resources to waste time worrying about prank phone calls. The deputy told me it was probably some overzealous fan who'd seen me on T.V. and was just too shy to actually speak once I answered." Olivia rolled her eyes. "They told me to change my number again, so I did."

There was a stretch of silence before Jake spoke again. When he did, he sounded angry. "Ryker didn't say a word to me about any of this. What did he tell you? Did he figure out who the caller was?"

Olivia scrunched up her nose. "I…uh…never actually told him about it."

Something flashed behind his eyes, but it was gone too quickly for her to decipher what it was.

"Why not?" he asked, barely controlling his anger.

She slumped back in her chair. "Jason's job is to keep terrorists from attacking the US, not babysit me. He'd done so much to help me already by finding this place and getting me a new job. I wasn't going to keep bugging him. Besides, I haven't had a phone call since changing my number the second time."

Jake rolled his lips in, and Olivia feared he was close to losing his control.

"Is there anything else, or are the phone calls it?"

His tone had changed, reminding her of the fierce warrior who'd led her through the jungle.

She didn't want to tell him. He'd already seen her as a helpless female enough for one lifetime. She didn't want to go back to that. Not with him.

Apparently, her hesitation in answering lasted too long. Jake expelled a loud, frustrated breath, his patience clearly wearing thin.

"I thought we were past this, Liv. There's something you're not telling me. The *real* reason you're answering your door with a fucking gun in your hand."

Olivia really, *really* hated how well he could read her because she didn't want to share the rest with him. Didn't want to appear any crazier than she already did.

Focused intently on her coffee, Olivia quietly answered. "Sometimes I feel like someone's following me. I haven't actually seen or heard anyone, but…I'll be walking down the sidewalk or to my car at work, and out of nowhere, the little hairs on the back of my neck stand up."

That same, funny look from before crossed his face. "Did you go to the police?"

"And say what? That I think someone might be following me? There's nothing they can do about a *feeling*, Jake. Besides, I've already been down that road, and I'm not too keen about repeating the trip."

He looked at her questioningly, so she said, "After you left, I…talked to someone."

"A shrink?"

"Yeah."

"Good."

His response took her by surprise. Sensing this, Jake went on to say, "That was some heavy shit that went down, Liv. Anyone would need someone to talk to after going through all that. So, what did the doctor say?"

Olivia lowered her chin a bit and broke eye contact, thankful that he at least didn't seem to judge her for having gone to counseling.

"Mild paranoia resulting from Post-Traumatic Stress Syndrome. The doctor said what I was feeling was normal."

"And what are you feeling?"

She was quiet for a few seconds, terrified of what he would think of her after all she was revealing.

"It's like my body knows someone's there, even though I can't see them, but—" she paused, shaking her head, and he took advantage of the silence.

Reaching out, Jake's large hand covered one of hers. "You went through hell, Liv. There's absolutely nothing to be embarrassed or ashamed of."

She pulled her hand away. "I'm not embarrassed," she bit out. *Liar, liar.*

Jake studied her for a moment, and Olivia assumed he was trying to decide on her level of mental stability. It irritated the hell out of her.

"I'm not crazy, Jake," she said defensively.

He shook his head. "Never said you were, sweetheart. Actually, I think I might be able to shed some light on this for you."

"Okay," she drug the word out, not sure she was going to like what he was about to say.

"Before leaving with the team, I…"—he gave a slight hesitation—"I told Ryker I wanted eyes on you. I pretty much ordered him to assign someone to watch you while I was away. To make sure you were safe."

He at least had the good graces to look guilty. *Well, that's something at least.* For a second, Olivia thought about making him dangle a little longer, but decided against it.

"I know."

Surprise flashed across his face. "You know?"

"Ryker assigned Mansfield and Brunor, the two agents I originally stayed with to be my protection detail. They followed me everywhere I went for the first couple weeks after you left. Jason told me it was at your request, but he wanted to make sure I knew the agents would be following me so I wouldn't freak out if I noticed them."

Rather than commenting on Ryker's sharing of that bit of information, Jake asked, "So, where were they the night Norman Rogers was waiting for you?"

"They were there. They stayed back, just as I asked them to."

"You did *what?*"

"I didn't want them scaring him and making the situation worse."

With disbelief, Jake shook his head and moved back into his chair. "You've got to be fucking kidding me."

"Norman never touched me or made any move to hurt me, Jake. The agents were close enough to intervene, if needed, and waited with me until the police came. Once the officers left to take Norman to the hospital, both agents cleared my apartment, and then went to their car. They watched my place from the street like they had the previous nights."

"What about after?" Jake looked toward the window next to them that showed her front yard. "Who's watching you now?"

He won't like this part. "No one."

As predicted, Jake's teeth clamped together as he asked, "Why not?"

"Because, I called Jason a few weeks ago and told him I

wanted the agents gone."

"Why the hell would you do that?" He asked the question as if she were stupid.

"I can't have those two following me around twenty-four-seven for the rest of my life, Jake."

"The fuck you can't. If they left a few weeks ago, then this feeling you've been having...like you're followed? It wasn't because of them."

Now, she understood the funny looks he'd given her earlier. Jake had thought her fears of being followed had come from her not knowing he'd told Ryker to have her watched and felt guilty. Too bad that wasn't it.

"I know," Olivia begrudgingly admitted.

She didn't want to share the rest, but decided it was best to just put it all out there now and get it over with. Like ripping off a bandage. "That's not all."

"Okay." He ran an aggravated hand over his jaw. "What else?"

"One morning, about two weeks ago, I was leaving for work. When I opened the door, I found a snake on the porch. It was lying on the mat right in front of the door."

He considered this for a moment. "Okay. Well, I know how you feel about snakes, but you do live in the country now. It could happen, right?"

"It could," she agreed. "Except it wasn't the kind of snake you'd find out here. Not even close."

His brows turned in and he leaned his elbows on the edge of the table. "What kind of snake was it?"

"A ghost snake."

Jake's forehead scrunched. "Never heard of it."

"That's because the species was only discovered a few years ago. Researchers found it in the Ankarana National

Park." She let that little tidbit sink in.

A few seconds later, as expected, Jake's brows shot up. "Madagascar?"

Olivia nodded then took a sip of her cooling coffee. "Before going, I researched the types of wildlife found there, just to be safe. I didn't want to be caught in the wrong company with my pants down, you know?"

The joke fell flat. She could easily see why Jake wouldn't find it amusing. She'd taken the time to research the country's wildlife but hadn't bothered to look at the crime statistics? *Brilliant.*

"Anyway, this particular article stuck with me because I remember thinking how cool it was that in this day and age we're still finding new species of animals. Finding one on my front porch, however—" she didn't need to finish.

Jake looked unhappy, to say the least. "Where's the snake now?"

She lifted her chin toward the large kitchen window on her left. "Most likely it's been eaten by a hawk or a buzzard. It was already dead when I found it. It's neck twisted." She shuddered at the memory. "I took a picture of it with my phone then used my grabber tool to pick it up and carry it out into the weeds. I showed the pictures to the police and told them what I'd found out about where it came from. They think it's someone's idea of a sick joke, but…" her voice trailed off.

"But you don't."

She raised one shoulder. "I don't know. Maybe. I mean, the snake was dead, and even if it weren't, they're not really a danger to humans, so maybe they're right."

"So, is that all?"

I wish. "There's one more thing."

He looked at her expectantly. Saying the words quickly, Olivia dropped the last bomb.

"Last week, while I was at work, someone broke into my house."

Chapter 3

"*What?*" Jake's eyes bugged out, and he shot up from his chair so quickly, it nearly tipped backward.

"Calm down, Jake. Nothing was taken or damaged or anything like that."

"So, how did you know someone was here?"

Breaking eye contact, she said, "Whoever it was...they left me flowers."

"Flowers?"

Olivia nodded. "Daisies."

His expression softened only slightly. "Your favorite."

Her gaze found his again. "You remember."

She absolutely would *not* tell him how she'd run through her house looking for him, thinking he was back and had brought her the flowers to surprise her.

Staring deep into her eyes, he spoke low. "Of course, I remember." Then, he blinked, and Warrior Jake was back. "And quit trying to change the subject. Someone broke in and left you your favorite flowers. Please tell me the police acted on *that*."

"They did what they could. Came out and took pictures.

Jotted down some notes. The deputies on duty suggested I get a security system, so I had that one installed, the next day."

Jake began to pace the length of her tiny kitchen. Just when Olivia was sure he was going to wear the finish off her hardwood floor, he stopped next to the room's edge and swung around to face her again.

So much anger flashed in his eyes that she actually recoiled in her chair. With his strong hands resting low on his hips, Jake was just this side of yelling when he asked, "Why am I just now hearing about this? Goddammit, Olivia. I should have known about this shit the *minute* it started. Why didn't you…"

Olivia's shoulders stiffened at his absurd outburst. Did he even hear what he was saying?

"Are you kidding me?"

Jake obviously didn't realize how unbelievable his comments were, because he kept his rant going.

"Fuck, no, I'm not kidding. I want to know why I didn't know someone was *stalking* you."

Olivia stood, her own fury flickering throughout her veins. "Okay. First of all, we don't even know for sure that there's a stalker."

He gave her new security system an exaggerated glance, and then looked back at her with disbelief. "Really." The word dripped with sarcasm.

"And *second*"—she went on, completely ignoring his interruption—"and most importantly…were you hurt while you were away?"

Her question took him off guard. His face contorted with confusion. "What?"

Olivia rolled her eyes. "You know, did you hit your head?

Are you suffering from some sort of traumatic brain injury or something?"

"Liv, what the hell are you—"

She cut him off at the pass. "Because it's the only thing I can think of that would explain why you're acting like such a moron right now."

His brows shot up. "*Moron?*"

Olivia crossed her arms at her chest and glared. "Total. Moron."

The look he gave matched her own. "Why? Because I fucking care about what happens to you? Because I actually give a shit that some asshole could be out there watching you, just waiting to hurt you, and I knew nothing about it?"

"Are you even listening to yourself, right now?" Not giving him a chance to respond, she continued her side of the yelling match. "Of course you aren't. You're too busy being a self-righteous prick to realize how ridiculous you sound!"

Jake's expression changed from pissed to surprised then back to pissed in less than a second.

"So, first I'm a moron, and now I'm a prick?"

"Damn right, you're a prick! You *left* me, Jake. You said you wanted me…that you wanted an *us*. You fed me that bullshit promise that you'd be here to help me figure everything out once we were home, and I was so pathetic I actually believed you. Right up until the moment you left without a single fucking word!"

Olivia walked over to dump her now-cold coffee into the sink. She sat the cup down with such force, she was surprised it didn't shatter.

Turning back around, her hands held the edge of the countertop behind her in a death grip while her mind raced to figure out what to say next.

She wasn't the one at fault here, and refused to stand by another second and let him make her feel as though she were.

"You know what, Jake? On second thought…"—Olivia gave a dramatic pause—"you're right."

It was surprising how calm her voice sounded, given the anger still coursing through her system. She tilted her head slightly, as though she were actually accepting her words as truth.

Not a chance! Olivia's fingernails tapped against the underside of the countertop as she spoke.

"I should have told you about everything. I mean, there were so many opportunities for me to do that, right? All those late night phone calls we've shared over the past two months. The times you called to check on me—"

Jake closed his eyes, his shoulders falling as some of the fight left his body. "Liv—"

"I guess I could have told you then, huh?"

Beautiful, tormented eyes met hers, and Olivia had to force herself to ignore the pain she saw there.

"Olivia, just…hear me out."

Ignoring his request, she snapped her fingers and smiled humorlessly. "Oh, wait! I remember now why I didn't tell you." Her gaze burned into his. "You. Never. Called."

"Sweetheart, would you please just listen—"

"No, *you* listen!" Her finger flew in his direction as two months' worth of hurt and resentment came rushing out full-force. "*You* left *me*, Jake. Not the other way around. After everything we'd been through. After everything you and I…"—she stopped cold, refusing to go in that direction—"you just left me there, with those agents. Those *strangers*."

Olivia continued on, not giving him a chance to speak. "I had no idea where you were. All I knew was that you were gone, and I had to pick up the pieces of my shattered life alone. How do you think that made me feel?" Her voice continued to rise until she was shouting. "Oh, and *hello,* even if I *had* wanted to call you, I couldn't because I had no way to get ahold of you!"

"*Bullshit!*" Jake yelled back as he took a step forward, his fisted hands at his sides. "You talked to *Jason.* If you'd told him what was happening, he would have gotten in touch with me, and you know it! I mean"—he stretched out his arms and motioned to her house—"he sure was willing to help you with plenty of other things while I was away."

Olivia swore she could actually feel her blood pressure rising. He did *not* just go there.

Refusing to even acknowledge his idiotic implication, she asked, "What then? Huh, Jake? Let's say I *had* told Jason what was going on, and he told you. You were on a *job*! What could you have done about it?"

Jake took a step closer to her. His voice grew louder, his words seeping through his teeth. "If I thought you were in trouble, I would have been here. I would have figured out something with the job, and I would have been here!"

"Which is exactly why I didn't call him!" Olivia's voice echoed throughout the tiny house.

For a moment, neither of them spoke. The silence was deafening.

"What?" Jake asked with little more than a whisper.

His brows drew together and something other than anger flashed in his eyes. Only briefly, but it was enough that Olivia recognized it. She'd hurt him.

The fact that she was scared and hadn't wanted his help cut him deeply. Jake was, to the core, a man of action. A protector. Especially to those he cared for.

Well, hell. As much as his leaving had hurt her, deep down Olivia never truly wanted to cause Jake pain. She did her best to explain.

"I knew if I told Jason what was going on, he'd tell you, and you'd go all Mr. Protecto on me." Jake opened his mouth to respond, but she didn't let him. "And despite the evidence from recent events, I'm not some weak, helpless, damsel in distress. Believe it or not, I *am* capable of taking care of myself."

The lines on his forehead smoothed quickly, and Olivia saw the muscles in his jaw bulge out. Rather than helping Jake understand, her explanation had clearly pissed him off even more.

Lovely. I just can't seem to win with him, today.

Jake spoke through his teeth again as he shoved his own pointed finger in her direction. "I have *never* thought of you as weak or helpless. You want to talk about evidence? The only evidence I saw in that fucking jungle was that you are the strongest, most capable woman I have ever known. But even if you weren't, it wouldn't matter, Liv. Nothing will *ever* keep me from worrying about you or wanting to protect you."

Olivia shook her head and smiled sadly. "That's what I've been trying to tell you, Jake. I don't need you to protect me. I've taken care of it. The police know about everything, and, as you so observantly pointed out," she motioned to her alarm system, "I'm taking extra precautions."

"That's all well and good, but—"

"But, nothing!" Olivia's voice rose with frustration again.

Trying to rein it in, she closed her eyes and inhaled deeply. *Damn it.* She hadn't wanted to bring it up.

At best, it would be awkward as hell, but Jake obviously needed to hear it, and she needed to let him off the hook so he could leave here with a clear conscience.

Then, they could both forget about it and go on with their lives. He'd go back to saving the world, and she'd be left alone, again. What else was new, right?

"Look, Jake. What happened between us in that hotel room, was…"—she paused as she tried to describe the most unbelievable experience of her life. There really were no words that could do it justice, so she settled for—"amazing. But, I'm mature enough to understand what it really was and what it wasn't."

His voice lowered, and he spoke with such calmness, it sent shivers down her spine. "And what exactly was it, Olivia?"

The truth was almost too painful to admit, but she forged on, needing to resolve this thing between them once and for all. Licking her lips again, Olivia began to babble.

"A one-time thing, right?" She shrugged one shoulder. "I mean, that's what I said that night. Hell, I pretty much begged you to make love to me. But, don't worry," she added quickly. "I'm not looking for more, I just…I wanted you to know why I didn't make that call to Jason about what was going on. I knew if I did, you'd leave your job and come rushing in to save the day, and I didn't want"—her voice broke and she swallowed hard—"I didn't want you coming here just because you felt obligated."

His eyes widened. "*Obligated?*" He practically spit the word out, as if it somehow left a bad taste in his mouth.

Olivia let out a frustrated breath. "Yes, Jake. Obligated. I know you. Hell, you said yourself, you're protective of me. I refuse to take advantage of that, and I'm sure as hell not going to be the type of woman to sleep with you, and then expect you to be at my beck after the fact. Especially when you obviously have a life that doesn't include me."

Jake flinched as if she'd just slapped him. "And what the hell is *that* supposed to mean?"

He was yelling again, and this time, a vein in his forehead and one in the side of his neck bulged from the pressure.

"It means"—she raised her own voice—"that you can't just show up here after two months of not even calling or sending a freaking text to see how I'm doing, and get mad at me for not running to you with every little problem that I have!"

"Mad?" He shook his head and his lip curled up in a sneer as he moved in on her. "Oh, sweetheart, I'm not mad. I'm fucking *pissed!*" His voice seemed to get louder with each word he spoke. "You damn well *should* have come to me with this. And news flash, Liv…having a stalker isn't a *little* problem!"

"I told you," Olivia shouted back. "I don't want you here just because you felt—"

"Obligated,*"* Jake threw the word back at her. "Yeah, I got that, Liv. But guess what? I'm not here because I feel obligated." He took another step toward her as they continued screaming at each other.

"Then why are you here, Jake?"

Tension rolled off his body as he continued to move closer. "You want to know why I'm here?"

Olivia jutted her chin up. "Did I stutter?"

His movement faltered slightly, but Jake quickly recovered. With one final step, they were standing toe-to-toe, and she had to tilt her head back to keep eye contact.

His hot, heavy breaths brushed across her face, and Olivia was sure her heart was going to leap out of her chest.

Determined to stand her ground and not let him

intimidate her with his size and stature, she stood still and waited for him to continue yelling. Much to her amazement—and total confusion—his scowl slowly turned up into a sinful, sexy grin.

No longer sounding angry, Jake's voice came out low and steady, and his eyes found her lips. He shook his head slowly. "God, I've missed that smart mouth of yours." He raised his hand to her face and traced her bottom lip with his thumb.

Olivia was so taken aback by his sudden mood change—it absolutely was *not* the jolt of electricity that thumb was sending through her system—that she was barely able to speak.

"Jake?" she whispered back. "W-what are you—"

The rest of what she was about to say vanished as he grabbed the back of her neck and crushed his mouth to hers. The kiss wasn't soft. It came out of the gate hard and fast, almost as though he were laying his claim.

Jake groaned as his tongue invaded her mouth. Olivia knew she should be pushing him away. Instead, she stood on the tips of her toes and wrapped her arms around his neck, pulling him closer.

Giving everything she had into that one, spellbinding kiss, she set free the desperate need that had been gnawing at her for the past two months,

It was too revealing. She was allowing him to see what she felt down to her soul, but Olivia couldn't find it in herself to care. She needed this. Needed *him*. Even if it was only for this brief moment.

He moaned again as he continued to devour her, and Olivia knew then, that he still wanted her just as much as she did him. Physically, anyway. Somewhere in the back of her mind, she wondered if that was enough.

As she continued taking what he was offering, her heart began to feel heavy because, deep down, she already knew the answer. And it broke her heart in two.

****

Jake pulled back, forcing himself to end the kiss. Their breaths were labored as he touched his forehead to hers, giving him a close-up view of her wet and swollen lips.

His cock twitched at the sight, and he wanted nothing more than to lift Liv onto the counter, drive himself inside her, and never let go.

He held back, though, having already broken the hands-off vow he'd made to himself on the drive to her house. But *damn*, the woman was sexy as hell when she was mad. Add to that her little quip about stuttering, and he'd lost it.

"*That's* why I'm here, Liv." He lifted a hand and gently brushed some hair from her face, tucking the wayward curls behind her ear. "Not because I feel obligated, but because I…"—he swallowed the words he was too afraid to say, instead giving her another truth—"I missed you." He leaned in, kissing her more slow this time, before breaking the kiss to admit, "I missed you so damn much."

Olivia ran a finger along his jawline, the simple touch as arousing as if her hand was actually touching his dick. Maybe even more so.

"I missed you, too, Jake."

She smiled, but her eyes looked sad, which bothered the hell out of him. Jake swallowed nervously, sensing she had more to say.

He didn't want to hear it, but that didn't matter. He'd hurt her by leaving without a word, and she had every right to feel whatever it was she was feeling. He just prayed he could make her understand.

"I'm sensing a 'but' coming."

She placed the palms of her hands on his chest, his body's reaction instant. He was already hard as a rock, his dick a throbbing club between his legs, but his heart was where he felt her touch the most. *Yeah, I am way the hell past screwed.*

"But, I—"

She seemed to be struggling to find her words. Good. At least it wouldn't be easy for her when she told him to go to hell.

"I lied," Olivia finally blurted out, her hands dropping to her sides.

Wait. She'd what?

Jake's mind raced, because this woman was the farthest thing from a liar. Him, sure. Her? Not a chance.

However, as he stared down into her eyes, those alluring swirls of greens and brown said she was telling him the truth. *Damn.*

Had she lied when she said she didn't regret being with him? Jake didn't think he could handle that. Anything but that.

Pushing past the lump in his throat, he nutted up and asked her, "What did you lie about, sweetheart?"

She glanced down at his chest, refusing to look him in the eye for this part. Definitely not a good sign. Jake held his breath and waited. *Please don't say you regret us, baby.*

"About not wanting more," she whispered.

At first she didn't say anything else, and he began to question whether he'd even heard right. Then, she looked back up at him and began talking so quickly, her words almost came out in one, long rush.

"I thought I could handle it, us…being together like that. I thought if I had you, even just that one night, it would be enough."

Her normally strong voice cracked slightly, and the tears beginning to well in her eyes tore at his swelling heart. Before he could respond, she rambled on some more.

"When you left, I thought maybe we really could go back to the way things were before. Like nothing had ever happened." She shook her head, almost frantically, her words falling out one right after another. "But, I can't. It's obvious you don't feel the same way, and that's okay. Well, it's not really *okay*, but I'll get over it. It'll take time, but I know I can move on, and one day we'll be able to be friends again. Until then, I just…I can't do this with you, Jake. I can't." She licked her lips and straightened her shoulders, drawing on her inner strength. "I *won't* be just a…booty call."

She wanted more? *That's* what she'd lied about? Jake's swollen heart pounded in his chest.

He wanted to do a fist-pump high in the air, or pick her up and swing her around like he'd seen guys do in those cheesy chick flicks.

Olivia Bradshaw wanted more. With him. *Hell, yes.*

He started to reach for her, but remembered what she'd just said about being a booty call. *Shit.*

He was really screwing this whole thing up. That was okay, because he was about to fix it, right the hell now.

Cupping her face with his hands, Jake tilted her chin up. He looked her square in the eyes as he spoke.

"Let me make something very clear. I would never, *ever* come to you for a booty call." He kissed her softly, his lips brushing against hers when he spoke again. "Not with you, Liv. Never with you."

Olivia's throat moved, and her eyes glistened. "It's just too hard, Jake. I know you don't feel the same way about me, but that's my problem, not yours. I'll...deal with it. Eventually."

She obviously wasn't listening. Jake opened his mouth to set her straight, but the stubborn-assed woman wouldn't let him get a word in edgewise.

"Look, Jake. I get that with your job, you sometimes have to leave at a moment's notice. I've always known that, even when I didn't know what your job really *was*. I also understand that whatever you and your team had to do this time was more important than staying with me. And that's okay, too."

Olivia stopped to take a breath. Her eyes filled even more, and the tip of her cute-as-fuck button nose turned rosy. She blinked, and a single tear fell.

"It was the fact that, after everything we'd been through together, you didn't even bother to tell me you had to leave. God, Jake. *That's* what hurt the most." Her chin quivered, and her voice broke. "You never even said goodbye."

"Ah, sweetheart. Come here." He pulled her in closely. Wrapping one arm around her waist, he cupped the back of her head and tucked it beneath his chin.

Jake felt her small hands grab the back of his shirt tightly, and he closed his eyes against his own emotions. It took him a full minute before he could talk past the softball-sized lump that had suddenly taken up residency in his throat.

He filled his lungs and prayed for the words to help her understand. Moving back just enough to look her in the eyes, Jake willed her to see the truth behind his.

"Leaving you that day was the hardest thing I've ever had to do."

Beautiful, tormented eyes stared up into his. "Then, why did you?"

She sounded so small and fragile, making him curse the circumstances behind their two-month separation once again. "I didn't have a choice. I had to leave with my team."

"Jason told me you had another job. He said it was important, but I still don't understand why we couldn't have talked for a minute before you left. Just long enough to at least say goodbye." Another tear fell.

He wiped it away before it reached her jaw. "My team and I left that day because we were going after the bastards responsible for your abduction. Time was of the essence, and literally, every second counted. You'd already been taken to the safe house when I found out I had to leave. I couldn't risk missing the opportunity to catch those assholes. Not even to try to find you to say goodbye. I'm sorry."

Olivia inhaled deeply, the movements pushing her soft breasts against his chest. Jake forced himself to ignore the way they felt.

Instead, he focused on the way her eyebrows turned inward, the soft skin between them wrinkling together in that adorable way they did. He wanted to kiss them. *Focus, McQueen.*

"I thought your team killed all of Cetro's men the day you found me. Well, except the two who took us, but we know for a fact they're…"

She didn't finish, which was fine with him. Neither one of them wanted to talk about the circumstances surrounding those two assholes' deaths. Jake sure as hell didn't want to think about how close he came to losing her that day.

"I'm not just talking about Cetro and his men, sweetheart. When we left Dallas two months ago, we were also going after the man who *hired* Cetro to take you."

Visibly shaken, Olivia pulled out of his arms and went back to the table. She plopped down in her chair, looking thoroughly confused. And scared.

She wrapped her arms around herself, rubbing them as if she were cold. "I-I don't understand. Someone actually...hired those men to take me?"

Following her lead, Jake reclaimed his chair as well. Propping his elbows on the table's wooden top, he fisted his hands together and said, "Most of what went down is classified. I can't give you all the details, but I'll tell you what I can."

She nodded her understanding.

"There was a group of men. Powerful men, with more money than God. Each month, they would put together the type of auction Cetro and his men were planning to take you to. One of the rich assholes saw your picture in the paper. It was with an article about relief workers offering aid to the victims of the hurricane."

Olivia absentmindedly nodded again. "I remember a few people taking pictures of us while we were working there. Some asked for our names and wanted to know where we were from. I thought it was great exposure for the program."

"I'm sure that was the intent behind the article, but the guy we went after saw it, saw *you*, and decided he...wanted you." Jake worked to bite back his anger, hoping she didn't notice how tightly his clenched fists had become. "He hired Cetro and his men to take you and hold you until the next auction."

Olivia thought for a moment, and then said, "Okay. So, I get why you left the way you did, but why were you gone for so long? Jason and the other agents acted like you'd only be gone a few days. And why couldn't you at least call or text me during that time to let me know you were okay?"

Jake understood her frustration. The two-day job had almost immediately turned into the mother of all cluster fucks. Ryker's contact was supposed to meet with the team after they'd landed that night. He never showed.

"The situation we were in was delicate. I couldn't risk either one of us by trying to contact you, even with a simple text. But, I swear to you, Olivia…when I left, I thought we'd only be gone a couple of days. A week, max."

With genuine concern, Olivia asked, "So, what happened?"

"Like I said, I can't tell you most of it, because it's classified. The rest…"—Jake sighed. "Hell, Liv. You've got enough bad shit stored up inside already. I refuse to add to it when it's not necessary. All you need to know is that my team did its thing. We found a way in, got what we needed, and took the organization down. Permanently."

Jake wasn't trying to be a chauvinistic prick. Olivia didn't need to know that, two days after they'd landed in Argentina—where they were supposed to meet Homeland's contact—Ryker had called with confirmation that his guy was found dead, his body dismembered.

He'd either been made as a snitch, or he'd pissed off someone in the group badly enough that they'd taken him out. In any case, the guy's death had caused Jake and his team to start from scratch, in turn, extending the length of the mission by a whole fucking lot.

Olivia covered her mouth and inhaled deeply through her nose. Her entire body started to shake, making Jake feel helpless.

He wanted to take her in his arms and promise that

everything would be okay. Vow that nothing bad would ever happen to her again. Instead, he stayed glued to his chair.

What she'd said earlier was true. She was a lot stronger than he gave her credit for, and didn't need him swooping in every time there was a problem. Even if every primal instinct he had was screaming at him to do just that.

As much as he hated it, Jake forced himself to give her a few minutes to process everything without him rushing to her rescue. Finally, her eyes met his.

"But you got him, right? The man who wanted to b-buy me?"

Jake nodded once, his voice deadly. "We got him."

She took in a cleansing breath and let it out slowly. "Did you kill him?"

Jake shook his head. She'd never know how hard it was for him not to put a bullet through the fucker's brain.

"Unfortunately, we needed the asshole alive so we could use the information he had to help shut the entire organization down for good."

Olivia sat quietly for a moment before asking, "And Cetro? Is he…"

"In a cell awaiting transport to the States. He's been in a Mexican prison for about six weeks now. A trial will be set soon. He's been charged with the murders of your friends and your kidnapping, along with human and drug trafficking charges, and a slew of other shit. Ryker's going for the death penalty, and he'll get it."

Jake didn't tell her he and his team found Cetro hiding out in a small village near the Texas border. Even now, the thought of him being so close to Olivia made his skin crawl.

"W-who was the man? The one who hired Cetro to take me?"

"I'm sorry, baby. I can't tell you his name. However, I can promise he will never be able to hurt you or anyone else, ever again."

Olivia stood and walked past him toward her living room, her body full of nervous energy. She ran a shaking hand through her hair several times, totally unaware—or maybe just not caring—that she'd pulled the elastic band loose from her ponytail.

The black ring went unnoticed as it fell to the floor behind her. She rubbed both hands across her face before turning back around.

"This is all so unreal. I can't believe there are people out there who'd actually do such despicable things to another human being."

Then, as if she'd suddenly realized something awful, a look of horror swept over her face.

Both hands flew to her chest, almost as if she were actually trying to reach in and grab hold of her own heart.

"Oh, God, Jake. You know what this means, right? It really *was* my fault. They were all killed because of *me*."

The guilt in her eyes as she referred to the other nurses and doctors Cetro's men had gunned down right in front of her gutted him.

Tears began to fall freely down her face, but she didn't seem to notice them. Jake sure as hell did. *Screw processing time.*

In an instant, he was out of his chair and pulling her into his arms. "No, baby," he said fiercely as he held on tight. "This was *not* your fault. The only ones to blame are Cetro and the other men we took down."

Jake spoke the truth, but knew Olivia would continue to blame herself. Time and support would help her come to terms with it all, but for two months she'd been forced to deal with it all on her own. A fact that shredded him.

He was here now, and for him, there was only one option. Jake had to make her understand. She had to let him back into her life, because if she didn't...if she spent one more second thinking she was alone in all of this, it would fucking destroy him.

With her head pressed against his chest, he said, "I know this is a lot to take in, Liv, and I'm so damned sorry for leaving you the way I did. But, after finding you alive in the jungle after I'd thought you'd been killed, knowing what you'd gone through...what they almost did to you..."

Damn it. Jake's voice broke, and he had to clear his throat to keep from breaking down.

"I had to make sure those assholes were put away for good. I needed to know they wouldn't be able to come after you ever again. The thought of that happening..."—He got choked up again, but pushed through it—"Sweetheart, that's what drove me onto that plane two months ago. It was the *only* thing that could have taken me away from you that day. I had to know you were safe, and that those bastards could never hurt you again."

Olivia continued to let him hold her like that, with the back of his shirt bunched in her hands for the second time in only a few minutes.

When she finally stopped shaking, she pulled back. Her eyes clear were and focused. Jake looked down into them and this time, he saw the one thing he'd prayed for...Acceptance.

"Thank you. For going after those men," Olivia offered solemnly.

Relieved beyond words, Jake kissed her forehead, then her cheek. His lips barely touched her ear when he whispered, "You don't ever have to thank me for that. Your safety is everything to me, Liv."

He moved in for a long, slow kiss. When it was over, he pulled back only slightly. Then, with his eyes locked on hers, Jake relinquished even more of himself to her. "*You* are everything to me."

After brushing some hair from her eyes, he cupped the side of her face. "I need you to believe that, baby. You have to know the only reason I left the way I did was to make sure the bastards responsible for taking you away from me never got the chance to do it again. I couldn't risk letting another team take over. *I* had to be the one to do it. Can you understand that?"

More moisture spilled from her forgiving eyes as she whispered the only answer he could bear to hear, "Yes."

Jake exhaled loudly, feeling as though a two-ton boulder had been lifted from his shoulders. "Thank God."

He hugged her tightly again. Knowing she not only forgave him for leaving the way he had, but that she actually understood the position he'd been in, made him want to cry like a baby.

His eyes stung, but he squeezed them shut to keep his tears from falling. After collecting himself, Jake put some space between them but kept his hands loosely resting on her hips.

"I promise I'll never leave you like that again."

There would be other jobs, of course, but he meant every word. No matter what he had to do, Jake would never leave without telling her goodbye again.

Chapter 4

Olivia could hardly believe what had transpired since coming home from work. In less than an hour, Jake had shown up unexpectedly, and they'd hashed out their issues—well, the most immediate ones, anyway.

She'd also learned that, without a doubt, all of the men responsible for what had happened to her were either dead or locked up for good.

She started to thank him again, but when she tried, the only thing that came out was a yawn. She covered her mouth until it was over. "Sorry," she said, embarrassed.

Jake smiled, and her heart did a complete somersault. "Don't apologize. Why don't you go get some rest?" She felt a sliver of panic until he said, "I'll be here when you wake up. Assuming you're okay with that."

Olivia knew they still had a lot to work through, but she couldn't bring herself to worry about that now.

"You'd better be," she said, giving him her first real smile in months. "I'm going to take a quick shower, first." She leaned up and gave him a sweet, chaste kiss. "Make yourself at home."

Not waiting for a response, she turned and headed toward the bathroom, her steps feeling much lighter than before. Olivia used her time in the shower to try to wrap her mind around everything she'd learned.

She understood now why things had happened the way they did. Jake had been out there fighting. For her, and for all of the women those bastards had hurt before her. For the ones they would have kept hurting, had he and his team not stopped them.

She knew enough from when Mikey and Jake served together to understand that, oftentimes, military men and women weren't allowed to share anything with their families about where they went or what they did. A mission like the one Jake's team had been on wasn't much different than that.

He and the others had left to take down some very bad men, and ensure her safety. How could she stay mad at him for that?

As she rinsed the conditioner from her hair, Olivia wondered how long he'd be able to stay before having to leave again. An uneasy feeling began to creep in at the thought, but she quickly shot it down. Jake was here now, and she was going to make the most of whatever time they had together.

After her shower, Olivia quickly dried off. Looking around her small bathroom, she realized the clothes she'd planned to change into were still lying on her bed. Right where she'd left them when the doorbell had rang. *Damn.*

She felt silly for worrying about it. The man had already seen every inch of her body. Still, she didn't want to push things too far too fast.

You are everything to me.

Those precious words kept rolling through her mind. It

wasn't exactly a declaration of love, but she'd take it...for now, anyway.

With a smile on her face and her towel wrapped around her body, Olivia opened the door and peaked down the hall toward the living room.

She didn't see Jake on the couch, and assumed he was probably in the kitchen or had gone outside to look around. Either way, the coast appeared to be clear.

In just three quick steps, she was at her bedroom door. Once inside, she shut the door, turned around, and ran straight into a solid wall of muscle.

Olivia let out a little squeak as Jake's hands grabbed her shoulders and pushed her flush against the door. The wood shook from the force of the impact.

He looked like he wanted to eat her alive. In the next second, she was surrounded by his warmth. With his forearms caging her in, Jake pressed the length of his hard body against hers. She almost forgot to breathe.

"Tell me to stop."

Oh, God. Jake's voice became so deep and rugged when he was turned on. It was as if he opened his mouth and sex came pouring out.

Olivia could feel her own arousal pooling between her thighs, and he wanted her to *stop* him? The man was insane.

"I wasn't going to do this," he continued before she could respond. "The whole way here, I promised myself I wouldn't touch you. I know we still need to talk about things, but...*Christ,* woman, what you do to me. It's like I can't think straight when you're around."

Jake brought one of his hands down and swept a strand of wet hair from her cheek. His touch was gentle, a complete contrast to the fierce emotions Olivia saw burning in his eyes.

"If you don't want this, I'll stop. But, you've got to tell me right fucking now, because honest to God, Liv. I don't know how much longer I can hold back."

"Don't stop, Jake." Her order was barely a whisper. "Don't you dare stop."

His control snapped then, and in an instant, his mouth was back on hers. He kissed and licked and nipped as if he was starved for her. Like he couldn't get enough.

His mouth moved frantically from her lips to her chin before leaving a wet trail down her neck. Electricity sparked everywhere his mouth touched her, his lips starting tiny little fires all across her sensitive skin.

Not wasting any time, Jake's hands moved down to where she'd knotted the towel between her breasts. With a quick flick of his fingers, the knot came loose.

He pulled back a step and the white terrycloth fell to the floor, pooling around her bare feet.

Jake stood there, drinking her in as if she were the most beautiful woman in the world. She was far from perfect, but when he Jake looked at her like that, Olivia couldn't help but feel as though she was.

"I'd almost forgotten how beautiful you are."

Unable to speak for the emotions running through her, Olivia continued to let him take his fill. Slowly—almost as if he were afraid she would break—Jake reached out and took her breasts into his hands.

Olivia's breath hitched from the contact. Continuing to knead the soft flesh, he bent down and gently took one of her nipples into his mouth. The warm, wet heat from his tongue sent shockwaves of pleasure through her system.

"Jake," she whispered his name.

While he sucked and licked, Olivia's fingers became

entangled in his hair. Eventually, he moved to the other breast where he repeated the same, exquisite torture.

With his mouth busy, Jake's free hand slid between her legs, his fingers playing her body like a finely-tuned instrument.

Gathering her own arousal, he began drawing lazy circles across her swollen clit. It was too much and not enough, all at the same time.

He continued teasing her with his gentle caresses as their tongues kept up with their erotic dual. Jake moved his hand lower, and Olivia cried out when he speared her sex with two, strong fingers. He began to thrust hard and fast, but it still wasn't enough.

"God, Jake! Please…I need you!"

Things were moving much faster than their first night together, two months ago. Not that she was complaining.

All at once, Jake pulled his mouth away and slid his fingers from her body. He placed his hands at each of her hips, lifting her as if she weighed nothing. And Holy God, if *that* wasn't hot as hell!

Olivia wrapped her legs around his waist and her arms around his neck. His jean-clad erection rubbed against her soaked core, but the friction wasn't enough to relieve the near-painful pressure there.

With his mouth back on hers, Jake spun them around and carried her to the bed. He laid her across it. Then, almost desperately, he stood and shed his own clothes.

Removing the protection from his jeans pocket, he held it up between the same two fingers that had just been inside her. Giving her a boyish grin, he wiggled them and said, "Boy Scout, right?"

Olivia chuckled, knowing he was referring to when they'd

been in the jungle, and she'd teased him about being prepared for anything.

Jake's smile faded as he rolled the condom onto his swollen cock. "I know I should take this slow, but—"

"I don't want slow," Olivia interrupted him. Her eyes wandered down to the object of her desire. "I just want you. Inside me." She looked back up into his eyes and added, "Now."

She knew she sounded bossy, but from the way Jake was looking down at her, he liked it.

With that damn sexy smile, he gave her a salute with what were quickly becoming her two favorite fingers. "Yes, ma'am."

He covered her body with his. Propped on his elbows to keep from crushing her, Jake used one knee to spread her legs further apart.

Eyes locked on hers, he eased into her in one, fluid motion. And just like that, all was right in her world.

****

Home. It was the first thought Jake had as he slid his body into Olivia's slick heat. Nothing had ever felt so good…or so right.

He moved his hips forward, burying himself as deeply as he could go. It still didn't feel like enough. With her, it never was enough.

Moving together, Olivia met him thrust for unbelievable thrust. Jake knew this first time was going to be quick, and sensed her urgency, too.

As their pace increased, her body began to quiver beneath his. Jake was already close, but he was determined to take care of her first.

Sliding one hand between them, he gathered some moisture onto his fingertips from where their bodies were connected. Pressing onto her swollen clit with just the right amount of pressure, Jake began moving his fingers in fast, tight circles.

He watched as Olivia threw her head back onto the mattress and squeezed her eyes shut. She moaned loudly, her nails digging into his back. God, he loved how uninhibited she was with him.

Jake clenched his teeth together. His lower back tingled, and his balls grew tight. Sweat beaded on his forehead, and he knew he couldn't hold out much longer. Thankfully, he didn't think he'd have to.

Olivia's breathing increased. Her entire body vibrated against his, and when her thighs squeezed his hips and her heels dug into his ass, he knew she was right on the edge.

"That's it, baby," he panted the words between thrusts. "Come for me."

Olivia cried out, her back arching off the mattress. Her inner walls clamped down on his cock, sending him straight into his own release. Jake grunted out her name as his own climax hit.

He continued thrusting wildly, as he came, determined to draw out every ounce of pleasure for them both.

Eventually, his movements slowed and he collapsed in a heap on top of her. After a few minutes—or hell, it could have been hours—he heard her sweet, muffled voice from below him.

"Um, Jake?"

"Hmm?" was all he could manage.

"I can't breathe."

"Shit. Sorry." With what little energy he had left, Jake lifted up, pulled himself out, and rolled onto his back beside her.

"So," Olivia spoke between heaving breaths. "Why exactly…did you promise…to keep…your hands to yourself?"

Jake turned onto his side, facing her. Apparently, she was still too tired to do the same, because Olivia only moved her head so she could see him better.

She was flushed, her eyelids heavy with pure satisfaction. Jake felt like the king of the fucking world, knowing he was the one to put that look on her face.

Lazily, he ran a fingertip down her arm, leaving goose bumps in its wake.

"I didn't want you thinking I was only here for a booty call." He raised one eyebrow and looked at her pointedly.

"Really?"

"Really."

Looking chagrined, she bit her bottom lip. "Oh."

"Yeah…*oh*." He leaned over and kissed her slowly. "You have to know I would never do that to you. This thing with us, it's not casual, Liv. Not for me."

She smiled, her relief obvious, and he felt like an ass for making her think for even one second that he felt otherwise.

"Me, neither."

"Good. And just so we're clear, there'll be no one else. Not for me," he kissed her again, just because he could, "and not for you." With a hard stare, he let her know under no uncertain terms, "I won't share what's mine."

Not waiting for a response—because nothing she could say would ever change his feelings about that—Jake stood up and started to walk out of the room.

"Where are you going?"

Without turning around, he spoke over his shoulder. "I'll be right back."

He went into the bathroom, found a washcloth, and put it under some hot water. After taking care of the condom and cleaning himself up, he rinsed the cloth out again and walked back into the bedroom.

She was still lying in the same spot. Her eyes were closed, and she hadn't moved an inch. Jake smiled, taking a second to appreciate the pure beauty that was his Olivia.

He hadn't lied about his reasons for trying to stay hands-off, but there was more to it. He hadn't wanted to take her again until he'd told her the truth about her brother's death.

That was before she walked into her bedroom wearing nothing but that damn towel. The second she did, he'd lost every ounce of self-control. With her, it seemed he had none.

Jake's original plan had been to show up, confess it all, and beg for her forgiveness. Then, he saw that damn gun in her waistband, immediately turning his entire focus to her safety.

The sex traffickers were no longer a threat. He knew that with absolute certainty. But knowing some other sick fuck could be out there, toying with her, put a knot in his gut.

Even if it was just some harmless fan, Jake still wanted to find the guy and pound his face in.

And he was still going to tell her about what really happened to Mike, but first, he needed to make sure she truly was safe. Once he was certain of that, he'd tell her everything.

For now, it could wait. She had enough to worry about, without adding his betrayal on top of it all. So, he'd keep his secret a little longer. For her sake.

Jake ignored the tiny voice in his head, calling him a spineless bastard and set about taking care of her.

"Spread your legs." His command was low, sensual.

Olivia's sleepy eyes opened half-way. "Again? Already?"

He chuckled and held up the washcloth. "I'm just going to clean you up."

"Oh, you don't have to…" she started to say. She actually looked embarrassed, which Jake found absolutely adorable.

When he placed the warm rag against her swollen mound, she closed her eyes again and moaned, all traces of embarrassment lost.

"I like taking care of you," he said softly.

She surprised him when she admitted sleepily, "I like it when you take care of me."

When Jake was done, he walked over to the clothes hamper in the corner of the room and tossed the washcloth in. He went back to the bed and slid his arms beneath Olivia's back and knees. She startled when she felt him picking her up.

"What are you doing?" Exhaustion had her words slurring together.

"You need sleep."

With her in his arms, Jake pulled back the top cover and sheet, positioning her so her head was on the pillow. He walked around the foot of the bed laid down beside her.

Already half-asleep, Olivia rolled over onto her side, facing away from him. He promptly reached over and pulled her back to his chest, spooning her. His cock twitched from the contact, but he ignored it.

Jake kissed the back of her head. "Rest now, sweetheart."

"Okay." After a few beats, he heard her soft voice again. "Jake?"

"Yeah, baby?"

"I'm really glad you're here."

He kissed her head again and gave her midsection a little squeeze. "Me, too, sweetheart. Me, too."

With his entire world wrapped up in his arms, Jake closed his eyes and fell asleep.

****

Olivia woke to a delicious aroma. She smiled, knowing Jake had taken over her small kitchen.

He'd cooked for her at her apartment a few times after Pops died. Each time, the food had tasted amazing. There really wasn't anything the man couldn't do.

She stretched. Muscles that hadn't been used in two months were deliciously sore. A wonderful reminder of Jake's other talents.

Flashes of their lovemaking played through her mind, and her smile grew even more. *Talented, indeed.*

Glancing at her bedside clock, Olivia did a double-take. *Holy crap!* She'd slept for ten straight hours.

Even more surprising was that she hadn't had a single nightmare. What a difference a day—or maybe she should say, *Jake*—could make.

Still wearing her stupid grin, Olivia quickly showered and dressed before making her way into her kitchen. She stopped when she came to the room's entrance.

Without a word, she crossed her arms at her chest and leaned against the wood trim. For the next few minutes, she stayed just like that, admiring the view.

Jake was standing at the stove, stirring something in a steaming pot. Dressed in the same jeans he'd worn earlier, he'd left the top button undone, and hadn't bothered with a shirt. Thank God for small miracles.

She took advantage of the moment, soaking in the site.

Slowly, her eyes worked their way down over his strong thighs. The denim was stretched tightly there, reminding her of the way those muscles had moved between her own legs just a few hours ago.

Olivia glanced lower and saw that his feet were bare. Her pulse quickened. She should *not* be so turned on, but cripes…even his freaking *feet* were sexy.

"Like what you see?"

When she met his eyes, she found them lit with smug amusement. Playing off her embarrassment from having been caught ogling, Olivia stood straight and started toward him.

"You shouldn't have let me sleep so long."

"I figured you needed it."

His bare shoulder lifted in a shrug, drawing her attention to the sexy-as-sin Delta Force tattoo on his left bicep. *Cool your jets, Bradshaw.*

"I must have."

She walked up behind him and wrapped her arms around his waist. The act felt so natural, as if they'd been together like this for years.

"What smells so good?"

"Spaghetti and meatballs. There's also garlic bread in the oven. Here,"—he turned around, and she loosened her grip without completely breaking her hold—"tell me what you think."

Jake lifted the wooden spoon to her lips, and Olivia opened her mouth to taste the red sauce.

"Mmm." She licked her lips. "Where did you learn to cook like this?"

Turning back around to keep an eye on the bubbling liquid, he said, "In the military, it was either MRE's or whatever the chow hall had to offer. Sometimes not even that. Even now, when my team takes a job, a decent meal isn't always an option. I like good-tasting food, and since there was no one else around to do it for me, I figured I'd better learn."

Olivia wanted to tell him he had to do all of the cooking from now on, but held back. That line was loaded with an assumed future and expectations he may not be ready for just yet.

"Well, since you're cooking, I'll set the table."

Forcing herself to move away from his delectable body, Olivia got their plates and silverware ready. She'd just opened a cabinet and was reaching up for two wine glasses when she felt his arms around her, pulling her back against his chest.

Jake's warm lips kissed the sensitive area just behind her ear. Smiling, Olivia closed her eyes and tilted her head to the side to give him better access.

"Better not start something you can't finish," she teased.

"Oh, there's no doubt I'll finish"—his stubble brushed her skin, sending waves of goose bumps spreading from head to toe—"but I'll make sure you go first."

Jake spun her around quickly, his words and the sudden movement causing her breath to catch. Her hands flew up to his shoulders, but the strong arms encircling her waist kept her steady.

Jake leaned in but didn't kiss her. Instead, he spoke in that panty-dropping voice again.

"You burn me alive with your touch, Liv." His lips brushed along her jawline. "You start a fire in me that I never want to put out."

Oh. My. God. Olivia was starting to wonder if too much pleasure could be lethal.

She tilted her head again, moaning as his open mouth landed on the place where her neck and shoulder met. His tongue darted out, and he licked her there before gently nibbling the delicate skin.

Olivia gasped, and felt his lips curve against her soft skin. *Damn him.* He knew he was teasing her, and she was incapable of hiding just how much she was enjoying it.

Reaching up, her fingers pulled on his hair. Even from behind the denim barrier of his jeans, Olivia could feel his cock twitch against her belly. His body's reaction to her was intoxicating, causing her sex to clench with anticipation.

"W-what about the food?" she murmured, eyeing the stove. She smiled when she saw the burners already turned off.

Jake lifted his head, his lips barely brushing her ear as he spoke.

"The food can wait, baby." He took her small lobe gently between his teeth. "I can't."

His words demolished her control. Olivia attacked with vigor, her mouth slamming roughly into his. Their tongues collided, twisting and thrusting violently.

Olivia was wild and crazy, and within seconds, they were in her living room, a trail of clothing scattered on the floor behind them. Thank God, she didn't have neighbors.

Standing in front of Jake, his back to her couch, Olivia used both hands to push against him. He could have easily stood his ground, but he let her take the lead and allowed his body to fall back.

A naked woman on a mission, Olivia quickly straddled him, lifting herself up just enough to be able to wrap her hands around his throbbing shaft. She started to position him at her entrance and then...

"Wait!"

That one word stopped her cold. Olivia looked down Jake, wondering why he was putting a halt to things.

"Condom," he ground out.

Oh. That.

"I'm on the pill," she blurted, more than ready to get the show on the road. "I, uh, got on it shortly after we got back. I was thinking that if we…well, anyway. I've been on it for almost two months, and I haven't been with anyone besides you in over two years. We all had to be tested before we left for Toamasina, so I know I'm clean."

His cock got impossibly harder in her hands. Excitement filled his eyes, and Jake looked up at her like a kid who'd just been offered his favorite toy.

"Homeland makes us test every six months. I hadn't been with anyone else for a long time before you, and there's been no one since. I swear on my life, I'm clean Olivia."

Smiling back at him, Olivia repositioned the head and sank down slowly. Very. Slowly.

****

"Ah, *fuck*," Jake croaked out as his dick slid into Olivia's tight sheath.

He knew his voice sounded strangled but *shit*. It was a wonder he could talk at all. He was just damn lucky he didn't lose it the second she filled herself with him.

Jake had never been this quick on the draw, but like everything else with her, sex with Liv was different. He'd also never ridden bareback, and holy fuck, it felt *amazing*.

She was hot and wet, her slick inner muscles squeezing him like a goddamn vice. He'd never been so turned on in his life. Even now, after having just gotten inside her, he was having a hell of a time not coming.

Then…she moved.

Determined to avoid complete and total embarrassment, Jake squeezed her hips, holding her still.

"Don't."

The order was gruff, his grip tight enough he'd probably leave bruises. His heart rate picked up.

He'd been so outraged at the ones that bastard, Cetro, had left on her before, but the thought of *his* hands marking Olivia as reminder of their shared passion…as wrong as it was, the thought filled Jake with a primal, male satisfaction that was better than any adrenaline rush he'd ever had.

What could he say? When it came to Liv, he was a total Neanderthal. And she was his vixen.

Ignoring his warning, Olivia shifted her hips again. His grip on her bare skin tightened and—*thank Christ*—she stopped.

"Sweetheart, if you move so much as a centimeter, I'm done for."

Olivia smiled in a way he'd never seen before, yet he knew exactly what that smile meant. Power. Right now, she held it all, and the little wench knew it.

She was on his lap, completely naked, with his bare, aching cock snuggled tightly inside her. Her hair was wild, her cheeks flushed, and her hard-as-nails nipples were right there for the taking.

Jake wanted nothing more than to lean forward and take one into his mouth. To flick it with his tongue while rolling the other between his thumb and forefinger, but he didn't dare. If he gave in to that urge, she would start moving again, and it would be game over.

The only parts moving now were their chests as air travelled in and out of their lungs. Jake's eyes never left hers. They were frozen, connected not only physically, but also on an emotional level deeper than Jake even knew existed.

It was the most intimate experience of his life. Jake's lips parted, and he was on the verge of confessing how he truly felt about her when Olivia broke the ribbon of intensity.

"What's the matter, Boss Man," she teased. "Can't handle me?"

Slowly and deliberately, Olivia rolled her hips forward. All thoughts of talking ceased.

Jake squeezed his eyes shut as that familiar tingling hit his lower back. His balls became so tight, he wouldn't have been surprised if they crawled right back up inside him. He groaned and dug his fingers a little deeper.

When he opened his eyes again, that smug smile was still there. He needed to take control of the situation...now, before it was too late.

Hold on, sweetheart. Two can play at that game.

Without warning, Jake lifted her up and off him, breaking their connection completely. She let out a little yelp as he flung her around so that she was now lying on her stomach across his lap.

Olivia's wide eyes looked up at him, all traces of smugness gone. Jake looked down at her, his smile just as arrogant as the one she'd given him just seconds before.

"You wanna play like that, Bradshaw? You'd better be prepared for the consequences."

She smiled back, clearly enjoying his playful attitude. "I'm not scared of you, McQueen."

One if his eyebrows rose. "Oh, really?"

Jake ran the palm of his right hand across the smooth skin

of her bare ass.

Her mouth dropped open. "You wouldn't dare." Olivia's words were a warning, but the heat in her eyes said differently.

It was the same heat he'd seen earlier when he'd threatened to spank her for trying to tell him she was fine. He had to admit, he'd fantasized about having her in this exact position. On several occasions.

As he continued to massage the perfect, heart-shaped ass just begging to be spanked, Jake decided it was time to put fantasy to reality.

In the same, teasing voice she'd used on him, Jake asked, "What's the matter? Scared you can't handle it?"

He knew she'd never back down from the challenge. What he didn't expect, was how hard he was praying she wouldn't.

Excitement flared behind her eyes and her cheeks became flushed. "I already told you. I'm not scared."

She wants it. "Oh, baby"—he squeezed one of her firm cheeks—"that was your first mistake."

Unable to wait any longer, Jake lifted his hand. He brought it back down with just enough force to make his palm sting.

Olivia gasped, and Jake watched her reaction closely. He'd rather cut off his own dick than actually hurt her.

She looked at him and smiled. Her face was flush, her eyes heavy with arousal. Jesus, she was so fucking turned on. *So am I.*

"More?" he asked, already knowing what her answer would be.

When Olivia nodded, Jake smacked her ass again. She cried out, the sounds of her pleasure echoing off the living room walls.

After a few more swats, he knew he needed to move

things along, or he was going to come all over her belly. Soothing the rosy skin beneath his palm, Jake slid his hand between her crease, and lower.

Understanding flashed across her face, and Olivia lifted her ass slightly to give him access. His fingers found her entrance dripping with excitement.

"Jesus, baby. You're so wet."

Olivia simply nodded again.

Jake grinned. "You liked that, didn't you?"

Another nod.

"Well, let's see if you like this."

Jake easily slid two fingers inside her. Olivia's eyes rolled shut, and she inhaled sharply. He moved slowly at first, then faster. Harder.

God, he loved how soaked she was. The sounds her arousal made as he continued to thrust his fingers in and out of her body was erotic as fuck.

Olivia began moving her hips against his hand even harder. She cried out again, and Jake could feel her inner muscles beginning to twitch against fingers. She was close.

Removing one of his fingers, Jake used the other to rub against her swollen clit. That was all it took.

With her head thrown back and her ass in the air, Olivia came harder than he'd ever seen her. She was still coming when he slid from the couch and re-positioned himself behind her.

With one knee on the cushion and a foot on the carpet beside the couch, Jake lifted her hips until she was on her knees. They'd have more room if he moved them to the bedroom, but he couldn't wait that long.

Olivia's hands gripped the arm of the couch as he slammed into her from behind. The sounds of skin slapping against skin filled the air, and after only a few more grunts and thrusts, Jake exploded, spilling himself inside her.

In that moment, he realized. It didn't matter how many times he had her, it would never be enough.

Chapter 5

Life was good. Olivia was surprised by the thought—and the smile that didn't want to quit—as Jake drove her to work three days later. Even more shocking was that she actually *believed* it.

There'd been no more phone calls, nothing sinister left on her porch. And even though they'd spent most of the last few days at home, when she and Jake did go out, she hadn't gotten the creepy stalker vibes once.

She was starting to believe that the police had actually been right. The phone calls, snake, and break-in were nothing more than childish pranks. That, or whoever had been infatuated with her had moved on. Jake wasn't as convinced.

"I have to go into the city for a meeting, so Trevor will pick you up and drive you home today."

Olivia looked at him. "Is that really necessary? I thought we agreed that everything that happened were just some sick pranks."

"No, *you* decided to chalk it all up as that. I'm not willing to take that chance."

"It's been two weeks, and nothing else has happened. Seriously, Jake. Trevor doesn't need to take time out of his day to babysit me."

Still concentrating on the road in front of them, Jake acted as if he hadn't heard a word she'd said.

"If I'm able to get away sooner, I'll drive you home. Either way, you're not to leave the hospital without one of us there to walk you out."

Olivia wanted to roll her eyes. "You don't think this is overkill?"

Jake gripped the steering wheel a little tighter before reaching over and grabbing her hand. Lacing their fingers together, he glanced over at her.

"I lost you once, Liv. I'm not willing to risk losing you again."

The sincerity in his gorgeous eyes did her in. "Well, crap."

Olivia sighed loudly and relaxed back into her seat again. Feigning frustration, she asked, "How am I supposed to argue with you when you go and say something sweet like that?"

One corner of Jake's mouth rose as he looked out the windshield again. "It's a gift. Might as well accept it now."

She pretended to glare. "Fine. Trevor can play bodyguard. But you're making it up to me when you get home tonight." Out of the corner of her eye, Olivia saw his smirk turn into a smile.

"Any thoughts as to how I can accomplish that?"

"I'll think of something."

Jake chuckled and raised the hand he was still holding to his mouth for a quick peck. "Oh, I'm sure you will."

Olivia thought for a moment before asking the question she was afraid to be answered. "So, this meeting. Is it about another job?"

"It is. I'd prefer to let Trevor take my place, but William

Cantrell personally requested I be there to oversee the details."

"William Cantrell," Olivia repeated the name as if she'd possibly heard it before. It took a few seconds before recognition hit. "Wait a minute. Are you talking about *Senator* Bill Cantrell?"

"The one and only. Apparently, he wants to hire us for extra security on his campaign trail, which starts in a couple of weeks. I'm meeting with him and the head of his personal security detail."

"Wow. That has to be good for business. Word of mouth alone from a guy like that could be huge for R.I.S.C."

"It definitely couldn't hurt." Jake turned onto the road leading to the hospital. "I still hate the idea of leaving you."

"Are you kidding? A freaking United States Senator wants to meet with you, Jake. Of *course,* you go. Besides, I'll be around other people all day long. I'll be fine." And then, because she couldn't help but ask, Olivia said, "So, this job. When would you have to leave?"

"I don't. Hill and Coop will be working this one."

At first, she was relieved, but then felt selfish. R.I.S.C. was his livelihood, and if they were going to make a go at an actual relationship, Olivia was going to have to get used to him leaving for it.

"Please tell me you aren't passing up this opportunity because of me."

Jake flipped on his turn signal before steering the truck into the hospital entrance. "This is a simple protection job, Liv. Hill will take point, but both he and Coop are more than capable of handling it."

Grant Hill was R.I.S.C.'s demolitions expert. The guy was a mass of muscle and definitely not someone Olivia ever wanted to tick off.

Sean "Coop" Cooper was one of R.I.S.C.'s snipers. He was also the only team member to be injured during her rescue.

A pang of guilt settled in Olivia's gut. "How is Sean? Are you sure he's ready to take on something like this?"

"Coop's leg is fully healed, and he's been released for full-duty by one of Homeland's physicians. He's been chompin' at the bit to get out and do something, even if it's just playing bodyguard. Both men volunteered for the duty, and honestly, after what we went through in Venezuela and then the two-month gig after, I'm ready for a break."

Jake stopped the truck in front of the ER doors. He got out and came around to open her door. Taking her hand in his, Jake helped her step down.

Olivia's heart did a little somersault. *Who says chivalry is dead?*

"I'll be back as soon as I can, but working out the logistics for a job like this will most likely take all day. Just remember what I said. If I'm not here, you don't leave this hospital without Trevor by your side. For any reason."

Normally, Olivia would be annoyed by the way he was ordering her around. Given his reasons for it this time, Olivia couldn't help but think it was sweet.

"I won't."

With one hand cupping her face, Jake spoke softer. "I'm serious, Liv. Be aware of your surroundings, even inside the hospital, and stick to Trevor like glue when you leave."

Grabbing his wrist, Olivia gave him a reassuring smile. "I promise."

Jake looked like he wanted to say more. Instead, he leaned down and pressed his lips to hers. All too quickly, he pulled away.

"You'd better get in there before I decide to throw you back into that truck and drive away."

Giggling, Olivia rose on her tiptoes and gave him another quick peck. "Drive carefully."

"I will."

She stepped around him, squealing when he swatted her on her ass.

Smiling, Jake said, "I'll see you soon. And remember...like glue."

Rubbing her rear, Olivia hollered out a sarcastic, "Yes, Dad!" before turning and walking through the ER's automatic doors. And for the first time in months, she couldn't wait for her shift to be over.

****

"Someone had better be dying."

Jake grinned as he drove away from the hospital. Derek never had been a morning person. "Hey, D. It's me."

A few seconds of sheets rustling and padded footsteps filled his ears. One cleared throat later, Derek sounded a bit more awake. "Boss?"

"Did I wake you?" Jake asked, even though he already knew he had.

"It's all good. What's up?"

"I need a favor. It's for Olivia."

"How is our girl?" D's southern drawl was more prominent now that he was relaxed.

"*Our* girl?"

"You nearly died trying to protect her. Coop caught a bullet for her, and we've all spent the last two months away from home so we could get the bastard who tried to buy her. Not to mention, I now have two assholes thanks to the new one Ryker ripped into us for going to bum-fuck Venezuela in the first place. So, hell yeah, she's our girl."

Though his words were in true Derek form, Jake found himself brushing off an unexpected wave of emotion that they had caused.

"Duly noted."

"Good. Now, are you gonna tell me why you called me at the ass-crack of dawn, on my day off, or are you waitin' for me to guess?"

"What's the matter? Did I interrupt play time? Let me guess…it's the blonde. No, wait. The redhead."

Jake could hear the man's smile through the phone. "What can I say? Unlike you, the rest of us haven't been lucky enough to find *the one*. And you know me. I like to collect as much data as I can before making a final decision. Especially somethin' that important. Consider this research."

To that, Jake had no response. He loved Olivia, and there would never be another woman for him. She was, without a doubt, the one for him. But, how did Liv feel?

These past few days had been nothing short of amazing, but what would happen when she learned the truth about her brother? And she would…soon.

As terrified as he was, Jake wouldn't take the next step without telling her everything. Olivia deserved to have all of the facts. He just needed to find the right time to tell her.

So far, that time had failed to present itself. Of course, Jake hadn't spent much time *looking* for that perfect moment, either.

He'd been too busy staring at her perfect ass...and those breasts...and the way she looked when she called out his name—

"Boss? You still there?"

Shit. Focus, McQueen. Jake cleared his throat. "Yeah. Sorry. Listen, I need you to put together some equipment and meet me at Olivia's place to install it. And I want it done ASAP."

"ASAP, as in..." Derek let his voice trail off.

"An hour. I have a meeting in three, and it's one I can't be late for."

There was a pause, and then, "What all are you thinkin'?"

"Security equipment. Cameras, lights, the works. I want them set up around the perimeter of her house. Definite focus on the driveway, front, and back door, but also some to show the surrounding land. She has a decent alarm system already in place, but it's not enough."

Derek's voice tightened, all traces of humor gone, "Did something else happen?"

Jake appreciated D's concern. During the short time they'd been around her, his team members all seemed to accept her as one of their own.

The guys had talked about her on several occasions while they'd been cooped up together the last couple months.

Derek and Trevor...hell, even Grant, on one occasion, had all made comments about what a sweet, strong woman she was. They'd mentioned how impressed they were with the way she'd handled herself with the whole Cetro mess.

Even Mac and Coop had agreed because they'd witnessed her bravery when she'd made a run for it at Cetro's camp before Coop got shot and they had to fly home. They'd all accepted her as his, which meant they wanted to keep her safe as well.

"Just taking precautions."

That first night at Olivia's—after the amazing sex and heated-up dinner—Jake had waited until she'd fallen asleep to call Derek.

He'd filled the genius in on what had been going on with Olivia while they'd been away, including the information she'd given him about Norman Rogers. Speaking of which—

"Did you find out anything more on Rogers?"

"Not that I could find. He's still a resident at the institution Olivia told you about. After looking more closely at his medical records, I don't see him being released any time soon."

That was good news, on two notes. One, Rogers was finally getting the help he deserved and, from the sounds of things, desperately needed. And two, he's also not a threat to Liv.

"So, just curious. Why the rush on the installation?"

"It's Liv's first day back to work since I got here. I'd like it done before she gets home."

"That way she can't argue with you about how she doesn't need it?" D's voice was laced with amusement.

Jake smiled. "Who says you're not a genius?"

"Um...no one." Both men laughed and then Derek said, "You aren't worried she'll be mad at you for, I don't know, overstepping your bounds with her house?"

"Let me worry about that. You just get the stuff together and get your ass here."

"Yes, sir, boss, sir!"

Jake pictured D giving him a mock salute. Probably the one-fingered kind. "See you in an hour."

****

Olivia glanced at her watch and smiled. She'd been busier than normal today, which had helped to make her shift go by fast. After giving report to the nurse taking over for her, she walked out into the ER's main entrance where, as promised, Trevor was waiting for her.

She pushed away the twinge of disappointment that it wasn't Jake standing there, but Olivia knew he would be back as soon as he possibly could.

He'd texted her a few times during her shift. Nothing important, just random messages saying hi or asking how her day was going.

Olivia had the feeling his true motive was to check and make sure she was okay, which made her love him even more. *Maybe it's time you told him.*

Trevor smiled and walked toward her. "Hey, there, stranger," he drew her into a friendly hug. "How are you?"

"I'm good." She hugged him back and then pulled away. "How are you?"

"Can't complain. You look great, by the way."

After being on her feet all day and running around like a mad woman, Olivia wasn't convinced he was telling the truth.

Of course, the last time Trevor saw her was the day they'd all come back home after she and Jake had narrowly escaped their captors. Olivia had been covered in bruises, then. Compared to that, she probably did look great.

"Thanks. You, too." Now, that was the absolute truth. Trevor was undeniably hot.

He kept his dark, wavy hair short and stylish. His bone structure was damn-near perfect, from his long, narrow nose to his chiseled jaw and chin.

There was a bit more scruff on his face than the last time she'd seen him, which only added to his ruggedly handsome appearance.

With his six foot-two, muscular frame, and his Hollywood looks, the guy could seriously be a model if he wanted to.

While Olivia thought him attractive—ahem, what girl wouldn't—she felt none of the panty-dropping vibes from seeing him like she did with Jake. Trevor was her friend and nothing more. Jake was…hers.

"How was work?" Trevor asked as he led her toward the elevators leading down to the parking garage.

"It was good. Busy, but good."

They continued with their friendly small talk as rode to the garage's first level where Trevor had parked his truck. They spoke as they walked, their voices echoing slightly throughout the concrete structure.

"I really appreciate you doing this, Trevor. I feel bad, though. I'm sure there are better things you could be doing."

"Nah." He smiled down at her. "As far as assignments go, trust me when I say I've had much worse. Besides, Jake texted me right before you came out. He's on his way back, and he's bringing food, so I'd say the trade-off was worth it." Trevor winked and gave her a boyish grin.

At that, Olivia smiled wide, too. They hadn't known each other all that long, but she felt very comfortable around him. He was handsome and sweet. He was also protective. All very much like Jake. Which made her wonder…

"So, tell me," she said, wanting to get to know the man more. "Why isn't there a Mrs. Matthews waiting at home somewhere?"

He laughed and shook his head. "Guess I just haven't met the right girl, yet."

"Well, I don't get it. You're good-looking, intelligent, and a total badass. I know I'm getting super-personal here, but you know pretty much all there is to know about my crazy life. So, it begs the question…how in the world are you still single?"

Trevor smiled again, but this time it didn't quite light up his face like before. Olivia feared she'd crossed some invisible, no-trespassing zone and instantly regretted asking something so personal.

She pulled her phone out of her pocket to text Jake, if for no other reason than to let Trevor off the hook for having to answer. Looking down at her screen as she walked, Olivia started typing a message to let Jake know they were leaving the hospital.

Still typing, she opened her mouth to apologize for prying when the loud pop of a car backfiring filled the otherwise empty air. Olivia involuntarily jumped, tossing her phone in the process.

"Shit!"

It landed a few feet in front of her, and she quickly moved to pick it up. Thankfully, it hadn't cracked. She stood and looked up ahead of them in the same direction the sound had come from.

"Holy cow, that was loud. That car must need some major work—"

Olivia turned to face Trevor as she spoke, only then realizing Trevor was no longer standing next her. She glanced down and gasped.

He was lying on his back, eyes closed, and he wasn't moving. Her heart nearly stopped cold when she saw where the bullet had torn through his shirt.

"Trevor!" Olivia screamed as she bent over his body.

"Help!" she yelled out. She spun her head around, trying to look for someone…*anyone* who could help, while assessing any immediate threat. "I need help, here!"

Olivia screamed the order at the top of her lungs, just as she had countless times while working in the E.R., but it didn't matter. The other doctors and nurses weren't around to rush to her aid this time. No one was around.

Looking back down, Olivia's voice broke, "Trevor?" He didn't respond.

With her heart in her throat, she checked for a pulse, and nearly cried with relief when she found one. "H-hang on. You're going to be okay. Just hang on."

Eyes still closed, his body was unmoving, but she couldn't seem to find any blood. At first, she didn't understand why.

Flashbacks from the attack at Toamasina threatened to consume her, but she forced them away. Trevor needed her here, not lost in the nightmares of her past.

Threat forgotten, Olivia's medical training took over, her sole focus on doing what she could to help him. With both hands, she grabbed the front of his dress-shirt and pulled, tearing it open.

Buttons flew around them, but she paid them no attention. Swiftly shoving his white undershirt up from the bottom hem, Olivia blew a sigh of relief when she saw the shiny gold end of a bullet sticking out from the black vest, just over Trevor's chest.

The Kevlar had kept the bullet from penetrating his heart, and she was so thankful he'd taken the precaution.

Fear continued to race through her veins, however, because even though the bullet hadn't gone into his body, Trevor was still unconscious.

Her years of working at the hospital in Dallas had taught

her the kinetic energy from a shot like that could cause serious internal damage, even with the vest.

"I'm going to get you help," she told him loudly, praying he could hear her.

Needing her phone, she stuck her hand in her pocket, but came up empty. Her mind raced.

Where the hell was it? Then, she remembered picking it up just before realizing Trevor had been shot.

Unsure of what she'd done with it after seeing him lying there, Olivia frantically searched the ground around her. A few agonizing seconds later, she started to stand and realized it had been under her the whole time.

With shaking fingers, she picked it up and began dialing the emergency room's direct number. She'd entered five of the seven numbers when a pair of strong arms grabbed her from behind. The phone clattered to the ground.

Terrified, Olivia started to scream, but the sound was cut off when one of her attacker's gloved hands pressed hard against her mouth. With his other arm wrapped around her waist, the man yanked her to her feet and began moving them both backward. Away from Trevor.

This can't be happening. Not again.

Olivia's heart pounded so hard inside her chest, she thought it would explode. Terror threatened to consume her, but she refused to let this happen to her again.

With as much force as she could muster, she twisted and bucked against the man's tight hold, but it was no use. The guy was too strong.

Turning them, the man drug her between a compact car and a white panel van. Olivia nearly laughed at how cliché it all was. Parking garage. White van. Bodyguard shot with no one else around to help.

The van's side door was open and the middle seats had been removed, leaving a dark, empty space. *Oh, God. Do not let him put you in there!*

As the man forced her closer, Olivia's feet scrambled to find purchase on the smooth, slick floor. Her heart sank when she glanced inside the van again, and saw a pair of handcuffs and a roll of duct tape lying on the vehicle's metal floor.

No! She'd seen enough TV to know, if he got her into that van, she was as good as dead. Or worse. She couldn't let that happen. She had to keep fighting.

The roar of her pulse was deafening in her ears as she bucked against the man. She attempted to kick back, aiming for his shins, but her feet only caught air.

When he tried to force her into the van, Olivia swung her right foot up, pressing it against the metal panel next to the open door. Using that as leverage, she pushed against it with her foot as hard as she could, throwing the guy's back into the other car's driver side mirror.

Her assailant cursed but didn't let go. When he attempted to push her into the van again, Olivia repeated the same action as before, but this time her shoe slipped.

Having lost her precious footing, she arched her body and threw her head back as hard as she could, praying she'd break the asshole's nose. She hit his chin instead, but from his reaction, it still hurt him.

"You bitch!"

Releasing her mouth, he grabbed hold of her ponytail, the back of her head burning as he pulled her hair hard. He yanked her head even further backward, toward his chest. She screamed as loud as she could, praying someone would hear her cry for help.

In an effort to relieve the burning in her scalp, Olivia reached back toward her attacker's wrists. Desperate to get free, her fingers frantically clawed at his leather-clad hands. She realized a moment too late, what a mistake that move had been.

Without warning, her attacker slammed her forehead into the unforgiving side of the van. Excruciating pain exploded inside her head and hundreds of tiny, white stars flashed before her eyes.

Olivia's knees buckled as she fought to stay conscious. She felt herself being lifted. The man had just started to put her into the van. when a loud roaring sound echoed off the walls.

"Let her go!"

A blurry, male figure holding what she assumed was a gun ran toward them. The man holding her froze for a split second, then cursed.

Just like that, Olivia felt herself falling.

Tossed like a rag doll, Olivia landed hard against the cold floor. Sharp pain shot through her left hip, ribs, and elbow, but she wanted to keep fighting. Was desperate to.

Rolling over, her hands slapped loudly against the concrete as she worked to get up onto her hands and knees. The pain and nausea slowed her movements to a snail's pace, and she was still struggling to stand when two deafening gunshots blasted through the air, back-to-back.

To her left, the man who'd tried to abduct her grunted loudly, his body jerking backward against the van. He was dead before he hit the ground.

"Olivia!"

Trevor's voice boomed as he kicked the dead man's gun across the floor, then squatted down next to her.

With a gentle hand on her shoulder, he sounded a bit

strained as he said, "Stay put, honey. Don't try to stand."

More than happy to oblige, Olivia plopped back down onto her butt, her entire body shaking from adrenaline and shock. She could hear Trevor on the phone calling for help but didn't pay attention to his words. He was okay, and she was okay. In that moment, nothing else mattered.

Chapter 6

"Shit. Fuck. *Fuck!* They got him, man! They got Carlos!" Marcus spoke too loudly.

Parked in the Emergency Room loading and unloading area, he and Marcus watched the scene from their rented SUV.

"Yes. They did," he answered his remaining partner quietly.

"So, it's over right? We're calling it off?"

He turned to face Marcus. "Why would I do that?"

The guy looked back at him as though he had gone insane. "Why would you—Carlos is dead, man! The whole plan hinged on him grabbing the woman for us. We're screwed."

"Actually…" he spoke calmly. "This works to our advantage."

"How in the fuck do you figure?"

"Drive," he ordered Marcus. "Take us to Carlos's apartment."

Forehead covered in sweat, Marcus argued. "Why the hell do you want to go there?"

"I'll explain on the way, but we need to hurry."

In an uncharacteristic moment of agreement, Marcus put the SUV into drive.

With one more glance at the flashing lights, he started to smile. Yes, Carlos's death would work out just fine.

****

"Where is she?"

Sitting sideways on the hospital bed, her legs dangling over the edge, Olivia heard Jake's voice seconds before the curtain giving her privacy flew to the side.

He stepped into the room, his presence instantly sucking all of the air out of the tiny space.

The expression on his face changed quickly from relief, to guilt, and then finally, rage. His gaze moved up to the icepack she was holding against her forehead.

"Liv." He rushed to her side, gently cupping the uninjured side of her face with his hand. "Baby, are you okay? How do you feel?"

"Like someone slammed my head into a van."

She tried to smile, but her joke fell flat when her voice cracked at the end.

Slowly reaching up, Jake pulled her hand and the ice pack away. When his eyes found the swollen bruise there, a muscle bulged in his jaw. He looked like he wanted to kill.

"Sweetheart, I'm about a second away from completely losing it, here. Don't bullshit me. What did the doctors say?"

Olivia's chest tightened, and her eyes filled. Jake's fear radiated through his touch, and she hated that he was so worried for her. She opened her mouth to answer, but Trevor walked in just then, beating her to the punch.

"That she has a mild concussion but is otherwise okay.

Her eyes slid over to Trevor. God, when she thought about how close he came to dying today—Olivia's bottom lip began to quiver.

"I'm fine, honey," Trevor said, sensing her guilt over what had happened. "I told you before, it's just a bruise, so you can quit looking at me as though I should be lying on a slab in the morgue."

Jake shook his head. "Jesus, Trev."

"No, he's right." Olivia, gave him a shaky smile and used her free hand to swipe at a tear. "We should just focus on the fact that we're both okay."

Maybe if she kept telling herself that, she wouldn't break down into a sobbing mess.

Returning his gaze to hers, Jake leaned in and gave her a gentle kiss before pulling away and whispering, "I'm so sorry, baby. I should have been here. I should have told Senator Cantrell to kiss my ass and stayed with you instead of worrying about the business."

"No, you shouldn't have," Olivia returned the ice to her head. "R.I.S.C. isn't just another business, Jake. What you and your team do is important. You were exactly where you should have been. Besides, if you'd stayed, it would have been you that man shot. And I seriously doubt you would have been wearing a vest." Olivia blinked quickly, forcing away more tears threatening to escape.

While waiting in the parking garage for medical help to arrive, Trevor told her he'd chosen to take the extra precaution at the last minute, thinking he should treat it as he would on any other job, just in case. *Thank God.*

Pushing her own guilt aside, she said, "You heard Trevor. I'm a little banged up, and yeah, I was beyond terrified. I'm still a little shaken, but otherwise I'm fine."

"A concussion is serious, Liv."

"I'm well aware of that, and I promise I will tell you

immediately if I notice any of the warning signs coming on. But right now, I just really want to go home."

Her head was throbbing, and she was a little nauseated, but she'd get a heck of a lot more rest at home than in a hospital with nurses constantly coming in to check her vitals.

Still battling with the decision, Jake asked, "What did the doctor say about you leaving?"

"That he trusts me to come back in if I feel worse. I've already signed the release form." He still didn't look completely convinced, so she added, "I work here, Jake. I know how this goes, and I really don't want it to be like when I first came back to Dallas, with everyone looking at me and whispering about what happened. Please...can we just go home?"

His face softened. Taking her free hand in his, he smiled. "Of course, sweetheart."

Jake then turned to Trevor, shooting off rapid-fire questions. "What are local authorities saying? Any idea who this guy was or why he went after Liv? And what about you...are you good with the cops?"

Trevor shoved his hands into his jeans pockets. "Liv and I have both already given our statements, which corroborated what they saw when they pulled the security footage from the garage. I've been cleared, and they've already declared it a justified shooting. The sheriff seems like a stand-up guy. Name's Mahoney. I told him I work for R.I.S.C. and shared the short version of what we do with him. Thought maybe he'd be more willing to share if he knew."

"And?"

Trevor gave him a smug smile. "It worked. The perp's name was Carlos Hernandez. His rap sheet's long, going all the way back to when he was in juvie. Started with petty stuff—vandalism, theft, that sort of thing. As he got older, things got more serious. Most recently, he's been in for assault and was charged with armed robbery. That should have put him in for a stretch, but the lucky bastard got off on a technicality."

"Yeah, well…looks like his luck ran out today."

Trevor grunted his agreement. "Before the nurses rushed in to take care of Liv, I snapped a pic of the bastard's face and sent it to Derek. If there's more to know about the man, he'll find it. In the meantime, Mahoney gave me Hernandez's addresses. I'm going to head over there now to see if they've found anything. I wasn't going to leave her until you got here."

"Thank you," Jake said sincerely. "Damn glad you were wearing that vest, man." The two men shook hands and shared a look that seemed to say it all.

"Oh, and the sheriff offered his personal apology for his deputy not taking Liv's complaints about the phone calls and the snake more seriously. The kid's been put on administrative leave, pending an investigation as to why he didn't."

This bit of news surprised Olivia. "Really?"

Trevor nodded. "Apparently, this isn't the first time the young deputy hasn't followed through like he should have. I have a feeling his career in law enforcement is going to be short-lived."

"I didn't want anyone to lose their jobs," Olivia muttered. "I just wanted the craziness to stop." Olivia started to slide off the edge of the bed, both men rushed toward her.

"Easy," Jake said as he took her elbow to steady her.

"I'll go get the wheelchair," Trevor offered.

"That's not necessary, Trev. I can walk."

Ignoring her, Trevor left the room. He returned less than a minute later with the chair, and Olivia didn't bother to argue. With these two, it was pointless.

As promised, Trevor waited until she was safe and secure in Jake's truck before leaving the hospital to meet the sheriff.

When Jake pulled into her driveway, she immediately sensed something was different. As they made their way to her porch, she noticed two new lights, one on each corner of the porch's roof.

"They're motion sensitive," Jake explained from behind her.

"There are two more on the back of the house, along with a small camera there." He pointed to the upper left corner of her doorframe. "They record a live feed, which is connected to yours and Derek's computers."

She turned to face him. "Why does Derek need a live recording of my front and back doors on his computer?"

"It's just as a backup, in case something happens to your laptop."

Olivia's heart felt heavy. Just this morning, she'd been thinking how good it felt to live a somewhat normal life, and now this.

"Don't be mad at Derek" Jake's hands rested on her tense shoulders. "He was just following orders. You can be pissed at me if you want, but I'm still not taking them down. Until we know more about this Hernandez guy and why he came after you, I'm taking every precaution I can to protect you. And even if it turns out he is our guy, the cameras are staying put."

That heavy heart began to thump harder in her chest. "What do you mean *if*? He has to be the one who did all those things. It's the only thing that makes sense."

"I'm sure you're right. But the fact is, you're out here all alone. And as much as I'd love to, I can't be here twenty-four-seven. Sweetheart, I need to know you're safe when I'm away."

The near-desperate tone of his voice tugged at her chest. Olivia took his hand in hers and gave it a squeeze. "I'm not mad at you or Derek. It was sweet of you both to do this. And to be honest, it does make me feel safer out here." She went onto her tiptoes and kissed him. "Thank you."

After stepping into her house, Jake shut the door behind them and entered her alarm code. Before she knew it, Olivia found herself wrapped in the warmth and safety of his strong embrace. She hugged him back with everything she had.

For a moment in that garage, she'd thought she would never see him again. Tears fought their way to the surface, but she refused to let them fall.

They stood like that for a solid minute before he released her.

"How are you feeling?" he asked, while taking one side of her face into his palm. "Any dizziness?"

"No," she answered honestly. With a smirk, she added, "I have a headache, but I'm pretty sure that's to be expected."

Staring into her eyes with an emotion Olivia didn't dare try to guess, Jake started to say something when his phone rang. Cursing under his breath, he pulled it out of his front pocket.

"It's D." Glancing back up at her, he said, "Why don't you go lie down and get some rest. I'll be back there in a bit."

Olivia wanted him to come with her, but refused to sound as needy as she actually felt.

"Okay."

After another quick peck, she turned and headed back to her bathroom. She stripped down and took a quick shower, needing to wash away the day. In the privacy of her bathroom, she finally allowed her tears to fall. Olivia cried quietly, not wanting Jake to hear. She refused to add to the guilt he already felt.

Back in her bedroom, Olivia pulled out the nightgown she'd worn in South America, the night she and Jake had first made love. She smiled, the feel of the smooth silk beneath her fingertips taking her back to that amazing night with him.

Not quite ready to go to sleep, she chose to sit in her overstuffed chair positioned near the one window in the room that faced the back yard. Desperate to fill her mind with more good memories, she reached over to the small bookshelf near the chair and picked up an old photo album before settling back against the cushions.

****

Jake slid his index finger over the screen and put the phone to his ear.

"Talk to me, D. What do you know?"

"The information I found matches what the sheriff told Trevor."

That was both good and bad news. "Okay, so the sheriff isn't holding out on us, but we still don't know why this guy tried to kill Trevor and take Olivia."

"Not yet, but they're bound to find somethin' once his place gets tossed. I'll let you know if anything else comes up."

"Roger that. Oh, and send me a copy of the security footage from the parking garage."

There was a beat of silence, and then, "Who says I have that?"

Jake smirked. "Just send it, asshole."

Derek chuckled. Jake heard a few clicks through the phone and then, "Done. You should be get it in just a few seconds."

Right on cue, Jake's phone vibrated with the notification. "Thanks, D. I appreciate it."

"I'd say anytime, but I'm hopin' we've seen the last of this shit."

"Yeah," Jake exhaled loudly. "You and me, both."

"Oh, and Jake?" Derek said at the last minute.

"Yeah?"

"That video…it's hard to watch, man. And I'm not the one in love with her."

Jake's chest tightened, but he didn't bother to denying it. "I know, but I still have to watch it. I need to know exactly what happened."

"I get it. Just remember…Trevor got the guy, and Olivia's safe there with you."

"Thanks, D."

Jake ended the call and pulled up his email. His finger hovered over the newest one, and his gut churned. He was about to see his friend get shot and the woman he loved get attacked and nearly kidnapped. Jake closed his eyes as his breathing picked up. He inhaled deeply and reopened his eyes. If she could live through it, he could damn sure do this.

His finger tapped the screen, and Jake watched his nightmare unfold. The whole thing only lasted about two minutes, but it felt like an eternity.

He was sick to his stomach, and his eyes and nose stung from his tears. It was one thing to hear Olivia and Trevor describe what took place, but to actually see it—*Jesus, baby, I'm so sorry.*

Jake wiped at his eyes and nose. He sniffed as he blinked quickly to stave off even more tears. The compulsion to kill the fucker hit hard. Too bad Trevor already took care of that.

Swallowing his anger and guilt, Jake called Homeland next. After ripping into Ryker for allowing Liv to turn away the protection Jake had ordered for her while he and his team were away, Jake proceeded to fill the other man in on everything that had happened to Liv. He then demanded that Ryker look into Carlos Hernandez as well.

Twenty minutes later, Ryker called him back with confirmation that Hernandez had no known ties to anyone involved in Cetro's human trafficking business. Nor, was he involved with any of the other men they'd taken down in connection with Olivia's abduction from Madagascar a few months back.

Jake had known the chances were slim, but when it came to Liv's safety, he wasn't assuming anything.

He'd just gotten off the phone with Ryker when Trevor called to inform him that Carlos Hernandez was definitely Liv's stalker. According to Trevor, the evidence recovered from the guy's apartment left no doubt.

The sheriff and his deputies found several pictures of Olivia from the past two months spread around the sick fuck's apartment. His computer's search engine was filled with inquiries on snakes indigenous to Madagascar, and there was a link to an underground site of sorts where one could illegally order rare animals—including the ghost snake— saved on the idiot's desktop.

As if that wasn't enough, they found a receipt for a large bouquet of daisies the same day Olivia reported her break-in. So, that was it. Case closed.

Why he chose to focus on Liv, they'd never know. Jake didn't care about the why's, though. Only that Olivia was here, with him. And she was safe.

He glanced at his watch. Nearly an hour had passed since Olivia had disappeared to shower and rest. Jake rubbed some tension out of his neck as he walked back to her bedroom to get some rest himself. The door was open just a crack, and there was a soft light spilling through it.

Slowly, Jake opened it and stepped inside the room. Instead of lying in bed, as he'd expected, he found her sitting in her oversized chair.

She was asleep, the light from a floor lamp positioned next to the chair. Trying not to disturb her, Jake reached over and turned the lamp off.

Jake started to close the curtains, but when he glanced back down at her, his hand froze, and he lost the ability to breathe.

The moonlight coming through the uncovered window illuminated her face. She looked like a vision. With her head tilted to the side, Olivia was resting against the chair's tall, cushioned back.

The dark waves of her hair cascaded down over her shoulders, and—*Fuck me*—she was wearing the nightgown from their night at the motel in Venezuela.

Jake's gaze dropped to her legs, and he swallowed hard, trying not to focus on the way one leg was bent and how the position had pushed the gown to well above her knee. He forced himself to ignore the ache he felt between his legs and how badly he wanted to touch her.

She'd been attacked. As much as he wanted her again, she needed her rest.

For the first time since entering the room, Jake noticed the small photo album lying in Olivia's lap. It was open to a page that held pictures of her, Mike, and Jake, and Pops.

They were from a camping trip Pops had taken them all

on when Jake and Mike were in high school. Jake smiled at the memory. Man, he missed that guy.

He ignored the guilt he felt for not coming clean to Olivia about what really happened to Mike. He also paid no attention to the little voice in the back of his head, telling him he needed to make that particular confession soon.

Jake already knew this. He just prayed he could find a way to make her understand.

Olivia looked so peaceful, he couldn't bring himself to wake her. Instead, he decided to put the book away, cover her with a blanket, and lie down on the bed alone.

Before leaving the hospital, the doctor had told him that they no longer woke concussion patients up every hour the way they used to, so he'd let her be. She needed to relax and get a good night's sleep.

Carefully, Jake reached for the book, but as he lifted it from her lap, Olivia came to. He sat the album onto the floor next to the chair and crouched down in front of her. She looked at him with sleepy, confused eyes.

"Jake? What is it? What's wrong?"

His brow creased. He hated that her first thought upon waking was that something bad had happened.

"Nothing's wrong, sweetheart. I didn't mean to wake you. I was just about to get you a blanket. But since you're up, you should know the sheriff's department confirmed Hernandez was the man who'd been stalking you."

She yawned, looking so damn cute, his cock twitched. Christ, it was like everything she did turned him on.

He was determined not to make a move on her tonight, but it was taking every ounce of strength he had not to push that nightgown up higher, put his head between her legs, and take her in his mouth.

"Okay," Olivia's sleepy voice interrupted his thoughts. "So, that's it, then. It's over?"

She shifted to sit up straighter. Jake nearly choked when the movement inadvertently pushed her nightgown even further up on her thighs, as he'd imagined doing himself just seconds before.

He knew she was completely unaware that, given his current position, he was now able to see the black lace panties, barely covering her, beneath it.

Clearing his throat, Jake forced himself to look back up into her eyes. The moonlight wasn't overly bright, but it was enough he could see the pain and fear that was still there.

"Yeah, baby. It's over."

He rested both hands on her knees, immediately wishing he hadn't. Not because he didn't *want* to touch her. Touching Olivia was his new favorite pastime, but he came in here to make sure she was okay, not seduce her.

Mustering up more self-control than he thought he had, Jake ignored the heat beneath his fingertips and focused on the task at hand.

"How are you feeling?"

"Better. A little sore, but I'm okay." She must have sensed the inner turmoil churning inside him, because she added, "Stop blaming yourself, Jake. This wasn't your fault."

He reached up and took her cheek in his hand. "Can't help it. I told you before, sweetheart. It's my job to keep you safe. It always has been, but lately I feel like I'm constantly failing you."

****

Olivia could barely swallow for the tightening of her throat.

She moved forward in her chair, causing his one hand to slide further up onto her thigh. Jake removed his other hand from her cheek and rested it high onto her other leg.

As always, his touch sent an electric current searing through her. It traveled up her legs, singeing the sensitive area between, and didn't stop until it reached into the depths of her soul.

Her fingers brushed against the scruff on his strong jaw. Looking into his tormented eyes, she said, "My hero. Always watching over everyone else. I can't help but wonder, though…while you're so busy protecting me, who watches over you?"

His eyes widened. His pupils darkened. And then, looking back at her with more emotion than she'd ever seen from another human being, Jake whispered, "I love you."

Olivia's tiny intake of air seemed to vibrate through the room. Shocked, she dropped her hand, letting it simply fall into her lap.

She'd wanted to hear him say those words for so long, and that moment had been so perfect…she had to have imagined them, right? This was too important not to be sure.

"Wh-what did you just say?"

For a second, he looked as surprised as she felt. Almost as if he hadn't meant to say it. Just when she was certain he was going to take those precious words back, Jake gave her that crooked smile she loved so much and shrugged.

"I said I love you." He exhaled loudly, as if he'd been holding the words back for an eternity. "God, Olivia…I love you so much it hurts And just so we're clear, this isn't a 'I-was-your-brother's-best-friend, you-and-I-have-known-each other-for-years kind of love'."

He dropped out of the squat onto his knees and took her

face between both of his hands. His gaze never strayed, and the blue in his eyes deepened with emotion. "This is a, 'you're-my-entire-world, I-can't-live-without-you kind of love'."

"Jake," Olivia whispered as tears began leaving sliver trails down her cheeks. She'd never been a crier, yet it seemed like that was all she did around him, lately. Jake simply thumbed them away.

"I'm in love with you, Liv. Have been for years."

Oh, my God! "W-why didn't you ever say anything?"

He looked up at her with such sincerity, Olivia's heart overflowed with love.

"Because, sweetheart. I don't deserve you. You should be with someone who can give you the world. A guy who won't leave you on a moment's notice to go somewhere you can't know even about for weeks on end. You should want someone who—"

Taking his hair in a death-grip between her hands, she interrupted him with a hard, fast kiss on the lips.

"I know exactly the kind of man I want to be with. I've been in love with you for as long as I can remember, Jake. I love *you*."

In that moment, Olivia's entire world shifted. Everything changed.

The looks they gave meant more. She could feel more in his touch. It was familiar, yet new. And despite everything else that was going on in her life,

Olivia's soul became filled with a sense of joy and peace she'd never known before.

Leaning up, Jake took her mouth with his, giving her every ounce of his love in that one kiss. Olivia did the same for him.

Without speaking, they both stood. Jake swooped her up into his arms and carried her to the bed, where he spent the rest of the night showing her just how much those three little words meant to him, too.

Chapter 7

"There's something I want to show you."

Olivia glanced down at the sheet covering his lower body and then back up at him. Feeling lighter than she had in months, she decided to play with him a bit.

"I hate to spoil your surprise, but"—she leaned closer, looked around her bedroom as though she were making sure no one else was listening and whispered—"I've already seen it." Laying back against her pillow, she grinned, adding, "But, hey… I'll be more than happy to look at it as many times as you need me to."

When she started to laughed at her own joke, Jake rolled on top of her, trapping her arms above her head. "You think you're pretty funny, don't you?" he teased.

Olivia bit her bottom lip and nodded. "Actually," she said, trying so hard to hold it in. "Yeah. I do."

She lost the fight and began laughing louder than before. Jake busted up right along with her. When their laughter died down, he wiped Olivia's tears of humor from her temples.

"Okay, funny girl. I'm being serious, now. I have something I want to show you. Some*place*, actually."

"Okay." She smiled up at him. "And where would one find this mysterious place?"

"Well, if you get that gorgeous ass of yours dressed, I'll show you."

And with that, Jake gave her a fast, hard kiss before hopping off of her and out of bed.

"Wait." She sat up, covering herself with the sheet. "We're going to...wherever we're going to...*now*?"

"Sure. You got someplace else you need to be?" Jake asked while he pulled on his jeans.

Olivia thought for a moment. Before Jake had gotten to the hospital, her boss had come into the examination room and ordered her to take the next two weeks off.

Thanks to all of the overtime she'd been working, Olivia had enough money saved up that she could afford it. So, she hadn't argued.

"Nope. Give me ten, and I'll be ready."

Jake looked at his watch. "You've got eight. And I'm setting the timer. Make it back early, and there might just be something in it for you."

Her eyes narrowed. "Challenge accepted."

Olivia quickly grabbed some clean clothes and ran to the bathroom. She made it back into the bedroom in seven minutes and fifty-three seconds.

Her prize? Three orgasms. Technically, she got two, but Olivia considered giving *almost* as fulfilling as receiving.

Nearly an hour later, she and Jake were still sitting in his truck when he flipped his turn signal and turned onto a paved, two-lane road.

"Are you actually taking me someplace, or are we just going to drive around in your truck all day?"

Keeping his eyes on the road, Jake smiled. "You really have no patience, do you?"

"I *had* patience." She turned her head and looked out the

back window. "But, I think it flew out the window somewhere back around mile marker fifty-two." She settled back against her seat, giving him a sarcastic grin.

Jake chuckled. "Smartass. As a matter of fact, we're just about there."

Five very long miles later, they turned on yet another paved road. This one had a sign warning trespassers that it was private land.

"Uh, Jake…" She looked over at him. "I think you took a wrong turn."

He smiled, "Trust me. I didn't."

Olivia looked at the sign as they passed by it. "But that sign said—"

"I know what the sign says. I'm the one who put it there."

"You did?"

They went around a corner and pulled up to a large, iron gate. It wasn't like one of those fancy ones with the great big initial in the middle like she'd seen on T.V. that shouted '*Look at me, I have money!*'

This one was practical. Efficient. It seemed to be saying something more along the lines of '*Keep away or I'll shoot your ass.*'

"What is this place?"

"Patience, sweetheart," was all he said before turning away.

Instead of entering a code to get in, as she'd expected, Jake leaned out the window toward a mounted box. It looked like a camera, but then, a horizontal red light appeared on the camera's screen. *No way.*

"You have a retinal scanner to get into your gate?"

She didn't care that she sounded impressed. That *was* impressive. Actually, it was really freaking cool.

Almost soundlessly, the gate in question answered for him when the two halves began to slowly open toward the paved drive in front of them. Jake, the smug bastard, gave her a smirk and a wink, before putting the truck back in drive.

"And here I thought I had a good security system," Olivia mumbled beside him. A small grunt was his only response as he drove them through the gate.

After a couple of curves and turns, the trees opened up into one of the most beautiful sights she'd ever seen. The cabin was breathtaking. It wasn't enormous or fancy, yet if Olivia had been given the opportunity to pick out the absolute perfect home, hands down, this would be it.

The ranch-style, log cabin stretched out in the middle of what looked to be an enormous piece of land. The porch was lit up and ran the entire length of the house. Olivia couldn't help but smile at the two wooden rocking chairs and small table, centered between two large windows to the right of the dark green front door.

The landscaping she could see was immaculate, its bushes and bright red flowers giving the place just the right amount of femininity. Down the hill and to the right of the house sat a large, rustic barn. There appeared to be a large fenced area behind it.

"Wow," she muttered, mostly to herself.

"Like it?" Jake asked from beside her.

Unable to pull her eyes away, she answered wistfully, "It's perfect." And it was. "What is this place?"

He turned his head toward her and reached for her hand. "My home."

She swiveled her head around, looking at him like he'd lost his mind. "Uh, did you forget? I've been to your home. Like, a million times."

Jake actually looked a little nervous when he said, "No. You've been to my apartment. This"—he motioned toward the cabin with his head—"is my *home*."

Olivia didn't know how to respond to that bit of news. She was still speechless when Jake came around to her side of the truck and opened her door.

Trying to process what he'd said, she silently followed him up the front porch and waited for him to unlock the door.

Once inside, Jake flipped on the light switch. Olivia thought she was surprised before, but that was nothing compared to what she felt now.

Her mouth dropped open as she turned in a slow circle, taking in the cabin's interior. The walls were unique. The bottom half were large logs like on the outside, and the tops were drywall, painted a neutral beige.

Absentmindedly, she noticed two newly patched holes on one of the living room walls, which hadn't been painted over yet, and assumed he'd been doing some work there.

The vaulted ceiling made the space appear much larger than it actually was, and an enormous stone fireplace nestled between two windows served as the focal point for the cozy living room. The dark leather furniture made Olivia smile because it was all so…Jake.

Olivia quickly took in the rest. Behind the living room area was the most beautiful kitchen she'd ever seen. Like the rest of the wooden furniture, the cabinets were made of a dark, solid wood. Somehow, the granite countertops, large bar area, and stainless steel appliances still worked in the otherwise rustic space.

Directly in front of her was a long hallway with several doors on either side and at the end was a set of large, double-doors. Olivia instinctively knew it was the master bedroom.

ANNA BLAKELY

Jake's bedroom. In Jake's amazingly beautiful house. A house she knew nothing about.

She turned to him and crossed her arms in front of her chest. "Spill it, McQueen."

He stepped closer to her. "I didn't tell you about this place because I…cared too much for you to."

Olivia started to tell him that made no damn sense, but he shut her down quickly.

"Do you want me to explain myself or not?"

Olivia huffed, "You've got about two seconds."

She saw the hesitation in his eyes just before he squared his shoulders.

"The truth is, I didn't tell you about this place before, because I knew if I did, then you'd want to see it."

"And that would have been a problem *why*, exactly?" she asked, clearly confused.

He lifted his hand and tucked a wayward curl behind her ear. "Because, sweetheart. I knew if I saw you standing here, in the one place where I truly feel at home, I'd screw everything up by telling you how I really felt about you."

And just like that, every ounce of anger was gone. Smiling, Olivia grabbed the back of his neck and pulled him down to her.

"I love you, too." As Jake's lips found hers, she began to wonder if someone's heart could actually burst from being too full.

****

Three days later…

"Are you sure you're okay with this?" Olivia asked him for

114

the third time since that morning.

Jake smiled and wrapped his arms around her waist. "I'm sure. It'll do you some good to get out of the house and have some girl time. Plus, I've got some stuff with the business I've been putting off for far too long. Phone calls, paperwork, you know…the *exciting* side of R.I.S.C." He made a gun gesture with his fingers and pretended to shoot himself in the head.

Olivia grinned. "Okay. If you're sure. I was surprised when Mac asked me to go shopping with her, since we'd only just met, but I'm actually kind of excited. I don't remember the last time I had a girls' day."

Jake hadn't planned on them staying at his place when he brought her here a few days ago, so they hadn't brought anything with them. After seeing it, Olivia hadn't wanted to leave.

With her blessing, Jake had called Mac—R.I.S.C.'s other sniper—the next morning and gave her Liv's security code and a list of things to pack. Later that day, Mac brought Liv's things to the cabin, and she and Liv hit it off instantly.

"Truth be told, I think Mac is more excited about your little outing than you are," Jake said, smiling. "I'm pretty sure she likes to shop as much as she likes to shoot."

That made Olivia laugh. "Yeah, I gotta say, when you first told me 'Mac' actually stood for 'McKenna', I was surprised. I was even more shocked when this petite, cheerleader-looking blond walked in carrying my stuff."

Jake chuckled. "She tends to have that effect on people."

Jake's doorbell rang, and he went to answer the door. "Speak of the devil."

"Hey, boss. Your lady ready to roll?" Mac greeted Jake with a smile, her blue eyes hidden behind her designer sunglasses.

"Yes, I am!" Olivia spoke up from behind him, not giving him a chance to answer.

Jake moved to the side to give Olivia room to get by. She stopped in front of him and raised up on her toes for a kiss. Even in heels, she still had to lift up to reach his mouth.

Mac mumbled something about waiting in the car, but Jake didn't pay much attention. He was too busy kissing his woman goodbye.

Goodbye. A sharp pang struck his chest as Jake thought of the conversation he had planned for them tonight.

It was another reason why he'd been more than happy to let her spend the day away from the cabin.

He needed time to plan. Strategize. Jake had to figure out a way to tell her about her brother that wouldn't end with her telling him she never wanted to see him again.

Jake deepened the kiss. If this ended up being their last, he was determined to take in every last drop of her love while she was still willing to give it.

"Wow. That was some kiss goodbye, soldier."

Jake forced a smile. "Have fun today."

She tilted her head, those little wrinkles forming between her brows. "You okay?"

"Yeah." He smiled wider. "I'm good. Now go," he swatted her butt, loving the cute, ruffled skirt she was wearing. She didn't dress up often, but man, when she did—*damn.*

"Have your girls' day. Drink overpriced coffee, eat tiny little pastries, and spend a ridiculous amount of money on a bunch of stuff you don't really need."

Olivia laughed as she walked past him. "Been on a lot of

these, have you?"

"I watch movies," he joked.

"Why, Jake McQueen. I never pictured you a chick-flick fan."

He gave her a real smile then. "Just go, before I give you another swat."

Olivia tilted her head and looked at him thoughtfully.

This time, his brow furrowed. "What?"

"I'm just trying to decide how long I would have to stand here before that happens." She winked and blew him a kiss, before walking out the door.

Jake laughed, but as he closed the door behind him, his smile faded. The woman he loved had no idea that, in a few short hours, her world would come tumbling down.

Chapter 8

An hour later, Jake stormed down the hill, wanted to howl out his frustration. He opened the man-door to the barn and headed toward his favorite horse's stable.

Riding always helped to clear his mind. Gave him time to think. And if he didn't think of something fast, he feared he'd lose Olivia forever.

Jake approached the familiar stall. Champ, his favorite horse, looked over at him, and he could have sworn the horse was glaring. Not that he could blame him. Jake hadn't been around much lately to give him the attention he should.

His hired hand—a trusted Army vet Ryker had put him in contact with—came once a day when Jake was away for work. He'd saddle Champ and Daisy up, taking each one for a ride around the property and made sure they were groomed and fed.

Since bringing her here, Jake had taken Liv riding, but that had been the first time in a long time he'd given his horses some quality attention.

"Hey, buddy." Jake reached out and rubbed Champ's coarse, brown hair. "You still mad at me?"

The horse blew air from his nose in a loud huff, but Jake

figured all was forgiven when Champ nudged his hand.

Drawing in a deep breath, Jake welcomed the smell of wood, hay, and horses. He smiled, loving the tranquility of it all. He was about to unlatch the stall door when the hairs on the back of his neck stood on end. Suddenly, Jake knew he wasn't alone.

He reached behind him, pulling the weapon he never left home without—not even to go for a short ride—from his back waistband.

With the safety off, Jake spun around, holding his gun out in front of him. He didn't see anyone, but that didn't matter. His gut told him someone else was there.

Keeping his back to Champ's stable, Jake held his gun with both hands, moving silently. His arms were steady as he pointed the weapon toward the front of the barn.

Jake's heart jumped when he heard a slight shifting sound coming from one of the far stalls. One that currently should have been empty.

Blood rushed past his ears and adrenaline shot through his system as Jake moved his finger to the trigger. He drew in a calming breath and held it. He was ready to fire when a familiar voice filled the tense air.

"You can lower your weapon, McQueen. I don't think Olivia would be too happy if you killed me."

Jake exhaled slowly, his heart working double-time to go back to its normal. He was re-positioning his gun against his back when the other man came out of the stable.

"Probably not," Jake responded. "Except you're already dead, so—" he let his voice trail off.

One corner of Mike Bradshaw's mouth turned up into a crooked smile. "Good point."

In spite of the impossible situation he was facing with

Liv—all thanks to the man standing in front of him—Jake couldn't deny he missed his friend something fierce.

Walking over to him, Jake extended his hand and said, "You're taking one hell of a risk coming here, Mike."

Olivia's 'dead' brother shook Jake's hand before pulling him in for a hug. The guy never had shied away from showing his emotions. *I guess some things never change.*

"Damn good to see ya, man," Mike said sincerely as his strong hands slapped against Jake's back.

"You, too." Jake returned the hug. They broke away, and Jake shook his head. "But, seriously, Mike. You really shouldn't be here. Olivia's staying here." Then, he quickly added, "Just for a few days. She's been pretty stressed, and I wanted to bring her here. To get away from everything."

He was rambling. *What the hell?* He and Olivia were both consenting adults. Not to mention the fact that her brother had allowed her to believe he'd been killed in a tragic training accident ten years before. So, Mike really shouldn't have a say in who she dated.

"I know. I saw her leave with that really hot blond."

Mike's eyebrows bounced up and down a couple times, and if he noticed Jake's overdone attempt to explain his sister staying at his place, he didn't say anything.

"You saw them leave?" Jake looked at his watch. "That was over an hour ago. What the hell were you doing, sneaking around my place for an hour?"

He'd set up the retinal scanner to detect Mike's eyes the last time his friend was here, so he didn't have to ask how he'd gotten in.

Mike grinned. "I'm not a complete idiot. What if they'd forgotten their purses or some shit and had to come back? And for the record, I don't sneak."

"What about your cover? How'd you manage the time away?"

"The opportunity finally presented itself, and I took advantage. I followed Olivia's story after Madagascar." The haunted look shadowing Mike's eyes was the same one that came over Jake's whenever he thought about her time there. "I knew she'd be okay after she came home. That you'd keep her safe. I just...I don't know. I guess I had to see her for myself. She wasn't at her new house or the hospital she works at now, so I figured this was the next best place to check. She doing okay?"

Jake didn't bother asking Mike how he'd been able to keep tabs on his sister while under cover. The guy had just as many—if not more—contacts than he did.

"She had some trouble when she first came home. Some jackass began stalking her, but Trevor took him out a few days ago. She's good now. Really good, actually."

Mike rubbed the back of his neck, his hand sliding beneath the ponytail he'd been sporting for the past several years as part of his cover.

"Damn, that girl never could stay out of trouble for long. So, where were she and Blondie headed?"

Jake wanted to laugh. It was a damn good thing Mac wasn't around to hear Mike's nickname for her. Otherwise, Mike really *would* be dead.

"Shopping." Jake grimaced. He'd rather face down the enemy with his bare hands than spend an entire day going from store to store, fighting the crowds.

Mike walked over to Daisy, the horse in the stall across from Champ. Rubbing her nose, he said, "They'll be gone for a while, then. I have some time." He turned to Jake. "Wanna ride?"

Jake contemplated this. It was risky, but it had been over a year since he'd spoken to Mike, and damn it, he'd missed him. He also knew how Mac shopped.

The kick-ass sniper could drop a man where he stood from over 2,000 yards without so much as breaking a sweat. She also could have coined the phrase, *Shop 'til you drop.* They should have plenty of time for a ride.

"Come on, brother," Mike prodded him. "It's been a hell of a long time since you and I rode together."

"Too long," Jake nodded in agreement.

Mike grinned. "Well, alright then."

After saddling the horses, Jake and Mike headed out the back of the barn and across the great expanse of his land.

Mike shifted on Daisy's back, his eyes darting out over the horizon and then back toward the cabin. No matter what he said about being safe here, the man still looked around for possible threats. That, and the sister who still thought he was dead.

"You're safe here, Mike," Jake assured him. "The land is secure, and we've got plenty of time. Mac's a soldier to the core, but I swear the woman could turn shopping into an Olympic sport."

Mike's broad shoulders relaxed, and he grinned. "Well, in that case," he let some of his southern drawl slip. "Wanna race?"

Jake's blood pumped with excitement. Nothing beat the rush of riding full-speed on his horse. An image of Olivia lying beneath him, naked and satiated, flashed through his mind. Okay, almost nothing. He grinned in spite of himself.

"First one to the pond just over that hill?"

Mike followed Jake's gaze to the large mound in the distance. "What's the wager?"

"We'll keep it low. Say, a Benjamin?"

"You're on."

Without warning, Mike spurred Daisy with the heels of his boots and with a "Ha!" he took off.

"Cheating bastard," Jake mumbled and shook his head, smiling.

He closed in on Mike, loving that he was able to spend time with his best friend again. Guilt tried to wiggle its way in, but he pushed it away for now, not knowing when—or if—they'd ever get the chance to do this again.

Mike had worked damn hard to get accepted into some of the most dangerous organizations in the world. Every day he survived without being made was like living on borrowed time.

He was the best there was for jobs like the ones he took on, but even the best could have a bad day.

The two men reached the pond at the exact same moment, but of course, each one swore his horse had gotten their first. After going back and forth a few times, they both finally agreed it was a tie and left it at that.

They dismounted and led their horses to the water's edge for a drink. Standing silently for a few minutes, both became lost in their own thoughts.

Jake wasn't sure what was going through Mike's mind, but all he could think of was everything that had transpired between him and Olivia during the past few months.

Lost in the moments they'd shared—both good and bad—Jake didn't know how in the hell he'd survive it if she left him, once he told her the truth.

Mike finally broke the silence when he cleared his throat. In a somber voice said, "Thanks for watching out for her, Jake. I know it sounds crazy given the situation, but I don't know what I'd do if I lost her." The man's voice was thick with emotion.

Trust me, buddy. I know how you feel. "I'm not going to let anything else happen to her, Mike."

Mike turned to face him. "I know you won't. And in case I've never said it, thank you. For watching out for her all these years. For saving her from those bastards and bringing her back home."

Jake swallowed back his own emotions. "Don't have to thank me for that, man. Not ever."

Mike tilted his head once and then went back to staring out over the beautiful horizon. Jake used the opportunity to take in just how different his friend looked.

It had been over a year since he'd seen him, and the guy was damn near unrecognizable. Of course, that was kind of the point, given the whole undercover gig.

Before going deep, Mike had always kept his hair military short and his face clean-shaven. Even in high school, he'd get a haircut the second it got long enough to start brushing the tops of his ears. Said it bugged the hell out of him.

The man standing before him, now, had a long, dark brown ponytail that reached down to the middle of his shoulders. His beard was unkempt, and the tattoos peeking out from under his short sleeves were some he'd never seen before. He looked like a total thug, but Jake knew that was far from the truth.

"It should have been me keeping her safe," Mike growled. "*I* should have been here to protect her." Even from the side, Jake could see the guilt in his friend's eyes.

"Kind of hard to do from the grave." Jake put his hand on the guy's shoulder. "I won't stop watching over her, Mike. Not ever."

He briefly considered telling Mike about his relationship with Liv, but decided not to, for fear his friend would return to his job distracted. Mike needed to keep a clear head.

Jake guessed it was why his friend had felt the need to see Olivia with his own eyes. Now that he had, Mike could focus on what needed to be done without personal shit getting in the way and putting him at risk.

Giving Jake an earnest nod, Mike looked at his watch. "Speaking of the little hellion, we should probably head back. I'm sure we have time before she gets home, but better not chance it.

The two men remounted and headed back toward the ranch. There was no racing this time. Their movements were slow and steady as they made their way back to the barn.

After a few quiet moments, Mike said, "So, don't bullshit me, Jake. How is she? Really."

Jake smiled, "She's good. No bullshit. Stubborn as ever, but she's good."

He opted to not share with Mike what had happened at the hospital. The guy was shouldering enough guilt already. He wasn't going to add to it unnecessarily.

The corners of Mike's mouth turned up in a sad smile. "Good. I'm glad." He was quiet for a time and then, "I've missed out on so much with her."

Jake waited a beat and then asked, "Was it worth it?"

Mike drew a deep breath in then let it out slowly. "If you'd asked me eight years ago, I'd have said yes. Hell, if you'd asked me two years ago, I probably would have said yes. These guys are bad news, Jake. I've been able to help put away some of the worst people out there. It's not just about selling illegal weapons and trading government information anymore. It's all about skin trade with these freaks. Fucking sick shit, man."

Jake understood his friend's anger all too well.

"The guy I'm in with now, Alexandar Volkov, is seriously bad news. And his sons are no better. Ivan, the oldest, is even worse than his old man. Total piece of shit. Uses his strip clubs as a way for his buyers to get a look at *merchandise* before spending their hard-earned money." Mike's words were laced with sarcasm. "Those women have no idea, either. They think they're just there to dance and maybe give a few private shows behind the curtains. Some are barely legal."

Continuing on, Mike's anger became more noticeable. "One night, they're on stage, the next they've suddenly 'quit' their jobs and moved on. Ivan is as good as his dad at making sure the stink from his shit doesn't touch him. He can't wait for the day Alexandar kicks the bucket so he can take over the family business. Mikhail, the youngest son, wants out, but he knows going against his father and brother would be suicide."

Mike took a breath and shook his head. "I've been working that angle for a while, and I'm finally close to breaking him. I can *feel* it. If I could just turn him, then good ol' dad and Ivan, along with the rest of the Russian bastards, will go down for good. But Mikhail's been too scared to give us anything concrete that we can use in court. Shitty thing is, I can't blame the poor sonofabitch."

Jake wasn't surprised that Mike was sharing such detailed information. Jake had the same clearance level as Mike, so Mike wouldn't be in trouble for reading him in.

"Couldn't you testify on what you've seen? From what you've just said, I would think you'd have enough to put them all away by now."

"I've got Mikhail dead to rights, which is why I've been

leaning hardest on him. Ivan…maybe, but not Alexandar. I'm tellin' ya, the guy's damn near untouchable. I could get the smaller fish, which would definitely hurt their empire, but my bosses want them all."

Mike ran a frustrated hand over his jaw. "And Alexandar Volkov isn't stupid. He's covered his tracks over the years and made sure nothing could be tied directly back to him. Well, almost nothing. We're so close, but I need Mikhail's help. I convince him, and we'll take Volkov down once and for all. Once the top falls, the rest will be scrambling to make deals. Problem is, even if I do get Mikhail to agree to everything, there's no guarantee that when the time comes he'll actually have the guts to take the stand."

Mike paused, lost in thought for a moment. "So to answer your original question, in the beginning, I was sure it was worth it."

"And now?" Jake asked, sensing his friend was struggling.

Mike looked over their surroundings and shook his head. "Now…" He inhaled deeply and let it out slowly. "Now, I don't know, man. Everything we've done has made a real difference to a hell of a lot of people. But you only get one shot at this, you know?" Mike was still looking out at the wide-open space longingly, and Jake knew his friend was talking about life.

"You could quit," Jake only half-teased. "Do some real work for a change."

Mike chuckled but, then, got serious fast. "I've been thinking about it. A lot, actually."

Jake swung his head to the side, surprised. "Seriously?"

Mike turned to him, not a trace of humor in his expression. "This cover has just about reached its end. If I can't convince Mikhail to help us soon, then they're going to either get someone else in who can or settle for what they can get with what we have now." He sighed, his eyes filled with resignation. "Either way, I'm done, Jake."

Jake recognized the look, and it wasn't a good one to have when working deep undercover. He'd seen a lot of guys burn out. They'd make a fatal mistake, or say fuck it, and join the other side.

Mike would never trade sides. Jake was as sure of that as he was his love for Olivia. But the guy was right. He clearly needed out of that life. Jake just prayed Mike could make that happen before he did something stupid like getting killed for real.

"So, what are you going to do?" Jake asked his friend. "It's not like you can just rise from the dead after ten years."

Mike shrugged one shoulder. "Maybe, maybe not. After all, it *is* the U.S. Government. They can always come up with some sort of explanation. And given everything I've done for them, you bet your ass I'll find a way when I'm ready. One thing's for sure, though. Whether I come back as Mike Bradshaw or someone else, it'll be for good."

Mike gave a brief pause then continued with, "It'd be one thing to do what you and your teams does. To be able to work a job here and there and come back home. To a *real* home and an actual life that belongs to you, and not some fictional character. Like this"—Mike glanced around at the property again— "You're gone when you're needed, but then, you get to come back to all of this. You've planted roots, man. Hell, I couldn't even tell you the last time I went on a date. An *actual* date with someone I liked, not a piece I was just using to gain intel."

Mike's hand scrubbed over his beard again. "Shit, Jake. I look back at my life, so far, and I've got nothing to show for it. Not personally, anyway. I'm thirty-four years old with no wife, no kids. Hell, my dad died, and I couldn't even go to his fucking funeral. Or Liv's for that matter. Though, thank Christ, that turned out differently."

Jake couldn't agree more.

"I don't know, man," Mike went on. The guy clearly needed to vent to someone he trusted. "I've left my sister alone all this time, even when she was going through her own hell, and for what? I mean, at least if I did what you do, I'd have the option to settle down somewhere. Start a family of my own."

Jake was surprised at that. Until recently, he'd never seen his job as one that was conducive to a long-term relationship, let alone a family. He was still worried about how they'd manage it, and wondered how Mike thought it could work.

"You think so?"

"Hell, yeah. It's no different than being career military. Better, actually. You guys are home a lot more and have the freedom to pick and choose the jobs you take. No government contract that owns your ass. It's your choice. You make the decisions."

Jake shook his head. "I don't know. I think about the situations we go into. Hell, my last job kept me away for two solid months. The thought of leaving Li...a wife at home to worry, or worse, take care of everything on her own if something happened to me?"

Damn, that was close. No telling how Mike would have reacted to that little slip. "I always figured it would be pretty fucking selfish to ask someone to live that way."

"Women are a hell of a lot stronger than we give them credit for, Jake. Shit, my sister's a perfect example. After everything she's been through, she keeps pushing forward. I don't know how she's done it all these years on her own."

This time, Jake couldn't hide his smile or the affection in his voice. "She's the strongest woman I know."

Mike tilted his head, and Jake worried he'd given himself away. He moved his eyes forward, doing his damnedest not to show how he truly felt about the guy's little sister.

Somber again, Mike said, "We almost lost her in that jungle. When I heard she was gone, what those bastards had done to her and the others…that was the closest I've ever come to blowing a cover."

Jake looked over at his friend and vowed, "I'd die before letting anything else happen to her."

Mike simply nodded. He may have 'died' himself years before, but Jake knew the thought of losing his sister for real was more than his friend could bear.

****

"I'm so sorry," Olivia whispered the apology to Mac as they drove down Jake's road. It was one of about twenty she'd given to her during the drive home from the mall in Dallas.

"Would you stop already? I keep telling you, there is nothing to apologize for. And if you do it one more time, I'll be forced to bring out that badass side of me you seem so fond of."

Despite the harsh words, Mac smiled at her and winked before rolling her window down and scanning her eye for entrance through Jake's gate. "I still can't believe that asshat came up to you the way he did."

Olivia gave her a quick smile back, still hating that they'd had to cut the day short because of her. It had started out great. Perfect, even.

In the first hour, they'd stopped for coffee and breakfast at a quaint little bakery then hit a few dress shops before heading to the mall.

They'd gone into one of the larger department stores. While Mac was busy trying on a pair of awesome boots with surprisingly high heels, Olivia had gone into another section nearby, looking for some new tennis shoes for work.

She was trying on a pair of her favorite brand when she caught a man staring at her.

Olivia had smiled politely, but only because they'd made eye contact. When she looked back up a few minutes later, he was still there. Staring.

It took about twenty seconds before she was overwrought with terror, flashbacks of being attacked assaulting her.

Her pulse had raced. A thin layer of sweat had formed on her brow, and she'd frantically looked toward Mac, praying she could get her attention, somehow.

When she realized Mac was too focused on the boots to notice her, Olivia had quickly turned and started walking toward the other woman. She kept her eyes looking straight ahead and not at the man who had begun to follow her.

He started to reach for her, and that's when she'd screamed. Olivia had yelled as if her life depended on it, and in that moment, she'd truly believed it had.

For a moment, she was back in Toamasina, being chased by Cetro and his men. She'd flung her arms out and swung her purse at the man trying to take her.

Except, he wasn't.

Olivia had been so busy trying to defend herself that she hadn't realized the guy wasn't actually attacking her.

Instead, he'd backed up a good five feet, and had been standing with his arms held up to show her and the other customers who'd stopped to watch the crazy lady in the mall that he meant her no harm.

Unlike Olivia, Mac had been of sound mind. She'd sped to Olivia's side, and quickly ascertained that there was no actual threat.

When Olivia had finally calmed down, she'd realized—with total humiliation—that the guy was actually much younger than she'd originally thought.

He very quickly explained to Mac that he'd seen Olivia on the news a few months before, and had simply wanted her autograph. Said he'd never met anyone "famous" before.

The poor kid had looked at her as if she was insane. Maybe, she was.

Mac parked the car close to Jake's truck, but didn't get out right away. Instead, she grabbed Olivia's hand.

"I won't say anything to Jake about what happened. It's your story to tell, if you choose. Just know that there's nothing to be ashamed of. Your reaction to that guy today was perfectly normal given what you've been through. I know from experience that terrible things happen to really good people, and there's not always an explanation or a reason why. Not one you can find, anyway."

Mac glanced away, and for a second, Olivia wondered if the other woman was referring to what she'd seen in her line of work, or if it was something more personal. She didn't have time to analyze things more because Mac quickly blinked, her eyes finding Olivia's once more.

"It takes time to sort it all out, and you, my friend, haven't had hardly any time at all to deal with everything that's happened to you. But I have no doubt that you'll get there."

Olivia wiped her leaking eyes again, grateful for her new friend. "Thank you," she said as she squeezed Mac's hand.

"Do you think you could, um…" Olivia turned and looked out the passenger window to the barn, sitting at the bottom of the hill. "Would you mind taking the bags in for me? I'd like to go see the horses. Clear my head a little before I go inside."

Jake had taken her riding, yesterday. The horses were truly majestic. Just being around them gave her a sense of peace, which was something she desperately needed now.

"Sure." Mac's smile was genuine as she added, "I can handle the boss, don't worry."

Olivia had no doubt that was true. It was hard to believe this petite woman with her cute dress and ponytail was a contract killer for hire.

Legal or not, it was still a scary thought. Olivia was just damn glad she was on Mac's good side.

The two women got out of the car, and Olivia headed down the large, grassy hill. She stopped suddenly, turning back toward Mac, who had almost made it to the porch steps.

"Hey, Mac?"

The blond warrior turned toward her. "Yeah?"

"Thank you. Maybe…I mean, when things have calmed down a bit, do you think you'd want to—"

"Name the time and place, and I'll be there," Mac interrupted with a smile. Then, she rolled her eyes dramatically. "You may have to sweet-talk my boss for me and convince him to give me the time off. In case you haven't heard, he can be a real hard ass."

Olivia chuckled as Mac winked and waved goodbye. By the time she'd made it to the barn, Olivia already felt a little better and had nearly forgiven herself for the insane reaction to being followed.

Maybe Mac was right. Who wouldn't be easily spooked

after everything she'd experienced?

Even so, she decided not to tell Jake. The last thing she wanted was for him to worry about her any more than he already did.

Olivia almost turned around to head back up to the house, but the temptation to pet the horses was still too great. She'd go in, say high to Daisy and Champ then head up to the house to find Jake. There were many ways he could make her feel better.

She smiled to herself, thinking she may even go a little crazy and keep her heels on for the first round.

Grinning at the images that thought created, Olivia reached for the barn's door. She stopped abruptly when she heard two male voices. One was most definitely Jake's, but the other was harder to distinguish.

Jake had told her that he had a guy who helped with the place when he was away for work, so maybe it was him. Or it could have been Trevor or another member of the team.

She hadn't noticed a strange vehicle in the driveway, but given her state of mind when they'd pulled in, that didn't really surprise her.

Olivia opened the door and started to go in. She smiled when she saw Jake walking toward her, but instead of smiling back, his eyes grew with that whole, deer-in-the-headlights look. Olivia had just opened her mouth to ask what was wrong when she saw him.

A pair of hazel eyes as wide as Jake's—and identical to her own—stared back at her. He had a beard and scraggly hair that had been haphazardly pulled back into a ponytail.

He was more muscular than he'd been when she'd last seen him, and his face was older now. Tanned from the sun with a few wrinkles that hadn't been there before.

But none of that mattered. There was no mistaking those eyes.

Unable to speak—or even breathe—Olivia stood frozen as the man smiled nervously and quietly said, "Hey, Junebug."

Her vision tunneled. The world began to spin around her. And within seconds, she felt herself falling.

Chapter 9

"Olivia?"

Jake's voice sounded far away, and there was an annoying tapping on her cheek. She tried to move away from it, to tell whoever was touching her face to stop. Instead, what came out was a low moan.

"It's okay, sweetheart. I'm here. Come on, now. It's time to wake up."

"Jake?"

Olivia's eyes fluttered open. Her head pounded, and at first, all she could see was a big, fuzzy blob.

As she continued to blink, Jake's face slowly came into focus. He smiled, but it didn't reach his eyes.

"Welcome back."

Her mind struggled to remember what had happened. She'd been shopping with Mac, then—*Ah, man*—her moment of total craziness at the mall.

They'd come here, to Jake's cabin. She'd gone down to the barn, and then…what? She couldn't remember anything after that.

Looking around, Olivia realized she was back in the house, lying on Jake's couch. He was crouched down in front of her, and he looked really worried. But other than a headache, she felt fine. She started to sit up.

"Easy." Jake slid his arm around her waist to help her. "Not too fast."

Once she was vertical, Olivia closed her eyes for a moment to steady herself. She actually felt okay, now. She looked back at Jake. *So, why does he look so worried?*

"What happened?"

The look Jake gave her was confusing, like a combination of guilt and relief. Which made no sense to her at all.

"You fainted."

Fainted? That couldn't be right. "I what?"

"You fainted," Jake repeated. "You don't…remember?"

He sounded hopeful. Or did he? Damn, she was confused.

"Quit messing with me, Jake. What really happened?"

He shook his head. "I'm not messing with you, Liv. You fainted. I got to you just before you landed. You're okay, though."

Olivia was getting aggravated. Mainly at herself, because she couldn't remember.

"People don't just faint for no reason, Jake. I certainly never have."

"Well, you know what they say. There's a first time for everything."

The low voice came from behind her, and suddenly, Olivia was back at the barn.

She was standing just inside the door, and someone else was inside. Standing next to Jake. *Mikey was in the barn with Jake.*

"It's not possible." She stared into Jake's eyes.

Jake whispered a curse before glaring at whoever was standing behind her. "I told you to wait."

In her peripheral, Olivia saw a man walk around the end

of the couch and stop next to where Jake was still squatted.

She licked her dry lips and swallowed hard, too terrified to look up. Jake reached for her hands, which were now in a white-knuckled grip on her lap.

"I promise I can explain everything, Liv."

Slowly, Olivia moved her eyes upward, her breath catching in her throat as she made eye contact with...*him*.

She couldn't bear to even think his name because it was impossible to believe. She swallowed again before speaking, trying to stay strong, but her shaky voice betrayed her.

"W-who are you?"

The man smiled, making him appear younger. "It's me, Junebug. Mikey."

Olivia's eyes shot back to Jake's. "Is this some kind of sick joke?"

His swallow was audible, his eyes too serious. "No, sweetheart. It's no joke." There was no mistaking the guilt in Jake's eyes.

Her questions came out one right after the other. "What is this, then? What's going on, Jake? I...I don't understand. Why would you do this to me?"

The man pretending to be her brother stepped forward. "Junebug listen, I—"

"Stop it!" Olivia yelled. "Stop calling me that! My *brother* was the only one who called me that, and he's dead!"

Hearing this man—whoever he was—use the nickname her brother had dubbed her with as a young child was unconscionable.

She was suddenly dizzy and nauseated and...*confused*. Why would Jake pull such a cruel, hateful joke on her?

Olivia felt her eyes fill, and when she stood too quickly, she started to sway. Jake stood with her, gently grabbing her elbows to keep her from falling.

"Baby, I know this is a lot to take in, but I promise, if you'll just let us explain…"

Jake may have continued talking. If he did, Olivia didn't hear a word he said. Glancing up at the other man, she could actually see her brother in his eyes.

No. Her mind refused to believe it. She blinked, sending tears down over her cheeks.

Jerking her arm free, Olivia yelled, "Please do, Jake! Please explain to me why you're trying to convince me that this man is my *brother!* Mikey died ten years ago!"

As the volume of her voice increased so did her tears. She turned and started to walk away, only stopping when she heard the imposter speak.

"I didn't die, Olivia. They just made it look that way."

Very slowly, Olivia turned around and moved back toward the man. She stopped directly in front of him and glared into those all-too-familiar eyes. He kept talking…or at least tried to.

"I've been working undercover and—"

Olivia didn't even realize she'd swung her arm until she felt the sting on the palm of her hand from where it had made contact with the guy's cheek. His head snapped to the side from the impact of the blow, which he simply took as if it were deserved.

Speaking in an emotionless voice that even she didn't recognize, Olivia said, "I don't know who you are, and I don't care. I just want you gone."

She turned and walked toward the hallway, wanting to get away from him, and—for the first time in her life—Jake, as fast as she possibly could.

"When you were seven, you broke Mom's favorite picture

frame. You threw your plastic Cinderella play shoe at me. You were mad because I'd pulled your new Barbie doll's head off."

Olivia stumbled to a stop but kept her back to the two men.

"And when you were thirteen, I caught you and Jennifer Green smoking cigarettes behind the garage. I made you both swear to me that you'd never smoke again, or I'd tell Pops."

Her breath hitched. She ignored the tears, now, not caring that they were running down the length of her neck.

It can't be. She'd *buried* Mike. She'd held her dad's hand as they stood over his grave and cried together. As they told him goodbye.

Olivia heard movement from behind her and knew he was stepping slowly toward her. She wanted to run, but her feet refused to budge.

She didn't turn around, though. Mostly for fear she'd start to believe the man's lies.

"I call you Junebug because when you were born, mom told me your middle name was June. It reminded me of June bugs, and the name stuck."

Olivia's hand flew to her mouth, holding back her sobs while the man continued to talk.

"The night before I left for boot camp, we both sat in your room on that God-awful boy band comforter of yours and made promises to each other. I made you promise to watch over Pops, to do good in school, and to stay away from that prick, James Marshall. You made me promise to make it through camp, and I swore to you, I wouldn't give up. No matter how hard it got."

Oh, God. How could this man know all of these things?

"You also made me pinky swear that I'd look out for Jake.

You told me I'd better make sure nothing happened to him, or you'd find a way to sneak onto base and strangle me in my sleep. Then, you said when you were finished with me, you'd find my girlfriend at the time, Tiffany Walker, and tell her about Michelle Haynes kissing me behind the concession stand after the Homecoming game."

A strangled sound escaped from Olivia's throat. Her mind raced with pain and confusion. She'd never told anyone else any of those things. Only Mikey knew, and he was dead. *Wasn't he?*

Olivia turned back around slowly. She had to wipe her eyes in order to focus on the man's face.

He was standing right in front of her, now. She studied him closely. The corners of his mouth turned up just enough to see the dimples in his cheeks, even beneath the dark beard.

He had her brother's strong cheekbones and a slightly crooked nose. Mikey had broken his once. He'd gotten into a fight after school when he saw a kid bullying a younger girl.

Her brother was a lot like Jake, even back then. Always protecting those he cared for and those who couldn't protect themselves.

She wiped her eyes again, her breath catching when she saw the small scar at the base of his bottom lip. Mikey had gotten stitches in that exact same spot when he was in high school. He'd been showing off for a girl in his class.

They were swimming in her backyard pool. Misjudging the distance he needed to jump away from the diving board, Mikey had flipped off of it, smacking his face in the process.

Later that night, he'd bragged to his friends about the three stitches he'd received...and the sympathy date he'd scored out of the whole ordeal.

Olivia's bottom lip quivered, and when she looked back

up into those eyes—her *brother's* eyes—she realized she was seeing them for the first time in ten, long years.

"Mikey?" she whispered his name.

He smiled wider, making his dimples cave in deeper. "Yeah, Junebug. It's me."

Olivia cried out and leapt into her brother's arms. She squeezed him as hard as she could, sobbing loudly, and not caring one bit.

For a moment, the two didn't move. They stood in the middle of Jake's living room, trying their damndest to give each other a decade's worth of love in that one hug.

When she eventually pulled back, Olivia ran her hand slowly across his hairy jaw.

"How is this even possible?"

Mike looked down at her and tried to explain. "Ten years ago, Jake and I had just finished a job with Delta. I went in for the debriefing, like always. But instead of the standard questions, I was put into a room with a man I'd never seen before. He was with a non-military government agency. Long story short, he was putting together a special team. An off the radar, deep cover team. Originally, I was told it would only be a year or two. But the government being what it is, ten years later, I'm still in."

Olivia was dumbfounded. "I can't believe this. All this time...I thought you were *dead*."

He looked at her regretfully. "It was necessary, Liv. For my safety, sure, but more importantly, for yours and Pop's. If the people I've been taking down knew who I really was, they would have been able to use you and Pops against me."

"But...I don't understand. *Why?* Why did you agree to do it?" Without warning, Olivia's joy over her brother being alive transformed into an uncontrollable anger. "We were your *family*, Mikey. I'm your *sister*. How could you just walk away like that? From me…from Pops?"

Mikey's look softened, but he only said, "I told you. It was complicated. The job was—"

"Fuck the job!" Olivia blurted out.

She ignored her big brother's raised eyebrows, knowing he'd never heard her curse like that before. Well, too damn bad. She wasn't a little kid anymore, and she was hurting.

"What about *me*? Do you have any idea what losing you did to me? Or Pops? It nearly killed him when that car pulled up to the house, and he saw the chaplain walking to the door."

She swiped more tears away, and for the first time since she'd stood from the couch, she glanced in Jake's direction.

"And what about *him*? Jake was your best friend, Mikey! Your *teammate*. How could you do that to him?"

She did a double-take, glancing at Jake again. To him, she asked, "And why aren't you as pissed off as I am? Why aren't you yelling at him, too? Or punching him in the face or *something!* You should be. He left you, too. He…"

Then, it hit her. She suddenly understood why Jake wasn't more upset, and that realization shredded her.

Feeling like someone had just kicked her in the gut with a steel-toed boot, Olivia inhaled sharply before whispering, "Oh, my God."

Panic filled Jake's eyes, and he quickly tried to explain. "Listen, Liv—"

She cut him off. "You"—she had to swallow before continuing—"you son of a bitch."

There was no mistaking the guilt smeared all over his lying face. "Olivia, please…just—"

"How long?" Her voice was surprisingly controlled now.

Jake's, however, was not.

"Sweetheart, just let me explain—"

"*Answer me!*" she screamed. Streaks of new tears marked her face. "How long have you known my brother was still alive?"

Jake took a deep breath then shattered her world. "I found out a month after his funeral."

Olivia let out a laugh of disbelief, and then covered her mouth, thinking for a moment that she was going to throw up.

"This whole time? You've known this *whole time*, and you never told me?"

"I couldn't—"

"*Bullshit!*" she yelled. Jake at least had the good grace to flinch from the outburst. "How many times, Jake? How many times did I cry on your shoulder? How many nights did I call you, bawling my eyes out because I'd had another nightmare about losing Mikey, and I couldn't go to Pops because I knew it would only upset him even more? *God!*" Olivia put her hands to her forehead. "I'm such an idiot!"

"You're not an idiot," Jake ground the words out.

Olivia ignored him. "I sure bet you had some good laughs after those phone calls, huh? Poor, clueless Olivia—"

"No, Goddammit, I *didn't* laugh. It tore my heart out to see you hurting like that. All those nights you called, I'd be up until daylight because I felt so guilty for not telling you the truth. I'd damn near decided to tell you, but—"

Mikey broke in, "Whoa, you were going to tell her? What the hell, man?"

"The dreams stopped," Jake said, ignoring him.

Olivia shook her head, and she smiled sadly. "They didn't stop, Jake."

Confused, he said, "But...you never called again. Not because of a nightmare, anyway."

Frustrated, Olivia had to force herself not to scream. "Because I realized you had a life and didn't need some college brat bothering you all the time! It was bad enough *I* couldn't sleep. There was no reason for both of us to be miserable. So, I just learned to deal with it on my own."

Jake stepped toward her, but she put her hand up to stop him and took a step back. Withdrawing from him like that hurt him. She could see it in his eyes, but she couldn't bring herself to care.

He fisted his hands at his sides. "Why didn't you tell me you were still having nightmares? I would have talked you through them. I would have figured out a way to—"

"Tell me the truth? Funny thing about that, Jake. I saw you even after I quit calling in the middle of the night. We've met for lunch how many times over the years? For God's sake, we were stuck in the freaking jungle together two months ago and thought we were going to die! I talked about Mikey then, and you *still* didn't tell me!"

She turned her back on them both and ran a frustrated hand through her hair.

"That wasn't the right time—"

Olivia swung back around. "I can't believe this."

The man she loved and the brother she'd thought was lost, were less than three feet away from her, yet she felt more alone than she'd ever been in her life.

Olivia looked back into Jake's eyes. "I thought that we..." She swallowed hard. "I can't believe I actually thought..." She swallowed again, this time to push back the bile threatening to fill her mouth. "God, Jake. I *slept* with you for Christ's sake!"

The memory of his hands running over her body, the pleasure he'd brought to her now tainted forever. He'd been lying to her that entire time about something so huge…something so unforgivable. It made her wonder, what else had he lied about?

"You said you loved me—"

"Hold up. You *slept* with him?" Mikey asked surprised, as if that was the most outrageous part of this conversation.

"Shut up, Mikey," Jake and Olivia both said in unison, never once taking their eyes off each other.

It was something they'd done countless times when they'd been younger. She would have laughed had the situation not been so totally screwed all to hell.

"So what was that? Huh, Jake? Did you sleep with me because you felt guilty for lying to me? Or did you just feel so sorry for me, that you thought you'd give me a few pity-fucks? You know, use my feelings for you against me to make yourself feel better? Tell me something…did it work?"

Jake's eyes burned into hers. He closed the distance between them in three long strides, and grabbed her shoulders, his grip just this side of painful. Even in the midst of this new insanity, Olivia knew Jake would never physically hurt her.

"Don't you *ever* say that again! Yeah, I lied to you, Olivia. For ten *fucking* years, I've lied, but I did it to *protect* you. To protect your brother and Pops. What happened between us had *nothing* to do with that. It sure as hell was more than some quick lays to appease my guilt."

Jake's nostrils flared as he drew in several quick breaths, the anger and pain in his eyes almost too much for her to bear.

"All I've ever wanted was to be with you. To give you

every part of me…the good and the bad. Holding this back, keeping this from you for so long…that was the worst kind of torture for me. So, no, Liv. The sex didn't *ease* my guilt. It made it worse. But being with you was worth it, because I love you, sweetheart. I love you more than life itself, so don't you *dare* stand there and cheapen what we have by saying it was just a few pity fucks."

Olivia wanted to believe him. With every fiber of her being, she wanted to believe him. Before today, she'd truly thought Jake loved her. Never, not in a million years, would she have doubted anything he told her. But now—

"Had, Jake. What we had. And I don't even know what that was anymore. But, hey…look at it this way. At least now you won't have poor Olivia to constantly watch out for. To always have to *protect*. You're off the hook. Yay, for you."

She jerked away from his grasp and turned toward the hallway to get her things.

"Olivia, listen to me. I know you're pissed, and you have every right to be, but you can't just leave like this."

Olivia stopped and threw her hands in the air, her frustration palpable as she turned to face them again. She'd been betrayed by the two men who always said they'd protect her, who claimed to love her, and it all came crashing down on her.

"I am so tired of men thinking they have the right to control me. To dictate how I live my life, or hell, whether or not I even get to *have* a life. First it was Cetro, then that crazed Carlos guy. Now you two want to stand there and try to explain away a lifetime of lies and pain and loss. And I'm supposed to do what, exactly? Just roll over like the good little sister and…whatever I was to you?" She gestured toward Jake. "Do you honestly expect me to just say, 'Okay, I understand. All is forgiven'? Well, fuck that. And fuck the both of you. This is *my* life, and I'll be damned if I let one more man decide what I'm going to do with it!"

This time, when Olivia walked away, neither man said a word. And when they heard the bedroom door slam shut, they both flinched.

Chapter 10

Jake was numb. He stood there with his hands resting low on his hips as he stared at those closed doors.

The last few days with Liv had been as close to perfect as he'd ever had. Just the two of them, talking and laughing. Making love for hours on end. Now, he'd be lucky if she ever spoke to him again.

Tears pricked the corners of his eyes as he pictured the way she'd looked at him when she realized he'd known about Mike all along. The betrayal she felt was a living, breathing thing.

For the first time in his life, Olivia had looked at him as if he was a stranger. The love they'd finally allowed themselves to embrace had been damaged, most likely beyond repair. He'd done that, and God, it *hurt*.

Jake rubbed his chest, pressing above his aching heart but found no relief. He closed his eyes and hung his head, his shoulders sagging as he continued to stand there, trying to make sense of what had just happened.

He'd done this to himself. To *them*, and he didn't know how to fix it. He'd find a way, though. He had to.

Maybe Olivia just needed some time to truly understand why he did what he did.

When Jake opened his eyes again, he saw a fist coming straight at him. Pain exploded in his jaw as Mike's blow struck, snapping his head to the side and nearly toppling him over. He grabbed the back of the couch to keep from falling on his ass.

"What the hell was that for?" Jake asked as he rubbed his tender jaw.

"That's for sleeping with my sister and, then, making her cry."

Mike punched him again. "And *that's* for keeping me in the dark about the two of you."

Jake righted himself and readjusted his jaw. He took several deep, heaving breaths and glared at his friend.

"Feel better now?"

Mike said nothing, at first. He just kept scowling at Jake as if he wanted to hit him again. Their staring contest finally ended when Mike's eyes softened, and surprisingly, the corner of his lips rose slightly.

"Actually, I do."

"Good," Jake said, his jaw throbbing, now. "I'll give you those two. Next time, I'm hitting back."

Mike chuckled and shook his head. "Yeah, well...what kind of big brother would I be if I didn't deck the man boinking my little sister?"

Despite their age and the fact that Mike had been noticeably absent from Liv's life for several years, Jake actually felt a little embarrassed that his buddy knew what he'd been doing with the guy's sister. *To* his sister.

Memories assaulted him, and that ache from before morphed into a sharp, searing pain.

"There was more to it than that, Mike. A *hell* of a lot more."

"I know," Mike said solemnly. "It's the only reason you're still standing." He came over and squeezed one of Jake's shoulders. "I always figured you two would end up together. Truth be told, there's no one else I'd rather have by my sister's side than you."

Jake reared back in shock. "Really?"

"Yeah, man. You think I never noticed the way you'd look at her when you thought no one else was paying attention? Why the hell do you think I asked *you* to be the one to watch out for her? And shit, that girl's been in love with you since she was old enough to know what love was. So, fuck, yeah, I always knew you were the guy for her. To be honest, I'm surprised it's taken you two this long to figure it out for yourselves."

Jake was speechless. All those years he'd kept his hands to himself, even before Mike's sudden 'death'. All that time wasted.

Well, shit.

"I'm pretty sure I just lost my chance with her, so—"

Mike actually chuckled. "Don't worry, brother. I'll go talk to her. She'll come around. Although, I'm almost certain you'll have to do a fuck-ton of groveling before it's all said and done."

Without another word, Jake watched Mike turn and head down the hallway toward his bedroom. He prayed his friend was right.

Because if Olivia decided she could never forgive him, Jake honestly didn't know how he'd move on from that.

****

Olivia sat on the edge of Jake's bed, her bags packed and sitting by the door.

She kept trying—with no success—to get her emotions under control. To make sense of what had just happened.

Her brother was alive. All this time, he's been alive. And Jake knew.

My brother's alive.

She was still struggling to wrap her mind around it all when someone knocked on the bedroom door. Not waiting for her response, the door slowly opened, and Mikey was standing there, looking at her with uncertainty.

Mikey's here. And he's alive.

"I come in peace," he said, smiling.

Olivia couldn't help it. She smiled back.

Mikey shut the door behind him and walked over to her. The mattress dipped as he took a seat beside her.

"Hey."

"Hey."

Olivia stared at him. She couldn't help it. He smirked and…God, she'd *missed* him.

His brows turned in. "What?"

She shook her head. "So many times I've wished I could see you again. Just one more time to talk to you and hug you and…tell you that I love you. And now, here you are and I…" Her eyes welled up again, and her throat became tight.

He took her hand in his. It was much bigger and rougher than she remembered. A man's hand.

"I really am sorry, Olivia. I know things haven't been easy for you. If it makes you feel any better, I *do* know how you felt. When I got word that Pops had died, it broke my heart. I *hated* not being able to go to his funeral. And then, when I saw on the news that you'd been killed, I…I lost it."

He blinked quickly, and Olivia realized he was fighting back tears. She couldn't remember ever seeing her brother cry, and despite the fact that she was still angry, she also felt badly for him.

Yes, it had been his choice to leave, but she knew what it was like to lose someone you loved. She hated that he'd had to experience that all alone, without family or friends there to comfort him.

"I nearly blew my cover, and I didn't even care. I wanted to come home sooner, but I'm still under Uncle Sam's fucking thumb. My contract isn't up yet, and if I break it before it expires, I'll be stuck in Leavenworth. Or worse."

She tried to sound understanding. "I-I know whatever you've been doing had to be important for you to leave us like you did. It's just that...damn it, Mikey, *we* were important, too."

"I know, Junebug. I know. And if I had it to do over again—"

She chuckled halfheartedly. "You'd do the exact same thing."

Her brother gave her a lopsided grin. "Probably. What I've been able to do has helped so many people, Olivia. We've saved countless lives. There's so much evil in the world, so many men and organizations out there, plotting against us. The people in this country have no idea, but I do. And the men and women I work with...we do everything we can to stop them."

Olivia squeezed his hand. "You're a good soldier, Mikey. A good man. You always were."

Mike raised an eyebrow. "You know who else is a good man?"

Olivia stood, immediately missing the contact with her

beloved sibling. "Mikey, don't—"

"No, Olivia. You need to hear this. The *only* reason Jake knew about me all this time was because about a month after I 'died'"— he used air quotes for emphasis—"Jake and a group of soldiers he was with were sent on a new mission. Their intercepted mine, and we ran into each other. It was fucking crazy odds."

He waited a beat and went on to explain. "We were in this remote, hole-in-the-wall place that wasn't even a blip on the fucking map, and I look up, and there he was. Staring right back at me. And he was *pissed*, Olivia. I've never seen him that mad before, not at me or anyone else. After he took me out back and beat the shit out me, he said he was leaving to call you."

At that, Olivia's ears perked up, and she tried to tell if he was lying. Which was ridiculous, given his entire adult life was based on nothing but lies.

As if reading her thoughts, Mikey said, "It's no bullshit, Olivia. Jake was determined to tell you I was still alive. He knew what my death had done to you and Pops, and it *killed* him to see you that way."

"If he was so determined, then why didn't he tell me?"

Mikey shrugged a shoulder. "I made him swear to me that he wouldn't."

Olivia's fists went to her hips as she stood there, her eyes shooting daggers into his.

"Oh, for God's sake, Mikey! You were two adults. How in the hell did you *make* him not tell me? What did you do, threaten not to be his best friend anymore if he did?"

Olivia knew her sarcasm probably wasn't helping, but damn it, this wasn't a joke. This was her life.

"No," he said, his expression deadly serious. "It wasn't the threat of losing my friendship that convinced him not to tell you. Would you like to know what did?"

"Not that it'll matter, but sure. Go ahead. Enlighten me," she snapped, then immediately felt bad, which pissed her off even more.

Of all the people in this house who should feel badly, it sure as hell should *not* be her.

"It was the threat to *your* safety that clenched it."

Olivia's forehead creased, her hands falling to her side. "What threat?"

Mikey shrugged that damn shoulder again. "I played the 'Keep Olivia Safe Card'. I knew Jake could never go against that."

"I'm sorry, the *what?*"

Mikey held out his hand to her, and surprising even herself, Olivia took it. He guided her back to the bed, and she sat down, again. Her brother looked at her with the sweet, loving eyes she'd remembered.

"I knew Jake's feelings for you went beyond a simple childhood friendship. So, I told him that if you knew about me and accidently said the wrong thing to the wrong person, then it would make you vulnerable. A target."

Olivia opened her mouth, but Mikey didn't let her talk. "You gotta understand, Sis. If any of the bastards I've helped put away ever found out who I really was, and that you existed…they'd use you to get to me in a heartbeat." He looked away for just a second before turning back to her. "It would have crushed me if that ever happened, but Jake? Something like that would fucking destroy him. I knew that, so I used it. I used his need to protect you, and his feelings for you against him to ensure his silence."

Olivia stared at him, letting the meaning of his words sink

in. "But we weren't...until recently Jake and I had never even—"

"It didn't matter." Mikey cut her off with a headshake. "I knew how he felt. And for the record, the *only* reason he'd kept his hands off you when we were younger, was because in high school, I told him I'd kill him if he ever touched you."

Olivia's eyes widened. "You did not."

He looked unapologetic. "I was your big brother. It's what we do." He glanced away before looking back at her again, his expression serious. "I'm so sorry for what you've been through. Jake and I, we never wanted you touched by our world. I didn't want you to know about the things we've been forced to do. Didn't want you to ever truly know the evil that exists out there."

Olivia couldn't help it. She laughed, thinking of everything she'd been through and how it had absolutely nothing to do with his or Jake's professions.

"Hell of a lot of good that did, huh?"

Mikey smiled back. "Trouble always did seem to find you. Looks like some things never change." His smile faded. "You know, I used to think there'd never be a guy good enough for you, but Jake loves you, Junebug. I know you're pissed, but that man out there would do anything in the world for you. Even risk everything you two have by lying to you, if that's what it took to keep you safe. He loves you *that* much."

She shook her head. "He couldn't love me and lie to me. Not about you."

"Damn it, woman! You are still as stubborn as a fucking mule. Did you not hear a word I just said? He lied to you to *protect* you, Sis." He put his other hand on top of hers. "Take it from someone who's missed out on that part of life. I've seen the way Jake looks when he talks about you. The way he

156

was looking at you when you walked in here and slammed the door like a little brat."

Olivia's mouth dropped open. "I am not a brat!"

Mikey smirked again, but continued on, "The poor guy looked like he'd just lost his entire world. Almost made me feel bad for clocking him like I did."

Her mouth opened even wider. "You *hit* him?"

"I'm your big brother, and I'd just found out he was boinking you. What was I supposed to do?"

She slapped his upper arm. "Boinking? Really? And you didn't have to hit him. I'm a grown ass woman and can sleep with whomever I want. You don't see me going around and bitch slapping all of the women you've—" She cut herself off.

With an understanding smile, Mike simply waited.

"Right. Never mind."

Olivia couldn't believe how easily it was for them to fall back into the playful sibling rivalry they'd always had, even after all these years. It was…weird. And wonderful.

Her heart was so conflicted. Happy, yet broken, all at the same time.

"Look, Liv. All I'm saying, is you need to forgive him. Try to understand that Jake did what he did, because he loves you more than anything in the world. He'd *die* to protect you."

Not ready to even consider hopping on the forgiveness train, yet, Olivia abruptly changed the subject.

"When do you have to go back?"

Mike checked his watch and sighed. "Soon."

"Well, then. I guess we should make the most of our time. We have a lot of catching up to do."

Mike put his arm around Olivia's shoulders and pulled her to him. He kissed the top of her head. "That we do."

Olivia turned and wrapped her arms around her brother's

wide chest, pulling him in for a hug.

"I've missed you so much. God, I love you. You big jerk."

Her bottom lip quivered as she cherished the feel of her brother's embrace. She didn't even try not to cry.

"Ah, I love you, too, Junebug," Mike said, squeezing her back. "Not a single day has gone by that I haven't thought about you."

"Me, neither," Olivia choked out, her tears soaking the front of his shirt.

They eventually pulled away from each other, Olivia and Mike both wiping tears from their eyes. They sat on Jake's bed and talked, using the next hour to try to catch up on ten years' worth of lost time.

Olivia filled him in on the cliff-notes version of her adult life, highlighting the most important parts, and Mike shared what he could, which wasn't a lot.

When he talked, he mainly used vague, non-specifics, but she got the gist. While she'd gone to college and become a nurse, her brother had been out saving the world.

Unable to put it off any longer, Mike stood and held out his hand.

"I hate to do this, but I really have to get back. If I'm gone too long, I'll compromise my cover."

Olivia tried, and failed, to squelch the sudden fear she had for her brother's safety. What he was doing was dangerous, and damn it, she'd just gotten him back. To lose him again…

No. She wouldn't go there. Life was too short, and she was going to enjoy the fact that, though she was still hurt from his deception, her brother was alive and well.

"When will I see you again?"

"Soon," he promised. "This is my last job. When it's over, I'm done. There are a lot of things I'll have to iron out, but

I'll be back in your life, one way or another."

Olivia didn't ask how he'd pull that off because it didn't matter. "Promise?"

He smiled. "I promise, Junebug."

She pulled him in for one more hug. "Be careful, Mikey. I just got you back, so don't go doing anything stupid like getting yourself killed for real."

He chuckled against her. "I won't." Mikey pulled back and gave her a look that reminded her of their dad. "And don't *you* forget what I said about Jake. I trust him with your life. You need to do the same."

"I do."

And she did. It was trusting him with her heart that worried her.

"I love you, Sis. I'll see you soon."

"I love you, too, Mikey."

With that, her brother turned and walked out of Jake's bedroom. Before she could close the door, Olivia caught a glimpse of Jake walking toward Mikey.

He looked at her, his face wrenched with pain. She quickly looked away before shutting the door.

Leaning back against it, Olivia sighed. She needed to clear her head and think about everything.

A ball of emotions, she realized the only way she could do that would be to have some time alone. Away from everyone else, especially Jake.

If she stayed here, Olivia knew he'd eventually break down her defenses. She'd end up forgiving him before she even knew whether or not she really wanted to.

Olivia went to her purse and pulled out her phone. She hated to bother her new friend, especially after totally botching their shopping trip, but somehow Olivia knew Mac would help her with what she needed.

After a long, cleansing breath, she tapped on Mac's name in her contact list and waited for the other woman to answer.

An hour later, Olivia was still hiding out in the bedroom when she heard the doorbell ring, followed by the door opening and Jake's muffled voice.

She grabbed her suitcase, shopping bags, and purse and lifted her chin before exiting the room. She didn't look back, not wanting to remember the wonderful nights, and mornings, she'd shared with Jake in his bed.

As expected, she found Jake and Mac standing by the front door. He was scowling at Mac, who looked completely unaffected by it. The other woman smiled at her, but Olivia didn't miss the pity in Mac's eyes.

She hadn't told her the details of what had happened. She'd never compromise her brother's safety like that— something both Jake and Mikey should have known.

It was one of the reasons she was so pissed off about being kept out of the loop. Olivia would have never said a word to *anyone* about Mikey still being alive. Too bad he and Jake hadn't trusted her enough to realize that.

When she called Mac, Olivia simply told her that she and Jake had fought, and that she needed to get back to her house so she'd have some time to think. It wasn't a total lie.

"You're leaving?"

Jake asked, his eyes locked on hers. He somehow managed to look like a hurt little puppy and a pissed-off pit bull all wrapped into one.

Ignoring the little voice inside her head telling her she should stay, Olivia said, "I need some time alone, Jake. To think about everything."

"Uh, I'll just…take these," Mac said as she reached for

Olivia's suitcase and bags. To Olivia she said, "I'll meet you in the car."

Olivia just stood there awkwardly, looking everywhere but at Jake.

"Olivia, look at me." After a few seconds, he added a sincere, "Please."

Hesitantly, Olivia's eyes found his, and she saw what Mike had been talking about. Jake *did* look like he'd lost his whole world.

She felt the same way. The only difference was, good intentions or not, Jake had brought this on himself.

His voice was low and overflowing with anguish. "The last thing I ever wanted to do was hurt you."

"I know."

Olivia's whispered response surprised her, mainly because it was true. Jake wasn't a vicious person. She knew he cared about her and wouldn't intentionally hurt her.

Except she *was* hurt, and like it or not, he was the cause.

He lifted his hand tentatively, but Olivia stepped out of his reach. If he touched her, she'd never have the strength to walk away.

Jake's eyes started to glisten as he lowered his hand back to his side. He hung his head, and Olivia felt his pain clear through her own battered soul.

"Baby, I'm so sorry."

His whispered words were so soft, she almost missed them. Olivia forced herself to ignore the hitch in his voice, but when Jake raised his head and those beautiful, sad eyes found hers once again...

God, were those *tears* trailing down his cheeks?

No, no, no.

She had to get out of here before she did something

stupid, like grab hold of his shirt, pull him to her, and never let him go.

"Goodbye, Jake."

The words felt as though they were being ripped straight from her heart. They were words Olivia never thought she'd say. Not like this.

She turned to leave, and this time, Jake did touch her. His hand flew out to gently grabbed her wrist.

"Liv, wait!" He sounded as desperate as she felt.

"I can't." She shook her head and felt her own cheeks becoming wet.

"I'll make this up to you, Olivia. I swear to God I will. I love you *so* much. Just…just tell me what to do, and I'll do it."

Olivia looked up at his blurred image and said, "You can let me go."

She knew her words held a double meaning, and they tore her heart in two.

Jake let her wrist go, but pleaded, "Baby, please. Don't go. Not like this."

She wiped her eyes, barely managing to say, "I have to, Jake." She sniffed. "And you have to let me. I need some time to deal with…everything. Cetro. Carlos Hernandez. My brother. *You.* I need some space, and you need to give it to me. So, please don't call me, and don't come by. When I'm ready"—her throat worked its way past the giant lump there as she swiped at her tears—"if I want to talk, I'll come to you. Until then, I just…I need to be left alone."

Olivia turned and walked out the door, afraid that if she stayed there one more second, Jake would start begging again. She wasn't strong enough to tell him goodbye twice.

Even with her vision blurred, Olivia found her way to

Mac's car. She buckled herself in.

When Mac asked if she was okay, Olivia's only response was to softly whisper, "Please. Just drive."

Chapter 11

Olivia had to hand it to Mac. The entire way home, the other woman never once asked what Jake had done to make her so upset.

When she pulled into Olivia's driveway less than an hour later, she put the car in park and turned to her. When Mac started talking, Olivia realized she hadn't asked, because she already knew.

"I've never been one to meddle in other people's business, but I will say this. With my job, I understand exactly why Jake and your brother kept this from you all these years. I also know what it's like to be betrayed by those closest to you. So, if you ever need to talk, about Jake or anything else, I'm here. And you don't have to worry about me running off and telling the boss anything you say, either. I don't play like that. Okay?"

Olivia nodded and smiled as best she could. Her tears had finally dried up, but Mac's offer of friendship brought them precariously close to the surface again.

"Thank you, Mac. I'll be fine. I just need some time to sort everything out." Olivia exited the car, grabbing her bags from the back seat.

She started toward her house when Mac hollered to her from the car. Olivia turned back around to see that Mac standing half-in and half-out of her car.

"I'll say this, and then, I'll be on my way. What Jake did, he had a good reason to do. Yeah, he's a man, and Lord knows they can all be idiots at times"—she rolled her eyes and paused—"but, here's the thing. Trust isn't something I give easily, Olivia. Especially when it comes to men. I trust Jake. And that man is head over ass for you. He'd do anything to keep you safe. So, whatever happens…whatever you decide, I hope you believe that. Because that's one truth I'm certain of."

Not knowing how to respond, Olivia simply thanked Mac again before climbing up her porch steps and going inside. Feeling both physically and emotionally exhausted, she locked her doors and set her alarm before heading for a long, hot shower.

Half way through rinsing the shampoo from her hair, she broke down again. Her body was wracked with hard, gut-wrenching sobs, which continued until the water had cooled.

She haphazardly dried off, not caring that her skin was still damp when she threw on a pair of sweats and an old t-shirt.

Olivia turned her phone off, shutting out the world, and fell into bed. Then, she cried herself to sleep.

****

Three days. It had been three very long, very fucked up days since Olivia had walked out Jake's door, taking the best part of him with her.

Desperate to numb the pain, he'd gotten completely shitfaced that first night. Later, when he laid down in his bed, the void there hit him instantly.

The bed was suddenly much too big. And too fucking empty. The worst part? Jake could smell her on his sheets.

Three days later, he still couldn't bring himself to wash the damn things.

Since then, he'd steered clear of the booze, but Jake hadn't found anything to ease the pain in his chest where his heart used to be.

In the end, by protecting Olivia, Jake may have lost her, forever.

Respecting her wishes, he hadn't called her. God, he wanted to. Actually, he wanted to jump in his truck, drive to her house, and knock her damn door down. Then, he wanted to kiss her until she finally agreed to forgive him.

Jake hadn't done any of those things. Liv had asked for time, so he was giving it to her. But goddamn, being apart from her was killing him.

He missed the hell out of her. And he was worried. She'd been through so much in such a short period of time.

Experience told him that she was probably still too pissed to talk to him right now, but she might be willing to talk with someone else.

Pulling out his phone, Jake tapped the second name on his favorites list.

"Hey, Jake," Trevor answered. "What's up?"

"I need a favor."

The last time he'd said those words to his teammates, they'd all travelled to Venezuela to take out Cetro and his men. Jake was well aware that what he was asking of his friend this time could be just as dangerous. Maybe even more so.

****

Work. It was exactly what Olivia needed. For two days, her existence had consisted of moping, crying, and sleeping. Wash, rinse, repeat.

She refused to do it for a third, so Olivia called the hospital and practically begged to return from leave early. Thankfully, they were busy and had an open mid-shift, so her boss agreed to let her come in.

After dressing in her light purple scrubs, Olivia threw her hair up in an unimpressive ponytail and glanced at her bedside clock. It was eleven o'clock, which meant she had two hours before her shift began.

Two hours would give her too much time to think, so she'd go in early. There was always something to do in an ER.

Even making beds or stocking supply carts would be better than sulking around her empty house.

Before Jake had come back, she'd gotten pretty good at spending time alone. Sort of. But now, everywhere she looked there seemed to be a new memory of the two of them together.

Mikey's little speech about how she should try to understand and forgive Jake's betrayal played on a continuous loop in her head, making it impossible to think about anything else. Hopefully, work would be the welcome distraction she desperately needed.

The sound of her doorbell startled her. On reflex, she started to get her gun, but stopped. The danger was over. Her stalker was dead, and Cetro and the others were all in jail.

Determined to live a normal life again, Olivia left her gun in her bedroom and went to the door. She looked through the peephole, surprised at who she saw on the other side.

Unable to keep her anxiety at bay, she entered her alarm code and unlocked the door in record time.

"Trevor? W-what are you doing here? Has something happened?" She hated how her voice shook.

Trevor's eyes went wide as he raised his hands, palms up, as if to surrender. "Whoa. Nothing's wrong. Jake's fine, I promise."

Olivia could feel the stress leaving her body and her shoulders relax. "Oh." She swallowed and nodded with a small smile. "That's good."

She absolutely would not think about how worried she gotten for the man who'd ripped her heart out.

He wrinkled his brow a bit. "Sorry. I guess I should have called first, but…"

"No," she said quickly, embarrassed by her reaction. "It's fine. Um, would you like to come in?"

Trevor nodded. "Thanks. I won't take up much of your time."

Olivia stepped aside to give Trevor enough space to step past her. At war with her thoughts, she ignored the disappointment she felt that it hadn't been Jake at her door.

It wasn't fair, given that she had told him to stay away. Still, part of her felt that if Jake truly loved her like he said he did, then he should be here, fighting for her. Fighting for *them*.

It was totally hypocritical and made absolutely no sense. Then again, love rarely did.

Shaking her head at her unreasonable thoughts, Olivia asked Trevor, "Would you like something to drink?"

Trevor smiled. "No, thank you. Actually, I was hoping"— he turned toward the couch—"could we sit and talk for a minute?"

Okay. Now he *was* starting to make her nervous. "Of course."

Olivia led them over to the couch where they both sat down. Glancing over at Trevor, she realized he almost looked uncomfortable, as if he were nervous, too.

Crap. This can't be good.

"I'm sure you're wondering why I'm here."

She smiled teasingly. "You missed my adorable face?"

Trevor chuckled. "Well, there is that."

He leaned forward, resting his elbows on his knees, hands loosely clasped together between them. "Okay, look. I know this is none of my business, and you have every right to say that, and then kick me out. But...I'm hoping you'll at least listen to what I have to say before you do."

He was her friend. The guy had risked his life—along with his team—to try to save her and Jake, and he'd taken a bullet to the chest while trying to protect her. She'd listen to anything he had to say.

"Okay. I'm listening."

The look of relief in his eyes was immediate, as was his tight smile. Trevor really was one of the good guys.

Even though she was still furious with Jake for what he'd done, Olivia couldn't help but be thankful he had a friend like Trevor watching his back.

Trevor filled his lungs before starting. "What went down between you and Jake is absolutely none of my business. I know that, but I was just hoping that maybe I could help you to understand *why* he did what he did."

"I already know why." Olivia tried not to sound too bitter. "He was protecting my brother."

Trevor nodded in agreement. "Yes, he was. But most importantly, Jake kept his knowledge about your brother a secret to protect *you*."

Jake and Mikey had both given her the same song and dance, but that didn't make her feel any better. Olivia gave Jake everything she had to offer, and he'd lied to her about Mikey. She didn't know how to get past that.

Shaking her head, Olivia said, "You don't understand, Trevor. This wasn't a little white lie that somebody tells someone they love like, 'No, honey, those pants don't make you look fat'."

Her obvious sarcasm had the corner of Trevor's mouth curving up slightly as he tried to contain his smile. Olivia wasn't smiling.

"This was my *brother*, Trevor. I thought he was *dead*." Her voice broke, but she kept on. "Jake knew how much pain that caused me, yet he still kept this from me for *ten years*. How do I even start to forgive something like that?"

She blinked quickly, determined not to cry. She'd shed enough tears over the past few months to last a lifetime.

All traces of his smile faded from his face, and Olivia got the feeling that whatever he was about to say wasn't going to be pleasant.

"One of the last ops I went on with Delta ended very badly."

Olivia wondered where he was going with his little trip down memory lane, but from his pained expression, she thought it best to just let the man talk.

"It was a joint operation between the CIA and the military. There was an agent assigned to our team. A woman named Lisa. She went on missions with us. Debriefed with us. As the Agency received vital intel, Lisa was the one who would relay it to our team. She also gave us access to two of her most important assets. She wasn't officially Delta, but by the end of the op, she was considered one of us."

He smiled sadly. "Lisa and I hit it off from damn near day one. We grew close, and I...I cared about her."

Olivia saw a strange sense of sadness mixed with regret when he spoke more about the woman. Clearly, this story had anything but a happy ending.

"What happened to her, Trevor?"

"Intel from one of the assets led us to the man we'd been after for almost a year. He was a member of a major terrorist organization responsible for the deaths of hundreds of innocent people. The asset somehow managed to find out where he and some other key players were hiding. It was an abandoned shack built against the side of a mountain in Syria. The night before the op, Jake came down with the flu, putting me in charge. I was the one who made the call to go in."

Trevor stood and walked over to her living room window. Looking out over her front yard, he went on.

"It was all a set-up. The asset was actually working for the man we were trying to take down. He led us into a trap."

"Like a double-agent?" Olivia asked quietly.

Jake nodded. "Lisa trusted him, and we got screwed." He took a deep breath and turned to face her. "Two of our men went in first. They said the place was clear and called for Lisa and her asset to come inside. Said they needed her to decipher something they'd found."

Over his shoulder, Trevor explained, "Lisa could speak and read several languages. It wasn't uncommon for her to translate documents for us during an op." Looking back to her window, he continued, "Per protocol for this mission, I stayed back with our other teammates, keeping an eye out for any incoming threats. I watched Lisa and her asset walk inside. Two minutes later, the building exploded."

"Oh, God, Trevor. I'm so sorry."

He turned back to her. "That wasn't even the worst of it. When we went through the rubble, we only found the two men from our team who'd entered the building first. They'd both been shot in the head."

"What about Lisa and her asset?"

"There was a tunnel built into the mountain behind the shack that led to a bunker. Our people didn't know it existed."

"Lisa?"

"She was taken into the bunker and through a second tunnel. There was a hidden exit at the end of that one. By the time our guys discovered it, she was long gone."

Trevor paused, his face hardening. "A video was sent to the CIA two days later. It was of Lisa. She was tied to a chair, and had been beaten. They received a new video every day for the next five days. I'll spare you the details, but by the fifth day, when we received confirmation she was dead, we were relieved. For her sake."

Olivia didn't even want to imagine what had been done to the poor woman. "I'm so sorry. You and your team must have been devastated."

Trevor nodded. "We were. And for a long time, I blamed myself."

"Why? You were only going off of the information Lisa's asset gave you, right?"

"Right. Except I didn't trust the asset. There was just something...off about the guy. I voiced my concerns multiple times to our commander and to Lisa. She always defended the man. Said he'd never steered her wrong. And the powers that be wouldn't listen to me because they were too focused on getting our target. No matter the cost."

Trevor walked over to the couch and sat down. "Instead of listening to my gut, I made the call to move forward with the op. I gave the go-ahead for Lisa to enter that building, and she died a horrific death because of it."

Olivia reached for his hand. "Trevor, what happened to Lisa was awful, and I can't imagine what you and your team went through. But it wasn't your fault."

He stared back at her, the sadness in his eyes heartbreaking. "I went through the pointless cycle of what-ifs. What if I had just waited a few more days until Jake was better? Maybe we would have learned about the tunnel and been more prepared? What if I'd listened to my instincts and demanded the CIA do a more thorough look into the asset's history and known associates? What if I had pushed the higher-ups harder? It went on and on."

Olivia understood completely. She'd played the what-if game ever since the day she'd been taken and her friends had been ruthlessly killed.

He blinked, and his glossy eyes found Olivia's again. "I blamed myself for a long time. The guilt ate at me. Watching those videos, seeing someone I cared about being tortured like that, and knowing there was nothing I could do to stop it." He shook his head slowly. "I've never felt so…"

"Helpless," she whispered for him, her face wet from tears she hadn't even realized had fallen.

Trevor's expression changed instantly. He squeezed her hand and looked at her apologetically.

"Damn, Olivia. I'm sorry. I didn't mean to upset you. After what you went through"—he released her hand to run his fingers through his hair—"Jesus, I'm sorry."

"It's okay," Olivia promised, sniffing as she wiped the

tears away with her hands. "That's exactly how I felt about what happened my group. I blamed myself for all of it, but Jake helped me see that there really wasn't anything I could have done to save them." She drew in a cleansing breath. "In my head, I know he's right, but my heart still hasn't fully caught up, yet. So, although our situations are quite different, I think I sort of understand where you're coming from."

His brows went together. "Yeah, I guess you probably do."

"What I don't understand," Olivia said softly. "Is what any of this has to do with me and Jake."

His look was piercing. "I didn't push Lisa into looking more closely into her asset. Every time I brought it up, it caused an argument. Same thing happened when I brought it up to the guys sitting behind their desks in Washington. So, I did the easy thing. I went against my better judgment, and I let it go."

"What I'm trying to say, Olivia, is that I don't know if it would have made a damn bit of difference if we'd waited. But if there was even a *chance* that waiting could have kept Lisa from being tortured to death and kept my men alive...I should have waited. No matter what the consequences were, personal or professional."

He let that sink in for a minute before asking, "Do you understand what I'm saying? I should have done whatever it took to keep her and the others safe. Even if that something would have ruined our chances at catching the bastard we were after. It was our job as a team to protect Lisa on our ops. Her safety should have trumped our objective, hands-down. No matter the cost."

Now, she understood. "I appreciate what you're trying to do, Trevor. I really do, but it's not the same thing."

Trevor shifted his weight so that he was facing her more directly. "See, that's where you're wrong, honey. You, Lisa…it's *exactly* the same. Jake and I are the same. So are Coop and Derek, and hell, even Grant. Guys like us, we're cut from the same cloth. Willing to protect the people we care about using *any* means necessary. I cared for Lisa, a lot, and I'll never forget her, but you? You mean a *hell* of a lot more than that to Jake."

Trevor waited, giving her the opportunity to speak, but Olivia didn't really know what to say, so he kept on.

"Honey, he did what he did because he was in love with you. Even way back then. He couldn't take the chance of something happening to you. Jake knew if you ever found out the truth about your brother it would probably ruin your friendship forever, but he still took that risk because he loves you, and the thought of something happening to you because he talked was unbearable."

When Olivia shook her head in disagreement, Trevor raised his voice slightly. "Look, Olivia. Jake had two choices. He could risk your being hurt or, God forbid, killed, or risk you hating him for the rest of your life. He chose the latter, because at least you'd be alive to hate him. Do you honestly think it was easy for him? That lying to you about something he knew cut you so deeply was a choice Jake made lightly?"

Olivia suddenly found herself on the defensive. Lifting her chin, she said, "Honestly? I don't know."

"Yes, you do," he said without pause. "And, so do I."

Trevor released her hand and stood. He walked toward the living room window, again, before turning and facing her. His hands rested low on his hips, his handsome face was dead serious.

"It takes a lot to scare me, Olivia, and I've got to tell ya.

The night Jake heard you'd been killed…he scared the shit out of me." His words made Olivia wince, but Trevor didn't stop. "I've been by his side through thick and thin, but I have *never* seen him hurting as badly as he was the night he thought he'd lost you."

Trevor moved toward her again, stopping to crouch down in front of her. Taking her hands in his, he said, "When Jake heard you were dead, it was like someone flipped a switch. Any light he had inside of him was just…gone. And honestly, I didn't think he'd ever get it back."

Trevor's image blurred behind her unshed tears.

"Then, we found you alive, and suddenly, that light was burning brighter than I've ever seen it."

"Trevor—" Olivia tried to stop him, but he wouldn't let her talk.

"Jake loves you more than anyone or anything on this earth, and there is nothing"—he squeezed her hands harder—"*nothing* he wouldn't do to protect you. That includes risking any chance he may have had with you by lying about your brother."

Olivia broke away from his grasp to wipe her eyes. Mikey had already told her that Jake lied to protect her, but for some reason, the way Trevor explained it seemed to have made more of an impact.

She hated it. Still wasn't ready to forgive Jake, yet, but the wall that had been erected the moment she'd seen her dead brother standing in Jake's living room began to crack slightly.

Olivia understood what Trevor was saying, but she still couldn't ignore the betrayal she felt.

She must have been silent for longer than she'd realized, because Trevor stood and began to walk to the door before she'd made any kind of response.

"I'll get out of your way." He turned and nodded to her scrubs. "I don't want to keep you."

Olivia had nearly forgotten about work. She stood and wiped her face with her palms as she followed him.

"Yeah, the hospital's short staffed, so I offered to cover the mid-shift today." She glanced down at her watch. "I don't have to be there until two, but thought I'd go in a little early." They stood in awkward silence before she said, "Thanks for stopping by, Trevor." She gently squeezed his rock solid bicep. "And thank you for telling me about Lisa. I can tell that isn't an easy topic for you to talk about."

His dark, tormented eyes stared down at her. "Definitely, not a story I tend to share."

Olivia didn't know what to say. *Honored* didn't seem like the right word for what she was feeling, but that's how she felt.

"Thank you for caring enough to share it with me."

"Don't take this the wrong way, but I didn't just do this for you. I love Jake like a brother, and I want to see him happy. I know you're still angry, but…you're a fool if you let him go. There's no better man out there. Definitely none who would love you more."

Olivia bit her bottom lip, unsure of the proper response to such a strong statement.

Seeming to sense her uncertainty, Trevor gave it one last shot.

"Just promise me you'll talk to Jake soon. At least give him a chance to explain his side of things."

She hesitated for a second, but finally agreed. "Okay."

He raised his eyebrows and dropped his chin, waiting for more. He reminded her so much of Jake, she actually chuckled and rolled her eyes.

"I *promise* I will talk to him."

Trevor smiled triumphantly. "That's all I ask. Thank you." He leaned down and kissed her on the cheek. "See ya."

Trevor made his way down her porch steps and was almost to his truck when Olivia yelled out, "Hey, Trev?"

He stopped and turned around. "Yeah?"

"Did you know? About Mikey, I mean."

Looking guilty but resolved, he said, "I did. I know you're probably sick of hearing it, but it was for your protection, as well as your brother's. I'd say I'm sorry, but the truth is, I'm not. I went against my gut once, and it cost me three friends. I wasn't going to lose another one."

Without another word, he got into his truck and started it up.

Knowing he was referring to her, Olivia stood at her door with a sad smile and a heavy heart. She watched as Trevor drove away, and thought about everything he'd said.

She thought about Jake, and wondered if it possible for them to recover from something like this.

Part of her wanted to say yes, but when she thought of all the times she'd cried on his shoulder—both literally and figuratively—the pain she still felt overpowered everything else.

Deciding to deal with it all later, she focused on getting ready for work. She quickly put on her tennis shoes and was headed back to her bedroom to grab her cell phone when her doorbell rang.

Given that she almost never had unannounced visitors, she assumed Trevor had returned to reiterate his point one last time. Olivia started talking before she'd fully opened the door.

"You do realize you've got to actually give me *time* to talk to Jake, right Trev?"

She said this in a teasing voice, but when she glanced up, Trevor's eyes weren't the ones staring back at her.

"I'm sorry, Miss Bradshaw. I'm afraid your time is up."

Chapter 12

Javier Cetro smiled down at Olivia. He looked just as she remembered.

Tanned skin. Dark, wavy hair. That jagged scar running from the corner of one eye to his jawline.

And those eyes. She'd never forget those cold, evil eyes. *Oh, God. Not him!*

Moving with lightning speed, she tried to slam the door shut, but Cetro stuck his large boot between the door and its frame. He pushed against it from the outside and Olivia lost her balance.

She stumbled over and back, falling against the end table next to her couch. The candlestick lamp there started to fall forward, but Olivia grabbed it. Screaming like a banshee, she swung it back around toward her attacker.

Cetro threw his arm up to block it. Instead of the lamp hitting his head as she'd intended, its base slammed into his forearm.

It went flying back toward her kitchen, landing with a loud clanging sound. Cetro growled, baring his teeth like some sort of wild animal as he continued his advance.

My gun. I have to get to my gun.

Spinning away from him, Olivia began to run through her

living room. She'd only made it a few steps when the full weight of his body slammed into her back.

They fell onto her coffee table, its glass top shattering the moment they hit. Olivia cried out, but then ignored the biting pain in her left arm as she scrambled to find a pointed piece of glass to use as a weapon.

Her fingers brushed over one almost immediately and she grabbed it. With as much strength as she could, Olivia flung her arm backward and jammed the large shard into the flesh of his upper arm. Then, she twisted.

The glass was cutting the insides of her fingers and palm, but she didn't care. This man had already taken so much from her. *I can't let him take me again.*

Cetro roared, his grip on her loosening just enough for her to wiggle out from beneath him. While he was busy pulling the glass from his arm, Olivia got to her feet and ran around the end of her couch.

She mentally kicked herself for not bringing the gun with her when she answered the door for Trevor earlier. She realized now, how incredibly stupid that decision had been.

If she made it out of this alive, she would never, ever keep her gun this far from the door again.

Gun...door...*Mudroom!*

Just then, Olivia remembered Pops' shotgun. She'd put on a shelf by the mudroom door when she'd first moved in, and had completely forgotten about it until now.

In a split-second decision, she decided to try for the shotgun rather than her pistol in the bedroom. Olivia made it halfway around the back of the couch, and was between it and the open entryway to her kitchen when Cetro surprised her by jumping over the piece of furniture.

He looked like some sort of action movie hero. Too bad

he was the villain.

Olivia screamed and jumped out of the way. He narrowly missed her, and she knew she needed to do *something* to put some distance between them if she had any hopes of retrieving her gun in time.

Grabbing the first thing she could find, Olivia picked up one of the wooden chairs from her kitchen table and threw it at him.

Anticipating the move, Cetro caught two of its legs with both hands and threw the chair to the side, causing it to crash against the front door. It broke into several pieces on impact.

Olivia tried to turn away, but she wasn't fast enough. Cetro's fist slammed into her left temple and cheekbone, and she flew sideways, grunting when her right hip hit the countertop next to her stove.

Her hand knocked against her coffee mug holder and several of the porcelain cups fell from the wooden stand. Some landed on the white countertop, others shattering as they hit the kitchen floor.

Ignoring the spots flashing before her eyes and the throbbing pain from the cuts on her hand and arm, Olivia fought to regain control.

Still stunned from the blow, her right hand bumped clumsily against her wooden knife block. The blades went flying over the burners on her stove.

Scrambling quickly, Olivia picked up one of the knives—not an easy task to accomplish with the amount of slick blood coating her palm and fingers. With a painfully tight grip, she held onto that knife for dear life.

Squeezing its hilt with all she had, Olivia took a deep breath, determined to hit an artery this time. She braced herself for the move, but before she had the opportunity to swing the knife around, Cetro was behind her. His body trapping hers against the counter.

He wrapped an arm around her chest, pinning her left arm against her own body, and used his right hand to grab the one holding the knife.

Yanking it back on her forearm, he slammed her wrist down onto the counter's edge. Olivia cried out, but somehow managed to keep hold of the knife.

It was her only defense. If she lost it, she was dead.

Cetro repeated the move. Over and over—each hit harder than the one before it—until she heard the sickening snap of her bones. Olivia screamed, nearly blinded by the stabbing pain.

The broken bones made it impossible for Olivia to keep hold of the knife's hilt. It bounced off the counter and fell to the floor with a clang, her hopes of surviving plummeting right along with it.

Olivia was then pulled back against his chest and spun sideways so she was facing her living room. With a hard push, she felt herself flying forward.

Unable to stop the motion, she cried out again when she landed hard, her injured hand making it nearly impossible to break her fall.

The side of her face throbbed from where he'd punched her, and her left arm was sticky and wet from the deep cut there. The pain in her wrist was the worst.

It felt like someone was poking it with a hot branding iron, and Olivia had to fight against the urge to vomit.

Unable to stop him, Cetro flipped her over onto her back. She did her best to fight him off. Swinging at him with her good fist. Kicking as hard as she could.

Even as she fought, Olivia knew it was useless. She was

going to die today. *I'm so sorry, Jake.*

Tears fell across her temples as she looked into the eyes of a monster.

"You may as well stop fighting, puta. I am not going to kill you. Not here, anyway. No, I have big plans for you. It's finally time you pay for what you've done."

Olivia opened her mouth to tell him to go to hell but was stopped by a second blow to her face. Then, there was only blessed darkness.

****

Normally, riding his horse took Jake's stress away. Today, however, as Champ slowly trotted him back toward the barn, his heart remained heavy.

From the moment Olivia left, everything had felt empty. His house. His bedroom. His heart.

He'd fucked up, and it may very well have cost him the most important person in his life. He should have told her. Should have told Mike to go fuck himself when he asked him to keep his secret all those years ago.

Mike had used Jake's feelings for Olivia against him. Had convinced Jake that, by keeping his secret, he was protecting her.

Sure, he understood Mike's position, but god*dammit*. There was more than one way a person could get hurt.

Good intentions or not, he still should have had the balls to refuse Mike's request. Jake should have trusted Olivia enough to tell her the truth sooner. Hell, he should have told her a million times before now, but he'd been too fucking scared.

She'd been through so much. He didn't think she could

handle learning her dead brother wasn't really dead, on top of everything else.

And that right there was the problem.

Jake had always underestimated Liv. So had Mike. They'd spent their lives trying to protect her the best way they knew how, but she'd been right all along.

Olivia didn't always need his protection. She needed a partner. An equal.

She needed someone to stand by her side, not in front of her while barking orders. Jake hadn't seen it that way ten years ago, so he'd gone along with Mike's plea for silence, to keep Olivia from getting hurt.

"Yeah, and how did that work out for you, asshole?" Jake chastised himself. Champ sneezed then shook his head as if he were agreeing.

"I know, buddy."

Leaning down, Jake patted the right side of his horse's neck with a gloved hand. "I really screwed up, didn't I?"

This time, Champ remained silent, and he figured that was about as good an answer as any.

He wondered if Trevor had made any progress today. Desperate, he wanted to call his friend and ask him what Liv had said. But, hell. He wasn't some junior-high kid asking his friend to pass notes to the girl he likes during study hall.

Jake had to keep *some* part of his man card, even if it was just a tiny, torn off corner. Damn, if his curiosity wasn't eating him up inside, though.

Back at the barn, he'd just finished brushing down Champ and was latching his stable's gate when Coop walked in.

Jake glanced up at the other man's face. Coop's expression had the hairs on the back of his neck standing on end.

"What's wrong?"

Coop's brows turned inward. "You talk to Ryker?"

Damn. Now those hairs were screaming at him. "No. Why?"

"You need to call him. Says it's about Olivia."

Jake's entire body immediately tensed up, his nerve endings tingling. "What about her?" he stepped closer to his teammate. "Is she okay?"

"Far as I know. Mac talked to her about two hours ago. She tried calling her just now, but she didn't answer. Mac wasn't overly concerned, though. When she talked to her before, Olivia was getting ready to go into work. Said she'd picked up an extra shift or something."

Jake relaxed his shoulders. Mac had talked with her recently, and she'd been fine. Plus, Trevor should have made it to Liv's house and been gone by now. He would have called if something were wrong.

"So, what's the problem?"

Coop shrugged a shoulder. "Don't know. Ryker just said to call him ASAP."

Shit. His shoulders tensed up again. Needing some uninterrupted time to think, Jake had purposely ignored his phone when he'd been out riding. It would ring, and he'd look to see if it was Olivia.

When it wasn't, he'd shove it back into his pocket. The way she'd left the other day, he didn't actually expect her to call. That didn't stop him from praying it was her each time his phone would buzz.

Not wanting to talk to anyone but her, he'd let Ryker's calls go to voicemail. Assuming he was calling about a new job, Jake hadn't bothered to check any of the other man's messages yet.

Ryker knew he'd taken himself out of commission,

though. Now, Jake had to wonder…why all the calls?

He'd been so up in his own head, worrying about pulling his ass out of the mess he'd made with her, he hadn't been thinking clearly.

He should have known, if Ryker was calling him on his down time, he needed to answer his damn phone. And Coop said it had to do with Olivia. *Fuck!*

Jake broke into a sprint, running from the barn to the house, his phone to his ear as he tried to get through to the Homeland agent.

The first three times he called, it went straight to voicemail. Jake didn't bother to leave a message. Instead, he ended the calls and immediately tried again.

By the time he reached his house, Jake's heart was slamming against his chest. Not from the uphill run, but because he knew in his gut that something was wrong.

On the fourth try, Ryker finally answered. "About damn time you call me back, McQueen."

"What do you know?"

"Shit, you didn't check your messages, did you?"

"Don't fuck me around, Ryker. What's happened?"

A loud sigh hit his ear. "You need to get to your girl, and stay with her."

Fear assaulted him, his steps faltering as he entered his house. "Why?"

Not that he needed a reason to keep Liv safe. Jake would always do that, but right now, he needed answers. He just wasn't ready for the one he got.

"Cetro."

Ryker's one-word response stunned him. Jake stopped moving altogether. He closed his eyes as he spoke. "Explain. And, I swear to God, Jason…you'd better not feed me any bullshit on this."

"The short of it? Cetro escaped, and word is he blames Olivia for his brother's death." There was a slight pause and then, "He's going after her, Jake."

Jake's eyes flew open. *"What the fuck?"*

Jake ran to his kitchen and grabbed the keys to his truck from the counter. He continued talking as he stalked down the hall toward what Jake called the war room.

Mac—who'd apparently come with Coop to deliver Ryker's message—abandoned the cup of coffee she'd been making, and she and Coop followed closely behind. They all went straight for the enormous safe at the back of the room.

"He's supposed to be locked up!" Jake growled. "What the hell happened?"

He quickly pressed his palm against the biometric scanner to gain access. A second later, the loud click told him it was unlocked.

While Ryker explained the very fucked up situation, Jake and the other two began choosing from the extra weapons and ammo available. Coop and Mac hadn't tried to ask what was going down, yet. They simply followed their boss's lead.

Needing them in on this, and not wanting to waste time repeating it all, Jake secured the extra pistol, currently in his hand, to the ankle holster beneath his pant leg before taking the phone from his ear and putting it on speaker.

"There was a major storm in the area where Cetro was being held." Ryker's voice echoed through the room, along with Coop's and Mac's curses. "The jail flooded and authorities were forced to evacuate all prisoners. Those in custody were being transported to another, more secure corrections facility nearby, when their van hydroplaned. They were going around a sharp curve and lost control. It rolled several times. Both the driver and the officer keeping guard in the back were pronounced dead at the scene, along with two of the other men in custody. Cetro survived, and somehow managed to get the guard's keys. He and another prisoner were gone by the time the wreck was discovered. The only other prisoner to survive was unconscious when emergency personnel arrived, so he couldn't give us any information."

"Ah, hell," A little bit of Mac's southern heritage slipped out with her frustrated response.

Coop let out a loud, "Sonofabitch".

Jake spoke to the other two as he secured the safe, and the three of them headed to Jake's truck. "Mac, keep trying Liv. Sean, call the rest of the team in. Have them meet us at her place. Mac can give you her address. Call Trevor first. He shouldn't be too far from there. Tell him to turn around. He's not to leave her sight until we get there. Tell him to sit on her if he has to."

Speaking to Ryker again, Jake asked, "How long ago did this happen?"

If it was within the last couple hours, there'd be no immediate threat to Olivia. He knew where Javier Cetro was being held, and it was several hours from them.

Even if the bastard had managed to find a vehicle immediately upon escaping, he'd still be hundreds of miles away.

They had plenty of time to make the drive to Olivia's hospital. He'd get her the hell out of there, and take her somewhere safe.

She'd probably put up a fight, but this was one time he would not back down. He'd sedate her ass if he had to. She may hate him, right now, but fuck it. At least she'd be alive.

Jake still couldn't believe he hadn't heard about this. He

hadn't been watching much television lately, so it was possible he'd missed what would have been a breaking news story.

None of his team had mentioned anything to him about it, either. Surely one of the other five would have heard about this. At the very least, Derek should have gotten some sort of alert, unless—

Jake realized Ryker hadn't answered him, yet. He looked at his phone, thinking maybe they'd lost connection, but the duration timer at the top of the screen was still counting up.

Ryker was still on the line, so why the hell wasn't the guy talking? A horrifying thought slammed into him, and Jake prayed his suspicions were wrong.

"Answer the fucking question, Ryker," Jake ordered with a barely controlled temper. "When did this happen?"

"I know you're upset, Jake, but I promise my people are on this."

Jake didn't miss the way Ryker had skirted around giving a direct answer.

After placing his weapons in the metal toolbox attached to his truck bed, Jake swung the driver's door open and jumped inside.

He slammed his door shut, and placed his phone on the dash holder before starting the ignition. Coop climbed in the passenger seat next to him, and Mac took the seat in the back.

"How fucking long?" Jake yelled as he spun his truck around and sped down his long driveway. The obvious silence was telling, making Jake's gut burn.

Ryker finally answered, "The storm hit a few weeks ago. Look, Jake—"

There was a lot of cursing in the truck, just then. The loudest coming from Jake.

"Jesus fucking Christ! You've known this psycho was running around free for weeks and you didn't tell me? Didn't warn *Olivia?*"

"Hell, no!" Ryker shot back. "I just found out about it an hour ago. Which, by the way, was when I started calling you. Apparently, it's an election year down there, and the authorities wanted the escape kept quiet."

Oh, God. Jake was sick at heart. Doing his best to focus on what would help Liv, he asked, "What's Cetro's end game?"

Ryker spoke quickly. "According to the prisoner in custody, the guy's gone completely off the chains. He blames Olivia for his brother's death. I remember from her statement when you guys returned from Venezuela that the boy was pretty much dead before she ever had a chance to try to help him, but she did everything she could to save him anyway."

"She did." Not that she'd been in a position to refuse.

When they'd been hiding out in the jungle together, Olivia had told Jake how, while being held captive by Cetro, she'd been forced to try to save his brother. The kid was wounded during a gun battle between Cetro's crew and the people they'd gone after that time. Despite Olivia's efforts, the young man had died.

"Right. So, Cetro's brother dies, and with you and your team's help, Olivia escapes. Fast forward a few days, and your team goes after him and the others. He's caught and taken to jail. The guy loses it. Uses his time in custody to plan his revenge against your girl. The wreck provided him with the perfect opportunity, and with the help of his new buddy, he tracks her down. Not hard to do for a man with his connections. He starts watching her, waiting for the perfect time."

Another thought occurred to him. "Jason, Olivia was

being stalked. She was attacked a few days ago while I was in the city taking care of some business." Something he still couldn't forgive himself for. "Trevor was with her. He was hit in the chest, but had on a vest. Olivia was banged up and almost taken, but Trevor woke up in time to take the guy out. Man's name was Carlos Hernandez. Derek didn't find anything, but there *has* to be a connection there."

"I'll have my guy look into it."

Jake's head spun as he continued to drive. He'd just stood there and watched as she walked out his door with Mac three days ago…alone.

His ears filled with the sound of his blood rushing through them. The phone calls, the fucking snake…he slammed the palm of his free hand against his steering wheel.

"Goddammit!" How had he not seen it?

Jake wanted to pull over to the side of the road and throw up, but he couldn't waste a single minute getting to Liv.

To Ryker, he barked, "We'll keep trying to get ahold of her. You hear anything new, I don't care how fucking small it is, you call me. *Immediately."*

"I will. And I'm sorry, Jake. I'd have called sooner had I known."

Without another word, Jake ended the call and immediately tried Olivia again. He didn't need Ryker's damn apology. He needed to know his woman was okay.

She didn't answer his call. He tried again and again, but always got the same result. The sick feeling that had started in his gut the second Coop entered his barn worsened with every second he didn't hear her voice.

Not giving up hope, he started to dial the hospital, but Coop's hand on his arm stopped him.

"Already called the hospital, boss. She's not there. She,

uh…she never showed for her shift."

Oh, God. Was he too late? Jake hit number two on his call list. Trevor answered immediately.

"Tell me you're there."

"Ten minutes out. You?"

Fuck. "I'm half an hour behind you."

Jake looked at his speedometer and pushed down his accelerator. The distance he still had to cover should have normally taken him another forty-five minutes at least, but Jake had been breaking land speed records since his tires hit the highway.

"I was there less than twenty minutes ago, Jake. I'm sure she's fine."

"The hospital said she didn't show for her shift, Trev."

Trevor waited a beat and then said, "Doesn't necessarily mean anything. She was pretty emotional when I left. Maybe she's taking some time to pull herself together.

Jake wanted to believe that. "Call the second you get to her place."

"Roger that."

Jake ended the call, and for what felt like the millionth time in the last ten minutes, he tried calling Liv again.

Chapter 13

Olivia woke from the vehicle's jostling motion. Her head and jaw were throbbing, and a sharp pain shot through her right wrist and up the length of her arm, any time she tried to move.

The cut on the inside of her left arm was still bleeding, but seemed to have tapered off some. Olivia knew she'd already lost a lot of blood, because the entire right side of her scrub top was soaked through, sticking to her skin beneath it.

Looking around slowly, she realized she was in the back of some sort of SUV. She tried to move again, but her hands were tied together in front of her with thick, coarse rope, increasing the pain in her wrist.

She started to panic. Wanted to scream for someone to help her. More than anything, she wanted Jake.

Images from her last day at his cabin began moving rapidly through her mind. It was like was watching them through one of those toys she'd had as a kid. The ones with the pictures on the slides. With each click, she replayed the scenes.

She was standing with Mikey and Jake in Jake's living room. *Click.* Talking with her brother in Jake's bedroom. *Click.* Jake standing at his door, begging her not to go as tears ran down his face. *Click.*

Feeling lost and betrayed as she walked out that door. *Click, click, click.*

Jake wouldn't be coming this time. There'd be no rescue, because she'd told him to stay away. Olivia could still see the devastating look on his face when she'd told him goodbye.

Tears filled her eyes, but only a few fell before she forced the rest away. Crying wasn't going to help. She had no way to call anyone, so if she was going to make it out of this alive, she'd have to depend on herself to do it.

Glancing over her shoulder, she looked at the top of the seat she was laying behind. No one was sitting there, and it was tall enough to conceal any small movement she made.

She listened, hearing Cetro's voice along with another man's. *Great. He brought a friend.*

Olivia couldn't understand what they were saying, because they spoke low, and in Spanish. As she continued to listen, Olivia became confident that they were the only two men with her in the vehicle.

Becoming more brave with her movements, she ignored the pain and began looking around as best she could for something, *anything* that could be used as a weapon to defend herself.

Of course, it couldn't be like the action movies she'd seen. or the mystery books she'd read, where the damsel in distress always found a tire iron or a screwdriver conveniently lying around. There was nothing Liv could see that would help her.

Her body rolled slightly as the SUV turned onto what sounded like a gravel road, and she had to bite back a moan. Not long after, they turned again, driving a short distance before stopping.

Olivia's heart rate was through the roof, and she had to force herself to take in deep, even breaths. Panicking right now would only ensure her death.

And she didn't want to die. There was too much left to do. So much she needed to say. *Not now, Bradshaw.*

Her problems with Jake would have to wait. Olivia needed to figure out what she could do to fight off two grown men by herself.

Assuming they were both armed, and she was tied up and injured, her choices slim to none. Even so, Olivia refused to give up. She may go down, but by God, she'd go down fighting.

Their doors shut loudly, and their voices travelled around the sides of the SUV toward the back. Olivia quickly shut her eyes and pretended to be unconscious.

The back of the SUV darkened with the men's shadows. She listened intently as they spoke. Thankfully, in English, this time.

"She's still out." She heard the other man say.

"Good," Cetro responded.

There was a short pause, and then, the other man asked, "What do you want to do with her now?"

"Finish your cigarette, then bring her inside to me. I don't want you smoking that thing in the barn. I'll go make sure everything's ready."

"You're the boss. Be there in a few."

Okay. So, she was in the country, most likely an abandoned farm away from anyone else. Olivia didn't think she'd been out for too long, so she couldn't be all that far from her house. At least she hoped this was true.

Please let someone come by my house.

Jake was a stubborn man. Maybe he'd ignore her request to be left alone, and finally decide to show up anyway. There'd be no mistaking that something terrible had happened there.

He and his team would haul ass trying to find her. They did it before. Olivia had no doubt, they could do it again.

She heard the grinding of gravel beneath the man's feet outside the back door. Time was running out. She had to come up with a plan.

The man hadn't been smoking in the vehicle, which meant he'd only lit up after he was outside. This bought her a few minutes, but that was all. She needed to *think*.

Allowing her eyes to open in narrow slits, Olivia could just make out the man's shadowy figure through the large back window. From what she could tell by his head and shoulders, she estimated that his waist probably fell at about the same height as the back latch.

That meant, the area right below his waist, would be at her eye level. This gave her an idea.

Mikey had talked to her a lot before he'd left for boot camp. During one of their more serious chats, her brother had turned almost deadly when he'd started talking about boys and how to stay safe while he and Jake were away.

She remembered squealing and begging Mikey to stop talking when he proceeded to tell her that a man's testicles were like plums.

If you squeezed one hard enough, Junebug, it'll pop.

Olivia had put her hands over her ears, but not before the visual image from their description had already sunk in.

Years later, an extremely drunk man came into the ER after getting a little too handsy with a girl at a bar. The woman had taken things into her own hands…literally…and Olivia realized her brother had been right.

The guy's left testicle had popped, just like Mikey had said it would. The man had been in so much pain, he'd passed out right there in the bar's parking lot.

Any second now, the man standing outside was going to open up the back hatch to get her out. Most likely, his crotch was going to be right on her level.

It wasn't the best plan, but it was all that she had. Olivia said a prayer that it would work, and she waited.

After what seemed like an eternity, Olivia heard the grinding of gravel, as if the man was stomping out his cigarette butt. She then heard him grab the SUV's back latch and pull.

Forcing herself to remain still, she kept her eyes closed, her breathing slow.

It was one of the hardest things she'd ever had to do, especially when she felt the man's hands on her, pulling her closer to the vehicle's edge.

Knowing he was about to lift her up, Olivia opened her eyes to slits again, and saw the man's zipper directly in front of her bound hands.

Thanks to her broken wrist, she'd have to use her left, non-dominant hand. Not the best option, but it would have to do.

As he started to lift her, Olivia said one final prayer, and grabbed hold of the man's crotch. She twisted and squeezed.

He cried out, and tried to drop her back into the SUV, but Olivia held on. She squeezed harder. The combination of the added pressure from her fist, along with the pull from her body falling was exactly what she needed.

She felt the pop, immediately followed by the man's strangled cry of pain. It was barely audible, as though he couldn't catch his breath.

When Olivia finally let go, the man fell to the ground and started gagging. Not wasting any time, she clumsily sat up, swung her feet around, and hopped down.

Her entire body hurt, and every time she jostled her wrist, she wanted to throw up. Even so, she ignored it all and began running.

Olivia followed what appeared to be a long driveway that connected to a gravel road at the end. If she could just make it to the road, then she'd have the thick patch of trees that lined it on the opposite side to use as cover.

Sounds of the man vomiting behind her reached her ears. *That's what you get, asshole.*

She kept running, hugging her broken wrist to her chest as she went. She'd already made it halfway between the car and the road. Just a little further, and she'd have a place to hide.

With a quick glance over her shoulder, she saw that the man was still down on the ground, and Cetro was nowhere in sight. *I'm going to make it!*

It became her mantra. Olivia told herself that, over and over, until her foot hit a larger rock at an awkward angle. Her ankle twisted and she went down onto her knees.

Unable to use her hands to break her fall, the jagged rocks dug into her flesh, ripping through her thin pants. Pain shot up through both legs. It hurt like hell, but she wasn't going to let that stop her.

Using her left elbow to balance, Olivia made her way back up to her feet. She'd just started to run again when she heard the man on the ground start yelling at her from behind.

"You stupid bitch! I'll fucking kill you!"

This was quickly followed by Cetro's loud bellowing voice. *"No!"*

On reflex, Olivia turned around to assess the threats behind her. She couldn't believe what she saw.

The man on the ground had his gun pointed directly at her

heart. Cetro had his gun aimed, too…just not at her.

He was marching hastily from the barn's large entrance, the barrel of his pistol pointed straight at the other man's head. She'd just started to run again, when the two men fired their guns simultaneously.

One of the bullets tore through the dirt and gravel by her feet. Olivia screamed and nearly fell over trying to avoid it.

She looked back as the man who'd tried to shoot her fell to the ground. Cetro had shot him in the head. *What the hell is happening?*

Not wanting to stick around to find out, Olivia started to run again. Cetro, the crazy bastard, ordered her to stop as another bullet hit the ground next to her.

"Fuck you!" Olivia yelled over her shoulder, still running.

He was going to kill her anyway, and a bullet was probably a lot better way to go than whatever else the sick bastard had planned for her.

He fired his weapon again and she felt a burning pain shoot across the outside of her left shoulder. She stumbled. *Shit, that hurt!*

"The next one will go into your leg."

Unwilling to give up, Olivia kept going, even though she knew he was gaining on her. Between the pain in her wrist, and the blood loss from the cut in her arm, Olivia was quickly losing steam.

She was hurting and scared. Even more than that, she was pissed. Enough was more than freaking enough.

If she was going to die—and this time it looked as if that was the case—she sure as hell was not going to make it easy on him.

"Go to hell!" Olivia yelled back, her voice shakier than she would have liked. "You want to kill me, then kill me. But, I'll be damned if I let you take me into that barn."

She stumbled, falling down to her knees again. *Get up, Bradshaw! Don't let him win!* Olivia tried, but tumbled to the ground once more.

When Cetro was almost next to her, she fully expected him to hit her. Or maybe kick her, like he'd done while she'd been held captive.

What she didn't expect was the snarling smile spread across his face as loomed over her.

"You will walk into that barn willingly. Then, you will do and say whatever I tell you to. You do this, and it all ends here. With you. If you do not"—he leaned down closer to her and yanked her up by her arm, causing her to cry out—"then once I am finished with you, I will find Jake McQueen and put a bullet between his eyes. After that, I will do the same to every man…and the pretty blond woman…on his team."

Olivia couldn't keep from gasping loudly. He knew about Jake? And the team?

Horrific image of Jake and the others, dead by this bastard's hand, flashed before her. Dear God, this man was pure evil.

Staring into a set of cold, unemotional eyes, Olivia tried to determine whether or not he was lying. He could be. Probably was. Unfortunately, there was no way to know for sure.

There was also no way in hell could she take that chance. Jake meant too much to her. So did the team.

She was faced with the worst kind of decision. Either go willingly into that barn, and let this man dish out whatever torture he had in mind before killing her, or fight him and risk him going after Jake and the others.

He may still do that, but if there was even a *chance* that she could prevent that, Olivia would do whatever she had to in order to—

Oh, God!

Realization hit with the force of a wrecking ball. Everything Mikey and Trevor had said about Jake and why he'd lied to her came rushing back tenfold. Olivia choked out a low sob as it all sank in.

She finally understood, but now, it was too late. She was going to die with Jake believing she hated him.

Another sob escaped because she knew Jake would spend the rest of his life blaming himself. That thought alone was worse than any physical pain she was about to endure.

At least Jake will be alive. He'll have a chance to move on. To be happy.

With that in mind, Olivia began walking back toward the barn. Her entire body hurt, but the jolts of pain were worth it if it meant saving Jake's life in the end.

****

Jake sped into Olivia's driveway. He slammed on the breaks, and put his truck in park behind Trevor's.

A large dust cloud bellowed up from behind him, and the vehicle was still rocking when he opened his door and raced toward the house.

Trevor stood on the sidewalk at the bottom of the porch steps, the look on his face confirming Jake's worst fears.

"Why the fuck haven't you been answering your phone? I've been calling you for twenty goddamn minutes!"

His friend remained quiet, which pretty much gave Jake his answer. With his heart in his throat, he made a move to go inside, but Trevor's palm slapped against his chest to stop him.

"She's not here, Jake." Jake's boot hit the bottom step, but Trevor pushed harder. "You don't want to go in there, man."

Somewhere in the back of his mind, Jake knew he was right. From the tortured look in Trevor's eyes, he knew that whatever was behind that door was bad. Really bad.

Still, he couldn't *not* go inside. Jake had to know. He needed to see for himself.

Shoving Trevor's hand away, he leapt over the rest of the small steps. Olivia's door was ajar, the place eerily quiet.

He raised his right hand and slowly pushed it open. It gave way with a soft creak, and his world came crashing down.

A strangled sound of denial escaped his throat as he took in the gruesome scene. Everywhere he turned, there were signs of a struggle.

A broken chair lay at his feet. Blood was on the floor, not far from where he stood.

Jake looked toward the living room, his knees shaking when he noticed the pile of broken glass that used to be Olivia's coffee table. His throat closed around a painful knot when he saw more blood there.

God forgive me. I've failed her again.

Woodenly, he stepped further inside. Turning to the right he noticed coffee cups and knives strewn across the countertop, stove, and floor. Broken porcelain crunched beneath his feet as he continued into the kitchen.

Jake ignored it. All he could focus on was the blood. *Olivia's blood.*

It was smeared all over the normally pristine countertops. Jake zeroed in on a particular steak knife lying on the floor near the edge of the stove.

Once again, Liv had been forced to fight for her life. This time, in the one place she should have been safe.

But it hadn't been enough. She was gone. *My world is gone.*

Jake's mind raced with questions to which he had no answers. They hit him at full speed, their effect dizzying.

Where was she? How long had she been gone? How badly was she hurt? *How could I let this happen?*

Stumbling out the door, Jake was down the steps before even realizing he'd walked outside. He passed by his teammates in a haze. Could hear their voices, but didn't bother listening to what they were saying.

He didn't care. All he could think about was the fact that the love of his life had been taken by a madman hell bent on revenge.

His breathing picked up. His heart raced. Liv was out there somewhere, and she was hurt.

That bastard, Cetro, had put his hands on her for the second time, despite Jake's promises that he would never be able to touch her again. *She may already be dead.*

Ah, Christ, he couldn't take this. The guilt, the pain, the fucking gut-wrenching fear for what Olivia may be going through was a living, breathing thing.

It was tearing him apart, piece by fucking piece. And it was all his fault.

"Goddammit!" Jake roared as his fist slammed into his truck's passenger-side door.

He felt no pain, only the fear that now consumed him to the point of madness. Chest heaving, he raised his fist again. When he started to swing again, his arm met with a strong resistance.

Ready to fight, Jake spun around, surprised to find Grant's hard eyes staring back at his. The other man must have arrived while he'd been in the house.

"Let me go," Jake growled menacingly.

With zero intention of following orders, Grant said, "Can't do that, boss."

"What the fuck do you mean, you can't do that?" Jake tried to jerk from the other man's grasp but was unsuccessful. "Let. Me. *Go!*"

Grant's only reaction was a curt shake of his head and a clear, "Not happening, boss."

Jake's nostrils flared as his breaths moved in and out in hard, fast puffs. He couldn't believe that, Grant Hill—of all fucking people—had his hands on him. Was *disobeying* him.

Jake opened his mouth to tell the asshole off, but the big guy didn't give him the chance.

"Don't do this to yourself, Jake. It's not your fault."

"The hell it's not!" Jake finally managed to pull from Hill's grasp. "She's *mine* to protect, and *I* let her go!"

"And she needs you, boss." This time, it was Coop who spoke up. "You're not going to be any good to her like this."

Jake looked at Coop then glanced around at Trevor and Mac who had all moved in closer, their faces covered with matching looks of concern. Finally, he looked back at Grant.

"That bastard has her, again. He's *hurt* her." His voice broke. Tears fell down his face, but Jake didn't care. "And it's my fault."

He looked back at the house, the images of what he'd found inside, forever burned into his mind.

"I swore to her that we'd caught him. I told her he'd never be able to hurt her again. And now he has her, and I don't even know if she's alive or—"

Trevor chimed in with, "She's alive, Jake. If Cetro wanted her dead, we would have found her body in the house. There would have been no reason to take her." Jake's friend took a step toward him. "But you losing your shit, right now, isn't going to help get her back."

Jake's mind cleared just enough to realize his friend was right. If Cetro just wanted to kill Olivia, he would have done it here and left her for him to find.

He was keeping her alive, for now at least, but *God*...Jake couldn't allow himself to think about what that bastard was doing to her. What he *would* do. Because Jake had no doubt that Cetro would kill her eventually.

"Boss, this isn't your fault any more than it is ours," Grant spoke up again. "Now, you can stand here feeling sorry for yourself, or you can get your head out of your ass and do what needs to be done to ensure that Olivia makes it out of this thing alive."

"You don't understand Grant—"

"Do you love her?" Mac's voice broke through.

Jake's eyes burned. He blinked back more tears. Turning to her, he whispered, "More than anything."

She gave him a small smile. "Then let's go find your girl."

Mac's blunt question and matter-of-fact attitude was like a slap in the face and a splash of ice-cold-water, all wrapped into one. And it was exactly what Jake needed.

Just like that, he was in battle mode. Except, "I-I don't even know where to start looking." He ran a shaking hand down his face before rubbing the back of his neck.

"I think I can help with that."

All heads turned at the sound of Derek's voice. Confused, Jake looked around, surprised when he saw D's car next to his.

Jesus, he must truly be losing it if he didn't even notice another vehicle pulling into the driveway.

"Did you check the camera feed yet?" Tablet in hand, Derek walked quickly toward them.

Shit! Fuck! Shit! He'd completely forgotten about the security cameras!

Jake's head swung around, his gaze landing on the one above Olivia's front door. The system Derek installed looked like a single camera setup, but was actually two. One lens faced her front stoop while a second one recorded her driveway.

Jake ran a hand over his weary face, again. Grant was right. He had to get his head on straight. Olivia didn't have time for anything less.

He turned back to Derek whose fingers were tapping away on the tablet's screen. Jake saw his teammate's face go slack, his complexion suddenly pale. "Ah, hell."

Jake's stomach plummeted. "What?" he demanded as he closed the distance between them. "*What?*" he growled again when Derek didn't answer right away.

Sympathy filled Derek's eyes as he turned the tablet so Jake could see its screen. His body tensed as he watched Cetro carry a bloody, unconscious Olivia outside. When they moved out of the camera's view, Jake tapped the screen to switch to the secondary camera's recording.

The bastard laid her down in the back of a white SUV. Cetro spent a couple of minutes bent over the back bumper before closing the hatch, presumably securing Olivia.

Jake's teeth clenched together so hard he was surprised they didn't crush into powder from the pressure.

His brow turned in when Cetro got in on the passenger seat, rather than the driver's. "He had someone with him," he said mostly to himself.

Squinting, he focused on whoever was behind the wheel,

but he couldn't make out any features other than the driver was obviously male.

"Probably the other prisoner he escaped with," Coop said.

They all watched, hovered over Jake's shoulders, as the vehicle quickly reversed out of the drive, and then took off toward the highway.

Forcing back the stark terror screaming through his veins, Jake restarted the video. This time putting all his effort into the details, as he would for any other job.

If he didn't, if he allowed himself to think about what Olivia could be going through this very second, he'd never make it another step.

"There!" Jake blurted. He looked up to find his entire team still surrounding him, having his back, as always.

His thoughts and vision blurred by emotions, Jake had missed it the first time. Pointing to the screen, he directed his words to Derek.

"Can you enlarge that?"

Derek took the tablet from Jake's hands, and in seconds, he had a clear picture of the SUV's front license plate. Another couple minutes, and he knew who it was registered to.

"It belongs to a rental company out of Dallas," D told Jake excitedly. "It was rented out under the name Robert Jones two days ago."

"Bob Jones? Really?" Mac asked sarcastically before muttering, "Guess Cetro doesn't have much of an imagination."

"How the hell is that going to help us find him?"

Jake could contact the state and local authorities to issue an APB, but by the time they got the word out, Cetro would be long gone, and Olivia would be dead.

The fingertips on Derek's right hand tapped against the screen with lightning speed. "It's a national rental chain."

Jake still didn't see his point "*And?*"

Head still down, Derek talked while he worked. "A few years ago, all of the major rental companies put GPS trackers in their cars. Too many people using fake ID's to rent them and then stealing their cars."

After another minute, D smiled and his eyes lit up with excitement. He turned his tablet around for Jake and the others to see. "I know where she is."

Knowing the others would follow, Jake sprinted to his truck.

Hang on, baby. I'm coming for you.

Chapter 14

The pain was excruciating. In her muddled mind, Olivia wondered just how much one person could suffer before it finally became unbearable.

As a nurse, she understood there were too many variables to accurately answer that question. What she did know was that she couldn't take much more.

Olivia wanted to think she could withstand whatever else the maniac decided to dish out but knew that simply wasn't true.

After having walked inside the large, decrepit building, Cetro had used the ropes around her wrists to hang her from a large hook that was connected to one of the barn's old beams. The pressure on her broken wrist was agonizing, and her shoulders burned from the constant pull. At least the large cut on her arm had finally stopped bleeding.

Olivia had passed out when Cetro first strung her up. Whether from the pain or blood loss, she wasn't sure. Though, she was awake and alert now, she kept her eyes closed.

Most likely, the bastard would want her to be aware of exactly what he was doing to her. If she could feign being unconscious for as long as she could, Olivia figured maybe it would buy her enough time. *For what?*

That little voice was right. It wasn't like anyone knew where she was. By now the hospital would have realized she hadn't shown for her shift. They may be a little worried when they couldn't reach her but would probably just assume she changed her mind and wasn't ready to come back after all.

And Jake...well, he'd have no way of knowing she was missing.

A different kind of pain hit. One she'd brought on herself. She'd been the one to tell Jake not to call or come by. Told him to give her space and not contact her.

I'm so sorry, Jake.

A sob built in her throat. Why couldn't she have seen what he and her brother had been trying so hard to get her to understand that day? Why hadn't she realized, then, that Jake had lied because he loved her, not because he'd *wanted* to deceive her?

Deep down, Olivia had always known Jake would never intentionally hurt her, yet, she'd thrown his betrayal in his face as if he'd done just that.

She'd let her anger and hurt feelings cloud what she knew to be true about the man she loved. And now she was going to die because of it.

A small whimper escaped before she could stop it.

"Ah, so you are awake," Cetro said, sounding pleased.

Olivia opened her eyes—no sense in pretending any longer—and found him standing a few feet away.

"Good. The show may begin."

The show? What the hell was he talking about? Unfortunately, Olivia didn't have to wait long for her answer.

Cetro turned back and moved toward a tripod that hadn't been there when she'd first come into the barn. Atop the metal legs sat a small video camera. Cetro reached up, pushed a button.

A tiny green light appeared. He was going to record her death? Jesus, he was even crazier than she thought.

Olivia knew she had to keep him talking, needing to buy as much time as she could. Even though she'd ordered Jake to stay away, eventually *someone* would realize she was gone.

Maybe Mac or Trevor would try to call or come by. They'd been so good about checking on her the past three days. Surely, they'd figure it all out.

The only question was, would it be in time to rescue her, or simply recover her body? Surprisingly, the question pissed her off more than it saddened her. Which meant her mouth took on a life of its own.

"What's the camera for, Javi? Is that the only way you can your jollies? Can't get off without watching yourself torture an innocent woman?"

Cetro stormed back to her, his hand moved lightning-fast. The skin covering her cheek burned from the blow and her eyes watered, but Olivia refused to cry. She would see him in hell before giving him that satisfaction, again.

The bastard actually smiled at her before turning back to the camera. "The camera will record your full confession."

Confession? "And what exactly am I supposed to be confessing to?"

He faced her again. When he spoke this time, his accent was even more prominent. It was as if his voice and his soul—if he'd actually had a soul—had both turned to stone.

"You will admit you killed my brother."

Olivia was unable to hide her surprise. Eyes wide, her voice rose at least an octave.

"*What?* I tried to *save* your brother. I didn't kill him!"

Ignoring her outburst, Cetro said, "My brother is dead because of you." His disgust for her was impossible to miss, and his next words dripped with sarcasm.

"Poor Olivia Bradshaw. America's sweetheart. A helpless woman who miraculously came back from the dead after such a tragic ordeal."

With crazed eyes, he stepped even closer to her, nearly spitting out his next words. "You are nothing more than a deceitful, murdering *bitch!* You may have fooled the rest of the world, but you do not fool me. You allowed a fourteen year-old boy to die. I know the truth." He glanced back over his shoulder toward the camera. "And soon every news station in the world will, too."

Oh, shit. He was going to try to torture a confession out of her, then send the recording to the news. Everyone she knew would see it. *Jake will see it.*

Even if Cetro stayed true to his word and didn't physically go after Jake, this alone—having to watch her torture and subsequent death—would kill him just the same.

"*No!*" Olivia screamed, fighting uselessly against her restraints.

She ignored the fire in her shoulders and the God-awful pain in her wrist. That didn't matter now. She had to protect Jake.

"*You sonofabitch!* We had a deal! You said this would end here. You said you'd leave Jake alone. You can't show him this! You can't—"

Cetro tsked, then spoke as if he were explaining something to a small child. "Actually, what I said was that I wouldn't hunt him and the members of his team down. He deserves to know the truth about the woman he was sleeping with, yes?"

Olivia looked him straight in his beady little eyes, not even trying to hold back her true feelings.

"You're nothing but a sick, twisted freak! It doesn't matter what you do to me. Nothing will change the fact that *I didn't kill your brother!*"

Olivia watched as he walked over to a table positioned up against one wall of the barn. From it, he picked something up, but it was only when he turned back around that she realized what it was.

Her heart raced dangerously fast, her breaths changing to rapid pants.

She tried to remain calm. To not show her fear. But the black, leather whip now in Cetro's hand made it impossible.

To keep from screaming, Olivia bit the inside of her cheek until she tasted blood. While he'd held her captive, she'd witnessed first-hand the kind of horror this monster was about to bestow upon her.

As much as she wanted to be, Olivia didn't know if she was strong enough to take it.

Walking behind her, Cetro began talking as though he were addressing an audience. He spoke of the injustice his brother had suffered. Ranted on and on about the pain his young sibling had felt, and the slow, agonizing death he'd been forced to endure.

All—according to him—because of her.

Olivia's entire body tensed when she felt a tug on the back of her scrub top, followed by more pulling, and then a ripping sound.

Cool air hit the newly-exposed skin on her back. He continued to cut until her top was nothing more than a pile of shredded material on the ground near her feet.

Wearing nothing on top now but her bra, Olivia wondered if she would pass out from fear before the true torture began.

Oh, God. Please don't let him do this.

Nearly hyperventilating now, her heart slammed against the inner walls of her chest as if it, too, were trying to escape the heinous actions of a madman.

"Are you ready to admit what you did?" he asked from behind her.

She could lie. Probably *should* lie. Even knowing the consequences, however, Olivia couldn't bring herself to deny the truth.

Refusing to let her last act on this earth be to tell a lie, she lifted her bruised chin, and stared straight into the camera.

With as strong a voice as she could muster Olivia said, "The only thing I did was try to save your brother's life."

The first strike of the whip was sudden, stealing her breath away. The searing pain was so fierce, her entire body felt the lick of its flames.

"Admit what you did!" Cetro yelled, but Olivia remained silent.

When the strips of leather slapped her skin for the second time, she couldn't hide the small cry that escaped from her tightly pierced lips.

She drew upon every ounce of strength she had, but by the third strike, the pain became nearly intolerable. Soon, Olivia's screams began filling the afternoon air.

****

Jake pulled his truck to the side of the gravel road and killed the engine. He and Derek got out and waited as Grant and Trevor did the same with theirs.

Everyone took care not to let their doors slam shut, unsure if Cetro had other men nearby. The team quickly assembled in small circle to discuss their plan of entry.

"According to this"—Derek addressed them all—"the vehicle is parked on the property just over that hill. It's abandoned farmland the bank took over when the owner died, a few years ago. There haven't been any recent offers or showings. And unless something's changed in the last month or so, which I seriously doubt it has, there's only one structure. An old barn."

Sometimes it scared Jake when he thought of all the things D could find out about a place or a person. He was just grateful as hell that Derek was part of their team. Especially now.

Though he was itching to quit talking and get to his girl, Jake knew it would be crazy to go barreling into the unknown. Not only would it risk his and the lives of his team, if they alerted Cetro and whoever else he had here, it would most certainly mean Olivia's death.

Like hell he'd risk her because he couldn't keep his shit together.

To the others, Jake said, "I called Ryker on the way here. From what he told me, I don't expect there to be a lot of men with Cetro. My guess is, when we get in there, we'll find him and Marcus Anthony, the other prisoner who escaped with Cetro during the storm. He's an African American male, age twenty-eight. Word is the two got pretty tight while they shared a cell these past couple months. But I don't want to take any chances and assume those are the only two."

Studying the map on the screen once more, Jake pointed and said, "Mac and Coop, I want you positioned here and here. Hill, you watch this side, and Trevor, you and I will approach from this area here. You go in through the barn's front doors, and I'll take the rear."

Then, speaking to the group as a whole, Jake added, "Olivia is the priority. Do nothing to risk her, got it?"

They all nodded in agreement and went to their prospective vehicles to gear up. They didn't have everything they usually did on a job, but it would have to be enough.

Not succeeding wasn't an option.

"Stay alert. Use your coms, and don't take any chances with your own safety. We get hurt, we're no good to her."

"We've got this, boss," Coop assured him.

Jake nodded once. "This ends here."

Several minutes later, Jake and Trevor broke through the property's eastern tree line. The barn Derek told them about was less than ten yards away.

The SUV they'd seen on Olivia's security footage was parked at the end of the gravel road leading to the building from the main road, and Jake nearly lost his footing when he saw the body lying on the ground behind it.

"Easy, boss." Trevor put his hand on Jake's shoulder. "Whoever that is, he's not Olivia."

Looking again, Jake could easily see the body was an African-American male. "I'd say we just found Marcus Anthony." Question was, why had he been killed?

As if reading his mind, Trevor spoke up again. "Probably outlived his usefulness. He helped Cetro get Olivia. Prick didn't need him after that."

Staying focused, Jake turned to his friend. "Listen. If something happens, and I don't—"

"Put that shit away," Trevor interrupted. "You're gonna go in there, take that bastard out once and for all, and then, we're bringing Olivia home."

Though he appreciated the guy's positive attitude, Jake had to say it. "Liv is the priority. If I go down, you get her the hell out of here."

"Jake—"

"Damn it, Trevor, just *promise* me!"

Trevor shook his head but said, "I'll protect her with my life, man."

Jake squeezed one of Trevor's shoulders. "Thank you."

"Screw that. You can thank me by going in and gettin' our girl back."

The two shared a look of understanding and proceeded to make their way to the barn. They were half way between the run-down building and the tree line they'd just come through when a terrifying scream cut through the afternoon air.

****

She was fading, fast. Olivia had tried to get through to Cetro, but there was no reasoning with insanity.

She'd gone into detail, explaining medically, why it had been impossible to save his brother. In one moment of desperation, Olivia had even tried empathy.

She'd shared how the loss of her brother had devastated her. How her life had been forever changed and how there was no way, she would ever want anyone—even a sadistic bastard like him—to suffer that same fate.

Eventually, Olivia realized there was no point in arguing. No amount of reasoning or empathy would make a difference.

Not one of the agonizing screams that had come with the strikes of the whip had fazed him. And there had been so many. As much as she wanted to fight it, Olivia knew her time was coming to an end.

Normally, she wasn't one to give up. But this situation was

as far from normal as anything could be, and she was tired. So very tired.

Tired of trying to convince a grieving sociopath she hadn't intentionally let his brother die. Tired of pretending to be strong, knowing all the while, she was crumbling with fear and pain inside.

Mostly, Olivia was tired of praying for a miracle that obviously wasn't coming. She simply couldn't do it anymore.

With what little strength she had left, Olivia lifted her head, and through swollen eyes, she stared straight into Cetro's.

"You can keep hurting me...or you can kill me. It doesn't matter. Nothing will bring...your brother...back. But if you're so hell bent on...blaming someone...for his death...you should go look...in a mirror."

She expected the comment to earn her another blow. Instead, she actually saw a brief flash of guilt. Unfortunately, it didn't last long.

"How *dare* you blame me for Miguel's death!" Cetro yelled, the veins in his forehead and neck bulging. "I raised that boy from the time he was just a toddler! I myself was barely a teenager. I gave him a home and food to eat. I taught him the ways of *life!*"

Olivia's outrage gave her a shot of adrenaline, and her voice came out a touch stronger. "You taught him how to...become a criminal. Your brother's blood...is on *your* hands...not mine."

The man glared back at her, his jaw clenching just before he turned and marched toward the table again. Olivia saw him pick up a very large knife before walking back to her, his eyes completely void of emotion.

She knew with utter certainty, that knife meant her

imminent death.

Cetro stood in front of her one last time. He didn't say anything, just stared expectantly. As if he were giving her one final chance to confess her sins.

She'd said all she had to say, and refused to waste what breath she had left on the man about to murder her.

When she remained silent, he walked behind her. This was it. This was how she was going to die.

Regret filled her soul and tears escaped her swollen eyes as she silently prayed Jake would somehow find a way to move on from this.

Cetro's hand grasped the back of her hair and pulled, so her neck jutted forward. Slowly, he pressed the knife's blade against her delicate skin.

Olivia prayed he'd make it quick. She felt a small prick followed by something warm dripping down between her breasts.

Closing her eyes, she brought to mind her most treasured memory.

It was the night Jake first told her he loved her. They'd made love, then, and though every time she'd been with Jake had been incredible, that particular moment between them had felt so magically different from all the times before.

Olivia held on to those images with every last ounce of strength she had. If she was going to die, she wanted her last thought to be about the love of her life. The man of her dreams. She thought of nothing else but…

"Jake."

His name was but a whisper. The single word a prayer that, even after everything, he would somehow know that she still loved him.

That, despite what she'd said to him, nothing would ever

change that. Not even death.

"Ah, yes. *Jake*," Cetro said from behind her. "The hero who saved you before. Too bad he won't be able to save you this time."

Surprising her, Cetro pulled the knife away from her neck as he continued to taunt her. With his mouth touching her earlobe, he asked, "What do you think he is doing this very moment? Hmm?"

A strange peace fell over Olivia as she waited for the end to come. She was hanging on by the barest of threads, each second pulling her further and further away.

She could still hear Cetro's voice, but his words fell on her ears as if they were travelling through a very long tunnel.

Unable to fight it any longer, Olivia slipped away into the peaceful abyss, Jake's beautiful, smiling face was the last thing passing through her mind.

****

Olivia's scream stopped both Jake and Trevor in their tracks. As the echoes faded, Jake's emotions hit him in rapid succession. Relief came first. If Olivia could scream, it meant she was still alive.

Next came the overpowering fear of not knowing what the bastard was doing to her. Finally, the ferocious need to find the sonofabitch and make him wish he'd never been born began to take over.

A hand on his shoulder and Trevor's low voice was the only thing that kept him from forging ahead recklessly.

"McQueen! You with me?" Trevor whispered loudly.

Jake blinked, only then noticing his friend was standing directly in front of him, now.

Not waiting for his answer, Trevor added, "Olivia needs you to be clear-headed. I know this is personal, but this isn't our first rodeo. You good?"

Jake swallowed. With a nod, he whispered back, "Let's do this."

After a quick check-in with the others, they continued toward the old barn. Trevor headed for the front as Jake made his way to the back.

As much as he hated to, Jake moved with slow, silent steps.

He could hear voices, barely able to make out what Cetro and Olivia were saying. A silent breath of relief escaped at the sound of her blessed voice.

She'd just said something about looking into a mirror. Her voice was strained and weak. Jake knew she was hurting, but—*Thank you God!*—at least she was still alive.

I'm coming sweetheart. Just a few seconds longer. I'm almost there.

He made his way around to the backside of the barn, where he silently moved through the opened doorway. Calling upon his years of training, he efficiently assessed the scene before him.

Cetro was standing in the middle of the barn's open space. Olivia hanging by her wrists in front of him. *Don't fucking think about that now. Just get the job done.*

The man had a fist full of Olivia's hair and a knife to her throat. He was leaning down, talking in her ear.

Silently, Jake made his way toward them, his mouth twisted in a feral smile as he heard the other man mention his name.

"Where is your hero now, hmm? Where is your precious Jake, just when you need him most of all?"

In a voice he barely recognized, Jake growled the last

words Javier Cetro would ever hear. "I'm right here, you sick fuck!"

The man's intake of air was sharp and sudden, but Jake gave him no time for further reaction. Swiftly securing the hand with the knife, he bent it back until he heard a snap, forcing the bastard to release the weapon. Cetro howled with pain.

Before the blade even hit the ground, Jake moved both hands up—one below Cetro's chin, the other grabbing the top of the bastard's head.

In one quick, sharp movement, Jake pushed up on Cetro's chin and twisted his head to the side. The satisfying crunch of bones was music to Jake's ears.

Jake let the asshole's lifeless body fall to the ground.

"I'm here, Liv! Please hold on, baby!"

Pulling his K-Bar from its sheath, he began sawing the thick ropes binding Olivia's raw wrists. "Ah, God, baby. I'm here, now."

Her head hung low against her chest, and she wasn't moving. Jake hadn't heard her make a sound since he'd slipped into the barn. Blood covered her back. The sight of those wounds alone was enough to bring him to his knees.

Jake had to work harder than ever before to remain focused on the task at hand. If he didn't, if he thought about what that monster had done to her, he'd go fucking insane. Allowing that to happen wouldn't help Liv, so with trembling hands, he continued working to free her.

"Jesus," he heard Trevor say as he entered the barn from the front, gun drawn. "Ah, Christ, Jake."

The agony in his friend's voice nearly tore him apart. "Help me get her down!" The panic in Jake's voice pushing Trevor's shocked form into gear.

The two men worked together to get her free. Trevor gently wrapped his arms around Olivia's hips and hoisted her up higher, making it easier for Jake to cut through the final strands of rope.

Olivia's arms fell limply to her sides, and her body dropped toward Trevor. He started to lay her down, but Jake shook his head in protest.

"Her back," he said, his voice cracking. "Let's take her outside."

Carefully, they transferred her into Jake's arms. He held on to his precious cargo and ran out of the barn as fast as he could, past the video camera he couldn't think about just then.

Trevor ran past him, sprinting to Derek's truck as he updated the team through his com. Jake didn't hear much of what was said, focusing instead on the precious cargo in his arms. Trev returned a minute later with a blanket in his hands.

He spread it out hastily, and Jake fell to his knees before gently laying Olivia down. He was unable to avoid the injuries on her back, but at least the blanket was clean, unlike the ground.

Jake reached over to check for a pulse, but when he saw the nick from Cetro's knife on her throat and realized just how close to death she had come, his hands began to shake too fiercely to try.

"Let me," Trevor said beside him.

Jake pulled his hand back and held his breath, praying she was still alive. He thought he'd seen her chest move to draw air, but his head was so fucked up right now, he didn't know if it she had actually taken a breath, or if his mind was only seeing what it wanted to.

"She's got a pulse," Trevor said excitedly.

Jake's relief was so staggering, he'd have fallen to his knees if he weren't already on them.

"Chopper's on its way," Mac hollered as she and Coop ran toward them from the south. "Ryker's medics are on hand. ETA four minutes."

Jake looked down at Liv. She was too still, and what little skin not covered in bruises or blood was too pale. Four minutes was too fucking long.

"How is she?" Hill asked gruffly as he came up from behind Jake.

"Her pulse is weak and thready," Trevor answered, his voice thick with emotion. "She's lost a lot of blood. Even with the chopper coming…"

He shook his head, his face contorted as he fought against the reality of the situation.

Trevor didn't finish what he'd been about to say. He didn't have to. Even with the chopper just minutes away, Olivia still may not make it.

Chapter 15

No. Fuck that. Liv was a fighter, and Jake would *not* let her give up, now.

"Olivia!" Jake's raised voice was gravelly, and he didn't even bother to hide the tears falling down his face. "Open your eyes." Jake gently shook her bare shoulders.

No response.

"Olivia!"

He didn't care how desperate he sounded. His entire world was bleeding out on the ground before him. He could practically see the life draining out of her, one agonizing heartbeat at a time.

Jake couldn't lose her. Not now. Not after all they'd been through. She would make it through this. He refused to entertain any other outcome.

While Jake kept trying to wake her, Trevor verbally assessed her injuries. "From what I can actually see, the cut on her arm is the worst. My guess is, her brachial artery's been nicked. She obviously has severe bruising, and, of course, multiple lacerations on her back." He clenched his jaw, pausing to reign in his anger.

"It looks like a bullet grazed her left shoulder, but the

wound is superficial. Her knees are scraped up, too. We won't know about internal injuries until we get her to the hospital." Trevor leaned over toward the side Jake was sitting on. "Ah, shit, Jake. The bastard broke her wrist."

Jake's eyes flew down to the wrist closest to him. He'd been so worried about getting her cut down and making sure she was breathing, he hadn't noticed how swollen and misshapen it was.

A tortured sound escaped his throat as he thought about her hanging from it. *God*, the pain she must have suffered.

He looked back up to her beautiful, battered face, wishing he'd made Javier Cetro suffer more.

He used that rage to push forward, refusing to let the bastard win. "Damn it, Liv. Wake up!"

Moving his attention back to her left arm, Trevor began to treat and put pressure on the deep wound there. A soft moan slipped out from between her lips and a surge of hope exploded inside Jake's chest.

"Liv? Baby, it's Jake. Can you open your eyes?"

For one long, excruciating second nothing changed. Then, her eyelids began to flutter.

"That's it, sweetheart. Let me see those gorgeous eyes."

Slowly, Olivia's eyes began to open. Her left one was so swollen, it only revealed a small slit. The other opened wider, and stared directly into his.

Jake hated the pain and fear he saw there.

"Jake?" she barely whispered his name.

He started to reach for the hand closest to him, pulling back at the last second, remembering it was broken. Instead, he gently began brushing some hair away from her forehead.

"Yeah, baby," his voice cracked. "I'm right here." More tears marked his face, but he made no movement to wipe them away.

Olivia closed her eyes, again, the movement sending her own silver streams down her temples. "Found...me," she rasped out.

It took a few tries before Jake could speak again. "Of course I did, sweetheart. I'll *always* find you."

Sounds from the approaching chopper quickly filled the air, but he didn't turn away from her.

She opened her one good eye. "C-Cetro?"

"Dead. I made sure of it this time. He will *never* hurt you again."

Olivia's lid fell shut, and her bottom lip quivered. "S-sorry, Never...should h-have...l-left...you. Under...stand—"

Jake reached across her torso and grabbed her uninjured hand. "No, baby. You have *nothing* to be sorry for."

The noise from the chopper cut off anything else he wanted to say. Jake and Trevor both arched their bodies over Liv's to protect her from the blades' powerful wind.

When it was somewhat calm, again, Trevor stood, jogging to the medics making their way across the grass.

Jake remained glued to Olivia's side, whispering comforting words. Loving words.

He kissed her forehead. "It's okay, now. You're going to be okay."

"H-hurts," she rasped, and Jake's nose burned as he tried to stave off the newest onslaught of tears.

"I know it does, baby. I know. But the medics are here now, and they're going to take you to the hospital. You'll be good as new before you know it."

Jake looked away from her for the first time since carrying her outside. He recognized Burns, one of Ryker's medics. Experience told him the guy knew his stuff.

Following closely behind Burns was taller, lanky man. One that looked too damn young.

As if reading his mind, Burns said, "This is Santos. He's good, McQueen. You can trust him."

Jake nodded and turned his attention back to Olivia, whose eyes had closed again.

The two men hurried to them. Jake scooted over to give the younger man room to work, but refused to completely leave her side. Burns looked at him knowingly.

"Trevor updated us on her known injuries, Jake. We'll take good care of her."

With swift, methodical movements, Burns and the other man took her vitals and started an IV.

Jake continued to smooth the hair on the top of her head, his touch a gentle reminder to her that he was still there.

Burns looked over at him sympathetically. "We need to move her. I'm not gonna lie; it's gonna hurt."

Jake spoke through his teeth. "Can't you give her something more for the pain?"

The older man shook his head. "Not without knowing the full extent of her injuries."

The thought of her enduring even more pain cut Jake to the quick. "She's hurting, goddamn it!"

Jake knew the man. Hell, Burns had even treated him a few times after he'd been injured on the job. That didn't keep Jake from wanting to rip the guy's head off, just then.

He started to protest some more, but a soft touch to his arm stopped him.

"S'okay, Jake." Olivia's eyes were still closed, but she'd definitely spoken to him.

"I can't stand to see you hurting, sweetheart." It was one hell of an understatement.

"I know"—she opened her good eye—"h-heart rate…already…s-slow. Pain meds could…m-make…worse. Probably p-pass out…anyway. Be…okay."

She closed her eye again, the effort behind her choppy words simply too great for her to bear.

Olivia had been beaten within an inch of her life, was barely able to even speak, and yet, she was trying to comfort *him*. Jesus, he was gut-shot.

More tears escaped the corners of his eyes. "I'll be right here. I'm not going anywhere, and neither are you." Jake leaned down and gently kissed her swollen lips. "You hang on, okay? This thing between us isn't finished. Not even close. So, you have to hang on, even if it's just so you can kick my ass later. You hear me, Liv? You. Hang. On."

"'K."

He could have sworn she tried to smile, but then, they were rolling her to her side and sliding the backboard beneath her.

Olivia's agonizing cry of pain gutted him. It was a sound he'd never forget.

As predicted, she lost consciousness. Jake was actually relieved that, at least for the moment, she'd found a short respite from the pain.

He and Trevor helped load her into the chopper, then Jake climbed in after. Trevor lifted his chin to the road where two black, heavily tinted, non-descript SUV's were pulling up.

Yelling over the chopper's growing roar, Trevor said, "There's Ryker. I'll handle things with him and meet you at the clinic."

Because these were Ryker's guys, Jake and his team knew Olivia wouldn't be going to a public hospital.

Homeland used a private healthcare facility located on the

outskirts of Dallas, which only a select few knew about. The staff included some of the most brilliant doctors and nurses in the country.

Jake nodded and turned his attention back to Olivia as the younger medic slid the bird's door shut. Burns wasted no time getting them off the ground.

While he flew, Santos began checking her vitals again. She lay on her back, quiet and still, until Santos began wrapping a splint around her broken wrist.

Olivia groaned, her brows turning inward with pain.

"Jake?"

She spoke so softly, Jake would have missed it had he not seen her lips move.

He leaned down closer, speaking loudly so she could hear him over the chopper's loud humming.

"I'm right here, baby."

Liv was quiet for so long he thought she'd gone back under. Then, he saw her lips move again.

He got even closer, his ear tilted just above her mouth. "What, sweetheart? I couldn't hear you."

"L-love...y-you."

Her words were broken from exhaustion and pain, but they were still the sweetest, most important ones he'd ever heard. Words he thought he'd never hear her say again.

Her image blurred behind his unshed tears. The stinging in his nose was back, and his throat closed up so quickly he had to swallow three times before he could actually speak.

"*God*, Olivia. I love you, baby. So much."

Once her mind was clear and she remembered what he'd done to her, she'd probably try to walk away again. This time he wasn't letting her go.

Jake blinked quickly, not because they weren't alone, but

because he wanted to see her more clearly. He leaned over her and kissed her forehead and lips before Santos placed an oxygen mask over her nose and mouth.

Her fingers squeezed his before going limp again. She actually looked at peace for the first time since finding her in that barn.

Sitting back in his seat more, Jake kept hold of her hand. Just as his shoulders began to relax, alarms started blaring all around them.

Santos sprang into action, checking her pulse and then immediately starting chest compressions. Jake nearly lost it.

Unable to do anything else, he got into her face and ordered her to be okay.

"Don't do this, Liv! Don't you do this! You fight, goddammit. You *fight!*"

For the umpteenth time that day, Jake felt as if his soul was being torn from his chest. Santos stopped the compressions to check for a pulse.

When he began rhythmically pressing down onto her chest again, Jake knew he hadn't found one.

Please don't take her. I can't lose her!

Jake panicked like never before. "You are not dying, Olivia! Do you hear me? You live!" His voice broke, but he kept going, "You fucking *live!* For me...for us!"

Santos paused and checked again. He was about to start compressions again when the guy huffed out a huge sigh of relief. He spoke to Burns in his headset. "Got her back, but pulse is weak."

There was a pause and then to Jake he ordered, "Sit back. We're getting ready to land."

Jake nodded, his eyes never leaving Liv's face. His movements became automatic as he slid back into his seat and buckled himself in.

How many more times would he have to live through thinking he was going to lose her?

For the next few minutes, he just sat there, emotionless and numb. Somewhere in the back of his muddled mind, Jake knew he was shutting down.

He'd thought he lost her once before and, up to now, thought that was the worst thing he could ever experience. He was wrong.

Witnessing the love of his life's heart stop before his very eyes had broken something inside him.

His mind and emotions became blanketed with just one thought—Olivia could still die today, and there wasn't a fucking thing he could do about it.

After they landed, the group of doctors and nurses Ryker had waiting for them on the roof whisked Olivia away. They pushed her into a large elevator, the doctor in charge shouting out orders as they went.

Jake jogged next to the gurney until he was literally pushed aside so they had more room to work. When the elevator doors shut, he found himself still standing on the roof with Burns and Santos, having no idea what he was supposed to do next.

When he refused to go into the surgical waiting room, the two medics took him to the hallway just outside the OR where Olivia was being worked on.

He mumbled a thanks to them both. They wished him luck, and went on their way.

For who knows how long—could have been hours—Jake simply stood there, staring at the OR doors. Wishing like hell he could go in.

A hand on his shoulder caused him to start. He was so

keyed up, his arm swung around before he'd even given it any thought.

"Whoa! Easy there, boss," a familiar voice said. "It's just me."

Jake blinked and stopped his fist mid-swing when he saw Coop standing in front of him. He lowered his hand without speaking.

"Everyone else is already in the waiting room, but I wanted check in with you and see how she's doing."

No one had come back out of those damn doors. Not even to give him an update on her status. Olivia could be gone for all he knew, but—

No. He couldn't think like that. He had to stay positive. For Liv.

Jake opened his mouth to tell him what had gone down in the chopper when both men heard footfalls. They turned to see Trevor walking down the hallway.

"How is she? Have they told you anything?"

Worry and guilt were written all over Trevor's face. Jake knew what he was thinking, because, hell, he'd thought it, too.

If Trevor had stayed just a little longer, he'd have been with Olivia when Jake got the call from Ryker. He would have stayed there until Jake could get to her, most likely deterring Cetro from making his move.

None of what had happened was Trevor's fault, but Jake knew his friend was shouldering some of the blame anyway. A part of Jake wanted to comfort him. As Trevor's boss— and more importantly, his friend—he knew he should say something to ease the other man's guilt.

Jake simply couldn't form the words. He couldn't find any words, for that matter.

All he could think about, all he kept seeing was Olivia lying lifeless in that chopper. He could still hear the alarms. Could see Santos frantically pumping her chest.

And Jake still felt as though he'd just lost the love of his life forever.

She was his soul mate. His other half. Against all odds, they'd found their way to each other.

Then, because he'd been a complete chicken shit and hadn't had the balls to come clean about her brother sooner, there was a good chance he'd lose her forever.

Jake's chest suddenly felt tight, like a giant vice had grabbed hold of his heart and was squeezing the life out of him. He rubbed at the skin there, and tried to force air into his lungs, but couldn't seem to get in more than a tiny breath at a time.

Overwhelming panic was spreading through every cell in his body, and he couldn't seem to stop it.

"Jake?"

Coop sounded worried, but Jake could barely hear him over the sound of blood surging past his ears. More voices travelled from down the hall.

"Boss, I'm so sorry." This came from Mac. "What can we do?"

"Hey, boss. How is she?" Derek asked anxiously. "She's gonna be okay, right?"

The whole team was here, now, practically talking over each other, with the exception of Grant. He remained stoically quiet, his big arms crossed in front of his chest.

Jake couldn't hear any of them. Jesus, what was happening to him? Was he having a heart attack? Is this what that felt like?

He was losing the last bit of control he had, and needed to

move, before he completely lost it in front of his entire team.

"Hey, man. You okay?" Coop asked warily.

"I…" Was that his voice? "I need to…"

Christ, he couldn't even form a coherent thought. Desperate, he looked around for a place to go. Somewhere to hide because, sure as shit, he couldn't let them see the breakdown he knew was coming.

There!

At the other end of the hallway were two doors. One with the universal symbol for 'Men's Room' on it.

Jake his rusty throat. "I just need…a minute."

Ignoring the worried looks of his team, Jake practically ran to the bathroom, thankful no one followed him. He pushed the door open with such force it slammed into the wall behind it.

Jake was heaving into one of the three toilets, before the door had closed completely.

Every lurch of his stomach brought with it a new memory of Olivia. A new fear that he'd be forced to live without her, for real this time.

This went on until well after his stomach was empty. Then, all he managed to accomplish was a series of wretchedly painful dry-heaves.

Several minutes later, the convulsing stopped. Woodenly, Jake reached up, flushed the toilet, and made his way to the sink to wash up.

He washed blood from his hands, which he'd forgotten was even there, and rinsed out his mouth.

As he wiped the water from his face, he stared at his reflection in the mirror. His hands were clean, with the exception of some blood still beneath his short fingernails, but his shirt and the top half of his pants were covered in blood. Olivia's blood.

The sight brought forth all of the emotions he'd been holding back, for Olivia's sake. Anger toward Cetro and himself.

Guilt over the whole situation with Mike, and for not protecting her like he'd sworn he always would.

Emotions as they slammed into him with a vengeance, and Jake could do nothing to stop them.

His fist shattered the mirror, shards smeared with his own blood clanged down into the porcelain sink below. It wasn't enough.

Lifting the large, metal trash can with ease and swung it around into the nearest stall, its side caving in as if it were an aluminum soda can. Used paper towels flew out, littering the cold, tiled floor, but it still wasn't enough.

Making a noise that didn't even sound human, Jake ripped the plastic paper towel dispenser from the wall and threw it across the small room.

A large patch of drywall tore away from the wall where it had hung. It cracked open as it smashed against the far wall.

Still. Not. Enough.

Jake looked around for something else to destroy. The only things feasible were the two sinks, their backs attached to the wall behind them. They'd have to do.

He grabbed onto the sides of the cold, smooth surface and growled as he pulled with all his might. The sink didn't budge, which only pissed him off even more. Jake yelled out as he tried again, but his efforts were in vain.

It became a challenge, then. A task he could focus on instead of thinking about the fact that Olivia was in that operating room, this very second, fighting for her life. *And mine.*

Jake gave another tug. A tiny spark of satisfaction crept in when he noticed the clear calking on the back of the sink begin to crack. Just a few more tries and he knew he could get the fucker loose.

He'd just started pulling again when he heard Hill's deep voice.

"Is that helping?"

Jake froze but didn't look up. He just stood there, staring down at the sink, his chest rising and falling with each heaving breath.

"Don't stop on my account," Grant added.

Jake swiveled his head around and gave the man a look that said he needed to shut the fuck up, and get the fuck out. Of course, the guy would pick today to become Chatty Cathy.

"What? You want to hit *me?*" Grant shrugged one shoulder and took a step closer. "Go ahead. Hit me."

Jake finally found his voice, though he didn't recognize it. "Get out."

Instead of leaving, Hill took another step closer. "Or what? You'll quit taking your frustration out on the bathroom and start fighting something that can hit back?"

Jake let go of the sink and in one long stride was toe-to-toe with his teammate. "Get. The. Fuck. Out."

"No."

For just a second, Grant's eyes flashed with what looked like sympathy or some shit like that. Whatever it was, Jake didn't need it. He sure as hell didn't want it.

His fists filled with the front of Grant's t-shirt. Jake pushed against the guy's chest until his back was against the same wall the door slammed into earlier.

"*Godammit*, Hill. I'm your boss, and I said to get out. That's a fucking *order!*"

"Well, it's a good thing I'm in here as your friend and not your employee. Besides, what are you going to do, fire me because I won't leave you alone to vandalize a fucking bathroom? Like I said, you wanna hit something...Hit. Me."

Jake's nostrils flared, and his jaw clenched tight. The two stood that way for a full thirty seconds before Jake shoved against Grant's chest with a grunt, releasing his hold.

Stumbling backward, Jake shook his head as if he were trying to convince himself this was all a bad dream, instead of the real-life fucking nightmare that it was.

"I lost her, man."

Grant's eyes grew. "What? I...I thought she was still in surgery."

Realizing how his choice of words sounded, Jake explained.

"She is," he said quickly. "I mean on the chopper. One minute she was talking to me, the next, her heart's not beating."

Jake wiped a hand down his face and grabbed the back of his neck. "Some medic half my age was doing chest compressions on her, and all I could do was sit there with my head up my ass and watch."

He moved his hands to his hips and paced back and forth, full of nervous energy. "And she's in there right now, fighting for her fucking life because *I* wasn't there to protect her."

"You know that's not true."

He stopped moving and faced Grant, yelling so loudly they could probably hear him in the operating room.

"She's *mine!* I damn well should have kept her *safe!*"

Jake waited for Hill to tell him it wasn't his fault again. How there was nothing he could have done to prevent what happened.

However, as the two men continued to stand there, Jake realized those things weren't coming. The guy wasn't even looking at him with the pity and sorrow he expected.

Instead, the big guy looked him square in the eye and asked, "What do you need?"

Jake stared at him for a few seconds. He was offering to help Jake, however he could. Too bad the one thing he truly needed, Grant couldn't give.

"I need to be able to *do* something instead of just waiting for someone to tell me what's going on."

Hill gave a slight nod. "The waiting's the worst. The waiting, the not knowing."

He pushed off of the wall and took a couple steps closer to Jake, but his eyes said he'd gone to a totally different place altogether.

"The fact that we are out there risking our asses to save strangers' lives almost every fucking day, yet the *one* person who matters most to you in the world, someone you'd die to protect, needs help in a way that you can't give."

Grant's forehead creased, and he shook his head. He blinked quickly and looked back up at his boss, almost surprised to see him there.

Jake knew where Hill had gone. He'd read what had happened in his file, but this was the first time the man had willingly shared something personal with anyone on the team. Even Jake.

"Your mom?" Jake asked quietly.

Hill nodded. "She died when I was nineteen. Cancer." One corner of his mouth twitched. "Of course, I'm sure you already knew that."

"I did, but thanks for sharing it anyway. And, I'm sorry. About your mom."

Shrugging, Grant mumbled, "It was a long time ago."

The room silent for a few seconds before Jake asked, "So, what did you do...when you lost her, I mean. How did you...cope?"

Though the other man never smiled, Jake could have sworn he wanted to. "I joined the military and started blowing shit up."

Barking out a surprised laugh, Jake said, "Yeah. That sounds like you."

Squeezing Jake's shoulder, Grant said, "Come on, man. I think you've done all the damage you can do in here."

Jake glanced around at his destruction. "Yeah. I'll let Ryker pick up the tab."

Grant nearly did smile, then. "Hell, yeah. Come on." He dropped his hand and reached for the door. "Let's go see about your girl."

Jake started to pass, but stopped just before the hallway. Of all the people he thought might come into that bathroom to try to save him from himself, Grant would have been the very last one he would have expected.

He turned to his employee. His teammate. And yeah, his friend. "Thanks, man."

Grant just nodded with a short grunt, and Jake wanted to smile. The Hill they all knew and loved was back.

The rest of the team was still waiting at the end of the hallway, and their eyes wary when they saw him.

"You okay, boss?" Mac asked almost hesitantly and lifted her chin toward the direction of the bathroom. "It sounded like a war zone in there."

Jake opened his mouth to talk, but Grant beat him to it. "He's fine. Now give the man some space. He doesn't need everyone smothering him for Christ's sake." He turned to

Jake and said, "I'm gonna go find some coffee. You want some?"

"Sure," Jake said, surprised at the offer. "Thanks."

In another unexpected move, Hill turned to the rest of the team. "Anyone else?"

"You're offering to buy us coffee?" Coop asked.

Before Grant could take back the offer, Derek stood from where he'd been camped out on the tiled floor. "I'll go. My ass is numb. I need to move around anyway."

Grant and Derek made their way down the long hallway, disappearing around the corner.

"What the hell was that all about?" Coop asked.

"Yeah. He actually, you know, talked. Like a person." Mac sounded genuinely surprised.

"Lay off Hill," Jake said, even though he understood exactly why they were shocked. "He's not a bad guy."

"I'm not saying he's bad. I mean, he's one of us, so of course he's bad*ass*, but I never thought he was *bad*. The guy just never talks. Then, he's with you in the bathroom, of all places, and comes out offering to buy everyone coffee. It's just...weird."

Mac was worried. Normally, she stayed pretty quiet herself, but she was rambling now, and Jake knew it was because she was concerned for Liv. They all were.

And though he still felt like it was *his* life on the line, Jake was suddenly glad they were all together.

Chapter 16

Jake, Mac, and Coop continued talking about nothing important, doing their best not to go crazy while waiting to hear something.

Grant and Derek came back a few minutes later, and while Derek joined right in on the conversation, Grant went back to being his silent, observant self.

Trevor brought Jake up to speed on Ryker's plan to clean up Cetro's mess. Thankfully, Homeland had the ability to make something like that go away without anyone being the wiser.

Of course, those who needed to know would be read in, and Ryker would make sure anyone left in Cetro's circle knew exactly what happens to those who come after innocent women. Especially on American soil.

Trevor also confirmed the other man with Cetro was, in fact, the other escaped convict. Somehow, Cetro had enticed Marcus Anthony to go with him and help with his plan for revenge against Olivia. Turned out, Marcus Anthony used to run around with Carlos Hernandez, Liv's stalker.

The theory was that Cetro had Anthony get in touch with someone he trusted to do the dirty work when it came to stalking and attempting to abduct Liv.

When Trevor tried to apologize for what had happened, Jake shut him down immediately. They couldn't start with the what-ifs. It didn't change anything and would only end up driving them both crazy.

In the end, the only one to blame was that sadistic fuck, Cetro. And he was finally burning in Hell.

Hours later, A white-haired man in surgical scrubs came through the swinging double-doors. He didn't look surprised to see them sitting on the floor, there rather than in the waiting room where they should have been.

Jake shot up, nearly stumbling in his haste. "How is she? Is she okay?"

The rest of the team got to their feet, as well, all surrounding him, ready to catch him if he fell. Figuratively and literally.

"I assume you're Jake?"

Jake approached the doctor with an extended hand. "Jake McQueen. I'm Liv's…we're…together." God, he prayed that was still true.

The man shook Jake's hand. "Agent Ryker told me you'd be here. I'm Doctor Wyrick."

"How is she?" Jake asked again.

The doctor removed his surgical cap and rubbed the back of his neck. "The surgery was tricky. The wound in Miss Bradshaw's arm went deep. There was a microscopic tear in her brachial artery. The angle and location of the tear was difficult to reach, and small tears like that are much harder to repair than larger ones. However, we were able to secure the artery and repair the torn muscles. With some physical therapy there shouldn't be any lasting impairments in that arm."

Jake's heart hammered against his chest. "So, she's going

to be alright."

"Aside from the artery, our orthopedic surgeon set and cast her broken wrist. She was lucky there, too. The break was clean and didn't require any pins. The cuts on her back were cleaned, and those that needed it were sutured."

He paused to take a breath. "All of her scans were clear and showed no signs of internal injuries. She'll need to stay here for a few days, but after that, I see no reason why she can't finish her recovery at home." The doctor looked around at the team and back to Jake. "I'm assuming she will have someone to help her?"

"She'll have everything she needs. Now, can I see her?"

Jake felt like he was crawling out of his skin with the need to see for himself, that she was okay.

"Miss Bradshaw is under heavy sedation to give her body time to start healing. She won't wake up for several more hours, but I'll take you to her." He looked around at the others, again, adding, "I'd like for it to just be you for now."

Fine by him. Right now all he cared about was seeing Olivia.

Jake started to follow the doctor but stopped and turned back to his team. "Thank you. For being here." He gave a quick glance to Trevor then Grant. "For everything."

Trevor, Derek, and Coop were smiling like a couple of goofballs. Mac's eyes looked suspiciously wet, and damn if Grant Hill's mouth wasn't turned up, just a bit.

Trevor smiled wide. "Go be with your girl."

A few minutes later, Jake was standing outside Olivia's room. He'd waited hours to see her, but now that he was about to, he found he was scared to death.

"My biggest concern is the amount of blood she lost," the doctor said beside him. "We gave her two units and will continue to monitor her cell count over the next twenty-four hours."

"But, she's okay, right? You said she was going to be okay."

"Physically, yes. I'm sure you're aware there are certain risks involved with any surgical procedure. But, barring any unforeseen circumstance, she should be fine."

Jake gave his thanks and reached for the door, but the doctor's next words stopped him.

"That young woman was put through hell."

Jake turned and spoke over his shoulder. "I know."

"I won't lie. She doesn't look good. The bruises and swelling will all go away with time, as will the cuts and scrapes. Some will most likely leave scars. Her back..." The doctor shook his head. "Tell me you got the bastard who did this."

A muscle in Jake's jaw bulged just thinking about it. Surprisingly, the doctor looked almost as pissed as he felt.

"I did."

Jake and Dr. Wyrick shared a look, and Jake knew the doctor understood exactly what he wasn't saying.

"Good. Now, go be with that young lady. She's going to need a lot of support to get through this. And I'm not just talking about her physical injuries."

"She'll have it. Trust me."

With one final nod, the doctor turned and walked away, leaving Jake at the door alone.

He took a deep breath, attempting to get his emotions under control before going in. Olivia didn't need the raging storm still bellowing inside him. She needed his help and support. His love.

Pushing everything else away, he slowly entered the room.

His heartbeat stalled when he caught his first sight of her.

The blood had been cleaned off, amplifying the bruises covering her face. Her left eye was still swollen but looked as though it had gone down slightly.

Her right arm was in a white cast from below the elbow down, and a sling held it in place as it rested on a pillow across her belly.

Her other arm was wrapped in gauze where the cut had been treated and sewn. An IV tube ran from beneath the tape on the top of that hand, up to the fluid-filled bag hanging on the metal stand positioned near her.

Tears pricked the corners of his eyes. The doctor had said she didn't look good, but he'd been wrong.

The bruised and broken woman lying before him was the most beautiful sight he'd ever seen.

Jake moved toward the left side of the bed, sliding a plastic chair as close to her as he could get it. Mindful of the IV, he reached through the metal railing to take her hand into his.

He exhaled long and slowly, as though touching her gave his lungs permission to breathe again.

He brought her hand to his lips, keeping it there. She was too cold. Too still. He needed her to wake up.

The doctor had said she would be okay, but until she opened her eyes, until he heard the sweet sound of her voice—

He used his shoulder to wipe a tear from his cheek. She'd been through so much. More than any one person should ever have to endure. Her sleeping image blurred as he leaned over the railing to kiss the top of her head.

Squeezing his eyes shut, Jake rested his forehead against her cool skin. He knew his tears were raining down on her, but he couldn't bring himself to move away.

"I love you, baby," he said with a broken whisper. "Come back to me soon, okay?"

Kissing her again, he could taste the saltiness of his sorrow. With her limp hand still in his, Jake sat back down. He wiped the tears from his face, but they just kept coming.

With his head hung low, Jake's entire body shuddered as he wept. He prayed for her forgiveness, and guidance on how to help her get through this.

Sometime later, Jake woke with a start. A soft moaning caught his attention, slapping the rest of the sleepy cobwebs away.

Olivia was having a nightmare. Jake watched her brow furrow. He felt her fear when the small hand he was still holding squeezed his tightly. Her legs began moving about as if she were running from something. Or someone.

Olivia mumbled something incoherent. Jake stood and began carefully caressing the bruised skin on her cheek with the back of his knuckles. He kissed her temple and whispered sweet, soothing words.

Before long, her jerky movements stopped. The creases on her forehead smoothed, and her entire body relaxed.

The cycle repeated itself several times throughout the night. At one point, it got so bad that the nurse had to inject a stronger sedative into Olivia's IV, and the doctor had to re-stitch the wound on her arm. She'd busted it open while trying to escape whatever hell she'd been trapped in.

The next thing Jake knew, a large hand was on his shoulder and a sliver of morning sun was peeking through the curtains. Through eyes that felt like sandpaper, he looked up and saw Trevor standing next to him.

"Sorry to wake you, but I thought you might want something to eat." He held up a fast-food bag with one hand, a large coffee in the other.

Jake ran a hand over his face and sat up from his slouched position. "Thanks," he said, reaching for the coffee. "I'm not hungry, but I'll take this."

Trevor sat the paper sack down onto the portable tray nearby, and pulled another chair closer. Sitting next to Jake, he looked at Olivia for a while and then, "So, how is she?"

"Doc says physically, she's going to be fine. But the other…" Jake trailed off, shaking his head. "I don't know, man. A person can only take so much, you know? She had nightmares all night. Never really woke up, but I know she was reliving everything. The doctors had to give her something stronger. She's just so—"

"Tough," Trevor finished for him. "If anyone can make it past all this, it's her."

Without taking his eyes off her, Jake agreed. "She's as tough as they come." Which reminded him—

"Where's the video?"

Trevor suddenly looked uncomfortable. "Uh…what video?"

"There was a camera in the barn. The bastard recorded everything he did to her. I want to see it."

Trevor's eyes flickered slightly and shrugged. "Asshole must have forgotten to hit record.

Jake's eyes narrowed suspiciously. "So, there's *nothing*?"

Trevor shook his head. "Even if there was, you wouldn't want to see that, Jake. Trust me. It's bad enough remembering the way we found her. The other…you can't un-see that shit, man. That crazy bastard is dead, and Olivia's safe. *Truly* safe. No sense in looking backward."

Trevor's gaze slid to Olivia's sleeping form and back to Jake's. A sadness was there when he spoke. "You've got a shot at something really good here, Jake. Don't dwell on the past. It's a waste of time and won't change what happened."

Jake studied his friend for a moment. "We still talking about Olivia?"

Trevor shrugged one shoulder and broke eye contact. "I just know blaming yourself for something you can't change won't do you or her any good." He looked back at Jake and gave him a sly smile. "And I don't want to see your dumb ass ruin the best thing that's ever happened to you."

Jake grinned for the first time in days. It felt odd…almost unfamiliar.

His mouth fell as quickly as it had risen. Studying Olivia again, he asked, "How do you know I haven't already?"

"When I was at her house, before, she promised she'd talk with you. That she'd listen and really try to understand everything. I believed her."

Jake's thumb absentmindedly caressed the top of her hand, to the side of where the IV was placed. "Doesn't mean she'll be able to forgive me for lying about Mike. Or that she won't blame me for this."

"You underestimate her, Jake. Sure, she was upset, but I saw the way she looked at you before that chopper came. Olivia still loves you. She's not going to blame you for what happened."

Jake closed his eyes and found himself back in that helicopter.

Jake?

I'm right here, baby.

L-love…y-you.

"Although, I do predict a massive amount of groveling in your future."

Jake did smile at that. "She's worth it."

He'd give her any damn thing she wanted, if it meant they could be together again.

With another squeeze, Trevor stood and carried the chair back to its original place. "I'll leave you to it, then. And don't be a bullheaded ass yourself. You need something, just ask."

"I will."

"I mean it, Jake." Trevor looked at him pointedly. "The whole gang's already said. Anything you or Olivia need, you'll get."

Jake's heart swelled, and his throat became thick. He was truly blessed to have friends like Trevor and the others.

"Got it."

With a single nod, Trevor turned to leave the room.

"Hey, Trev?"

The other man turned back toward him. "Yeah?"

"Thanks."

With another solemn nod, Trevor walked out the door.

Jake leaned up and kissed Olivia on the lips. She didn't move.

"He's right, you know. You *are* the best thing that's ever happened to me." He kissed her cheek, and whispered in her ear. "I love you, baby. I'll be here when you're ready to come back to me."

He settled back down in his chair. The hard plastic bit into his back, but he'd sit there until Christmas if he had to.

When Olivia opened her eyes, Jake needed his face to be the first thing she saw. He needed her to know she was safe, and he was here for her.

With a prayer in his heart that she'd find a way to forgive him, Jake took hold of her hand and sat back, prepared to wait for as long as it took.

****

Everything hurt. As Olivia lay in a state of semi-awareness, she tried to remember why. When no answer came, she began mentally cataloging the worst of it.

Her right wrist ached and felt much heavier than usual. The left side of her face felt sore and swollen, and she had a marching band stomping around in her head.

The bass drum was beating to the rhythm of her heart, and Olivia wanted to shove her foot through its center to make it stop.

Her back felt as though she were lying on a bed of broken glass, several places on her skin stinging and pulling.

As she began to regain consciousness, she realized she was in a hospital bed. She just couldn't remember why. Unfortunately, the blessed ignorance didn't last long.

It came back to her in waves. Initially, it was like the tiny ones that hit your toes as you first make contact with the water. Then, they began to grow in size and ferocity, each one stronger than the next.

She remembered getting ready for work. The attack at her house. Waking up in the back of an SUV. Fighting off Cetro's goon and hanging from that hook, helpless while at the mercy of a madman.

Olivia remembered thinking she was going to die and damning Cetro to hell for what he'd threatened to do. How, even though they'd had their first big fight, Olivia knew with certainty that her death was going to destroy...

"Jake."

The beeping from the heart monitor sped up with every beat of her heart. She felt trapped. She needed to wake up and get out of this bed.

She needed to go find Jake. Olivia had to let him know that she understood, now. That she forgave him and still loved him. Still wanted forever with him, if he'd have her.

Something glorious happened next. Over the beeping of machines, she heard Jake's voice. His excited, worried, *amazing* voice.

"Liv? Baby, did you say something?"

He's here! Oh, thank God!

She had so much to say to him. So much to apologize for. Olivia felt his fingers tightened around hers.

"Open your eyes, sweetheart. Talk to me."

She wanted to. More than anything she wanted to see him again, but her eyelids felt weighted.

Working to peel them open, her body fought against the strong painkillers the doctors must have given her. When Olivia heard a moan, it took her a second to realize it had come from her.

"You can do it, baby. That's right. Come back to me."

Quick flashes of light felt blinding as her eyes finally began to open. They felt scratchy and dry. At first, everything around her was blurry, including the shadowed figure hovering over her. She blinked a few times to clear her vision until finally, she saw him.

Jake was leaning over her, his one hand holding her uninjured one. With his other, he caressed the top of her head with such gentleness it brought tears to her eyes.

"H-hi."

She was surprised by how sore her throat was, how ragged her voice sounded.

Jake choked out a sound that was something like a half laugh, half sob. He smiled, but he looked so tired and weary. There were shadows under his eyes, and from the growth covering his strong, handsome face, Olivia knew he hadn't shaved in a while.

She was so busy noticing how exhausted he looked, it took her a second to realize there were tears sliding down both of his cheeks.

Her heart hurt. For him. For herself. For all of the pain they'd both been forced to endure.

She started to raise her casted hand, wanting to somehow ease his pain, but it was heavy, and she was too weak to try to remove the sling.

Jake brought the hand he was holding to his cheek, uncaring that his emotions were literally spilling over her.

"Hi, sweetheart."

He drew in a stuttered breath then let it out slowly, looking down at her through those red-rimmed eyes. All she could do was stare back.

They stayed like that for a precious moment, and Olivia relished every second of it.

She was alive. Jake was here, and she was okay. Well, maybe *okay* was a bit of a stretch.

She hurt like hell and knew that when she actually allowed herself to really think about all that had happened, she'd probably break down into a total mess.

For now, though, Olivia was determined to remain focused on how lucky she was to be alive and to have the man she loved by her side.

A trickle of doubt starting creeping its way in. Did she still have him? He'd saved her life, but that didn't mean he still wanted to be with her.

Jake would never allow *anyone* to suffer unjustly if he was able to prevent it. It's who he was. And she'd walked out on him. Just left without giving him the chance to explain.

An image of Jake's tortured face hit her so hard she had to close her eyes, again. In her mind, she saw Jake looking at her and crying like he was now. Except there was no joy in his eyes. No relief. Only misery.

"What's the matter, sweetheart?" Jake's question snapped her back to the present, his brow creased with concern. "Are you hurting? I'll go get the nurse and tell her you need more pain medicine."

"N-need...t-talk." She was trying to tell him they needed to talk, but she couldn't get much out past her scratchy voice.

Jake reached over to the plastic pitcher sitting on the tray next to him. He filled the insulated cup next to it and secured the lid. Sliding the bendable straw between her lips, he held the cup steady for her.

The cool water felt amazing on her dessert-dry throat.

When she was finished, he returned the cup to the tray before getting up and turning to leave the room. Olivia saw him wiping away his tears as he walked. She had to stop him.

Yes, she hurt, but she needed to tell him before the nurse came back in. Whatever they were giving her was sure to put her back to sleep, and Olivia couldn't bear the thought of Jake spending one more second thinking she didn't still want to be with him.

"I couldn't...let him...hurt you," she rasped.

He froze when he heard her broken sentence. Spinning back around, Jake looked at her questioningly.

"What? What do you mean, sweetheart? Couldn't let who hurt me?"

Olivia swallowed, her throat still feeling dry. She had to get through this. "C-Cetro."

Jake took a tentative step back toward her, his expression a mixture of confusion and...fear? "What do you mean you couldn't let him hurt me?"

"I tried to f-fight him off...when he came to my house. But he..." She swallowed again. "He was too strong." A tear slipped from the corner of her eye down to her pillow.

"I know you fought, baby. I saw your house." A muscle in that strong jaw of his bulged. "There was never any doubt that you gave him hell. But what did you mean about him hurting *me*? Besides the obvious."

Jake glanced at her broken arm before zeroing in on her bruised face. His eyes darkened with sorrow. "I didn't think I'd survive it...knowing he had you again."

Olivia shook her head, immediately regretting it. She had to get through this. He needed to understand.

"I'm talking about...after. When I tried to run. He told me to get up...and walk to the barn. I told him to go to hell. I didn't know exactly what he had p-planned, but I knew it couldn't be good. So...I refused. I told him...just to kill me, right then. He said"—she paused, licking her dry, cracked lips—"he said if I didn't go in there willingly that he'd find you."

Jake's eyes widening with horror and disbelief. "No."

Olivia knew Jake was going to be royally pissed at what she was about to tell him, but it didn't matter.

She had to make him understand that *she* truly understood why he did what he did. This was the only way she knew how to do that.

"H-he said if I fought him anymore...he'd go after you and your team...when he was done with m-me."

"No." Jake's eyes filled as he emphatically shook his head.

"He swore if I stopped...trying to run, it would end...with me. He promised...he'd leave you...and the others, alone."

"*No!*"

Jake took a step forward. He was mad, but his eyes held something besides just anger. Tears were streaming down his face, again, but he didn't seem to notice.

"Don't say it. Don't you dare say you went into that place and let him *torture* you to try to save me! Tell me you didn't do that, Liv. *Swear* to me that's not what happened."

"H-had to."

His face nearly crumpled with obvious pain and guilt. "Jesus, Liv, he was *lying*! A man like Cetro can't be trusted any farther than you could throw him!"

Jake ran a frustrated hand through his hair and swore. "It wouldn't have mattered what you let him do to you, that bastard still would have come after me. But you still...after what I did to you? *Why*, baby? Why would you do that?"

Through her own tears, she quickly finished what she was desperately trying to say.

"I had to, Jake," she said, her voice breaking. "Because if there was even the slightest chance he was telling the truth, I had to protect you. Don't you see? I get it now. I understand why you lied about Mikey. You didn't have a choice." Then, she whispered, "And neither did I."

She held out the hand with the IV attached and waited, praying he'd understand. "I did it because...I love you."

****

No, no, no!

Jake looked at Olivia's outstretched hand as if it were a snake preparing to strike him.

Not because he was afraid to touch her. Hell, all he'd ever wanted was to be able to touch her freely. For her to be his and for him to have the right to hold her in his arms whenever he wanted. But her admission had just knocked him flat on his ass.

Jake hung his head, his eyes squeezing tighter, causing more tears to fall. He worked to control his breathing for fear he'd hyperventilate and pass out on that damn hospital floor.

Christ, Liv. Baby, what did you do?

With every step closer to that barn, Olivia had to have known the worst was yet to come, and she'd done it anyway.

To protect him. To protect his team. He didn't know how to process that.

He'd lied to her for an entire decade. While he was supposed to be her best friend, and even later when they'd become lovers, he'd continued to betray her undying trust.

Then, she'd left him. Had turned her back on him and walked out of his life—was that just four days ago?

Jake had deserved every bit of her wrath. What he didn't deserve was her sacrificing her fucking *life* for him! *Not for me, baby. Never for me.*

Olivia started to lower her hand and Jake realized he still hadn't taken it. The movement brought him back just in time to see loss and heartbreak behind her eyes.

"It's okay, Jake. I understand. After the way I treated you, the things I said. I don't blame you for not...wanting me...anymore."

Not want her? Jake was dumbfounded. What the hell was she talking about? He opened his mouth to ask her, but she continued on with her absurd line of thinking.

"Especially now"—she looked at her lap—"I...can't see m-my back, but I can f-feel what he did to me. I know I'll have s-scars, and I don't blame you for not w-want—"

Jake rushed forward and snatched up her hand. "Look at me." He wasn't gentle in his command.

After a moment's hesitation, she lifted her head. The heartbreak and pain reflected in her eyes was almost enough to end him. He had to set things straight. Right. Fucking. Now.

"I love you. I've always loved you, and I will *always*. Love you. For the last, I don't even know how many years, your face is first thing I picture when I wake up in the morning. You're the last thought I have before falling asleep at night. I've wanted nothing more than to have the right to hold you and kiss you whenever I damn well please. I only held off because of the fucked up situation with Mike, but now, you know about that and"—he looked at her tentatively—"you say you understand."

"I do understand," she whispered.

The tightness in his chest eased for the first time in over ten years.

"Good. Because I refuse to hold back anymore. I love you, and no amount of scars will *ever* change that." He narrowed his eyes at her. "Quite frankly, the fact that you could even think they would pisses me the hell off. Any scars you have will only be proof of how strong you are. How brave you were to have fought against that monster."

Jake ran one of his hands down his face before continuing. "Jesus, woman. I swear to God if you *ever* do anything like that again, I'll tie you down and never let you leave the house. That shit isn't going to fly, understand? You don't sacrifice yourself for me. That's *my* job, do you hear me? It's *my* place as your husband to protect you. It'll be—"

Olivia's eyes grew wide. "Husband? Jake, what are you—"

Only then, did he realize what he'd said. Funny, though. He didn't regret it for a second.

Okay, maybe the *way* he'd said it and the fact that they

were in a hospital room and she was tied up to a million different machines wasn't the ideal proposal, but damn if he'd wait another second to lay claim on her. He wanted the entire world to know she was his.

His grip on her hand softened, and his thumb began caressing the inside of her delicate wrist. Careful of her bruises, he moved his other hand up to the side of her face.

"I know I'm screwing this whole thing up by doing it here. Like this. You deserve flowers and candlelight and...shit! I don't even have a ring, yet." He looked at her apologetically. "I swear, I'll get you one as soon as I can. Until then, just know that I love you, Olivia. I want to marry you and have babies with you."

He took a breath and kept going. "I know it won't always be easy. In case you missed it, I'm an overprotective asshole. And in the interest of full disclosure, you should know that's not likely to change. In fact, after this, I'll probably get a lot worse. I'm going to hover and worry. Your safety and the safety of our children will be above anything else." He took another breath and let out everything else he'd ever wanted to say and more.

"I wish I could promise that nothing bad will ever happen to you again, but you and I both know that's not realistic. We'll need to have a good, long talk about my job and what it all means, but...sweetheart, you're my *life*. Without you, nothing else matters. I know you're going to have a lot to deal with from all of this, but I will be by your side every single step of the way. This isn't like last time, sweetheart. I won't be taking an active role in any jobs for a while, so you don't have to worry. I'm here for you. Only for you."

"I'll listen if you want to talk. I'll go to counseling with you, and I'll hold you through any nightmares that may come.

I'll make love to you over and over again, and eventually, with time, we will replace every one of your bad memories with good ones. Together."

Jake was rambling, but he meant every single word. He kissed the back of her hand and then, "So, what do you say, Liv? Will you marry me?"

He looked into Olivia's eyes and waited with baited breath, praying she would say—

****

"Yes," Olivia whispered.

Her heart soared, her head dizzy from the sudden turn of events. She brought her good hand up to cover his. "Yes, I'll marry you, Jake. You're all I've ever wanted. I love you so much. And I'm so sorry. I shouldn't have left the way I did. I should have listened to you and Mike when you tried to explain. I…"

"Shh." Jake moved a finger to her lips. "Baby, stop. You have *nothing* to apologize for. I was an ass, and you reacted accordingly."

"But—" she tried to interrupt, but he just shook his head.

"No buts." He moved his finger and began caressing her cheek with the back of his knuckles. "The rest is in the past. All you need to focus on now, is our future."

Olivia knew they'd never forget what had happened. As Jake carefully brought his lips to hers, she also knew that— despite the horrors she'd suffered the past few months—she was the luckiest woman in the world.

Epilogue

"It's time."

Olivia turned away from the floor-length Venetian mirror to find Trevor standing in the doorway.

He looked ravishing in his black tuxedo. He truly was movie-star handsome, and Olivia knew that any woman out there would be very lucky to have him.

The moment was bittersweet. She'd always pictured her dad as the one who would give her away on her wedding day. Then, after learning that Mike was still alive, she'd desperately wanted him to do it but had no way of contacting him.

Unfortunately, he was still finishing up his last undercover job. He'd promised they would see each other again soon. That had to be good enough.

For now, her man was waiting for her outside. She was certain of it. She'd heard stories of other brides who were so scared of being left at the altar that they couldn't relax until they actually saw their groom.

Not Olivia. She had no doubt that Jake was out there, waiting to become her husband.

The past six months had passed in a blur. Between moving into Jake's ranch, her rehab and counseling appointments, and planning a wedding…the days had flown by. Some nights were still rough, but the nightmares came less frequently now, and Jake had been by her side through it all.

Both to her delight and dismay, Jake had taken a leave of absence from R.I.S.C. He still took care of the day-to-day decisions, but wouldn't play an active role in any dangerous jobs that had come their way for a while.

At first, she'd cringed at the idea that he would take time away from the job she knew he loved simply because of her. It didn't take long, however, before she realized just how much she enjoyed having Jake McQueen at her side every day and in her bed every night.

The first two months consisted of a lot of personal, in-your-face care since she needed help cleaning and dressing the wounds on her arm and back. Once most of her injuries had begun to heal, Olivia had wanted Jake to touch her in a way that wasn't clinical. He'd adamantly refused for fear he'd hurt her.

After weeks of frustration and waiting, and after preparing a few tricks of seduction up her sleeveless teddy, Jake had finally relented, letting go of that famous control of his.

At first, she was self-conscious about her back, but Jake quickly put her at ease when he lovingly kissed every single one, reminding her repeatedly how strong and brave she was.

Olivia hadn't thought that part of their relationship could get any better than it had already been. Boy had she been wrong. Tonight would be no different.

After their simple ceremony behind Jake's ranch, they would go to whatever hotel Jake had chosen. He'd let her plan the wedding with the agreement that he got complete freedom to plan their honeymoon. Olivia trusted him completely, so of course she'd agreed.

Their honeymoon was to be celebrated at an undisclosed

location. Jake had wanted to surprise her, and no amount of begging and pleading had worked. Not even in bed.

So, tonight—wherever they were staying—she and Jake would make love for the first time as husband and wife. It would no doubt, be a night she'd never forget.

Olivia smiled and started toward the doorway, wrapping her fingers around Trevor's extended elbow. She was so thankful he'd agreed to give her away.

She and Trevor had become even closer friends these past few months, and Olivia couldn't imagine her life without him.

"Thank you."

"No, thank *you*. I'm honored you asked me to give you away today."

"No, not for that. Well, that, too, but I meant for making me see things through Jake's eyes."

Trevor's eyes became tormented. "I just wish I wouldn't have left so soon. If I hadn't, then maybe…"

Olivia squeezed his forearm. "You have to stop blaming yourself, Trevor. If you'd stayed, Cetro would have just waited and come after me a different time. Besides, it's over. You guys found me, and Cetro's gone for good. I'm marrying the man of my dreams today, so, no more talk of drug lords or anything else like that. Today is all about being happy."

"And are you happy?"

Her face lit up. "The happiest. Although, I do wish my husband-to-be would have let up on the whole security thing today."

Understanding filled Trevor's face. "He just wants to keep you safe, Liv."

"I know, and I love him for it."

"So, what's the problem?"

"Well, given his propensity to keep today all-things

R.I.S.C., Mac and Ryker's secretary, are the only other females here. I mean, no offense to either of them, but it seems a shame to waste a handsome man such as yourself on a woman who'd probably kick your ass if you tried anything with her, and a sweet grandma."

Trevor threw his head back and laughed. "I didn't know you were so concerned with my love life."

"It's your *lack* of a love life that concerns me."

He shook his head and grinned. "Well, don't let it."

"Look, I know I'm the one who just imposed the whole, no-negativity, rule, but you can't let what happened to Lisa keep you from going after what you want. You're an amazing man, Trevor. You deserve to be just as happy as Jake and I are."

"I know."

"I'm serious. You...wait. You know?"

He chuckled. "Seeing you and Jake fighting for each other the way you have. Going through everything you went through, and still coming out on top..." he trailed off.

"Yes?" she prompted.

He shrugged, looking adorably embarrassed. "I guess it's made me think, maybe I can have that, too. You know?"

Olivia grinned. "I do."

"Hey, you're supposed to be saying those words to Jake, not this guy."

Olivia gasped and spun around, her long, lace dress making a swishing sound as she moved. "Mikey!"

Even in her three-inch heels, Olivia ran toward her brother and jumped into his arms. He held her tightly, slipping his hands beneath her fingertip-length veil so he didn't pull it from her hair.

Mikey then spun her around a couple of times before

carefully placing her feet back on the ground.

"I can't believe you're here! What about your assignment?"

Her brother shrugged. "It's over. I completed my last contract with Uncle Sam. I'm officially a civilian, now."

She *really* looked at her brother, surprised she hadn't immediately noticed all the changes.

His brown hair was shorter, more like when he was in high school. The beard was gone, making him look much younger than when she'd last seen him. And he was wearing a tux that matched Trevor's exactly.

Noticing her assessing gaze, Mikey teased, "Word is some jackass out there is waiting to marry my only sister. I couldn't let that happen without me, so what do ya say?" He lifted his elbow much like Trevor had. "You ready?"

She was still trying to process the other thing he'd said. Not sure she'd heard him right, Olivia asked, "You're...*done*? As in, no longer undercover?"

He smiled. "Yep. I'm free to go and do whatever I want."

"How? I mean, not that I'm not thrilled, but you 'died'. How are you going to explain that if you see someone you—"

"The official story is, I suffered a serious head wound in the supposed training accident I had ten years ago, and then went into a coma. My ID got inadvertently switched with another soldier who died...although, not really. They made that guy up to fit the story."

She raised a brow. "Really? A ten-year coma? *That's* the best they could come up with?"

He chuckled. "I know, right? It's like something out of a damn soap opera script. But, hey...what can I say? It's the government."

"That'll work? You won't be in any danger by exposing yourself like that?"

266

"Well, I don't plan on exposing myself to anyone. There are laws against that, you know." He winked, and Olivia smacked his arm.

"Owe! What was that for?"

She rolled her eyes. "For being a perverted, twelve-year-old boy, that's what."

Mikey laughed loudly, as did she. It really didn't matter what the story was. Olivia was just thankful she had her brother back. For good, from the way it sounded.

Smiling so wide it almost hurt, she started to take his arm again but hesitated at the last second. She turned to look over her shoulder, but Trevor was already starting to talk.

"It's okay, Liv. This was the plan all along."

Her brows rose at that. "Really?"

Trevor smiled. "Really. It was all Jake's idea. He wanted to surprise you." He looked over her to Mikey. "Although, I was beginning to think you were going to be a no-show."

Mikey chuckled. "I was, too. The paperwork on my last case took a lot longer to wrap up than I expected. Barely made my flight."

To Olivia, Mikey said, "I've already missed too damn much. Seeing my baby sister marry my best friend? I wouldn't have missed that for the world."

Despite her heroic efforts, a tear slipped from Olivia's eye. Mikey swiped it away gently and asked again. "You ready?"

She smiled and whispered back, "Ready."

The ceremony was perfectly simple. Only Jake's team, Jason Ryker, his secretary, Brenda, and the preacher Ryker provided were in attendance. Mac served as her Maid of Honor and Trevor was Jake's Best Man.

Olivia cried as she recited her vows. Jake kept it together. Barely.

When it was his turn to speak, there was no mistaking the love he felt. Not only from the beautifully written words he had composed but also in the way those blue eyes shone with unshed tears. Tears of love. For her.

Feeling giddy, Olivia started a little when she felt something gently touch her cheek.

"I don't know what put that smile on your face, but I sure hope it has something to do with me."

Olivia lifted her head from Jake's chest as they continued to dance. She found those same blue eyes staring back down at her, the corners crinkled with amusement. She smiled even bigger.

"It has everything to do with you."

His own smile grew, and she suddenly found it hard to breathe. Warrior Jake was fiercely handsome, but smiling, happy Jake was absolutely stunning.

"I was just thinking that I never want to forget how magical this all is."

He leaned down and kissed her as their bodies continued to sway back and forth to the slow love song.

"You won't," he spoke against her lips. "And neither will I."

He pulled back a little and used his fingertip to gently swipe a curl from her forehead. "There's nothing that could make me forget how lucky I am to have you as my wife, Liv. To know that this is the face I will always come home to." He hugged her closely, whispering in her ear. "These are the arms I'll fall asleep in. Wake up in." He pulled back slightly. "I love you so damned much, baby. I promise I will do my best to show you every day for the rest of my life."

For years he'd been her best friend. Then, he became her real-life hero. After that, her lover. And now...now he was her husband. Olivia's heart felt as though it would burst.

"I love you too, Jake. I always will."

He leaned in for another kiss. This time his voice was deeper, his loving tone laced with heat.

"What would you say if I asked you to start the honeymoon early, Mrs. McQueen?"

Olivia lifted onto her tiptoes and took her own kiss, still astonished that she'd have the right to do that any time she wanted for the rest of their lives.

She raised an eyebrow and gave him her own wry smile. "I'd say…race you to the car."

****

Didn't catch the first half of
Jake and Olivia's story?

See how it all began in:

Taking a Risk, Part One
Available at Amazon Books

Keep reading for a sneak peek of

Beautiful Risk

Excerpt from

Beautiful Risk

Book 3 in the R.I.S.C. Series

Available at Amazon Books – Spring 2019

Excerpt from

Beautiful Risk

"Just grow a pair and ask her, already," Derek said loudly.

"Shh! Keep your voice down, dipshit," Trevor warned his friend. "She'll hear you."

Good. At least then she'll know you've got a thing for her."

"I don't have a...*thing* for her." It was the first lie Trevor had ever told his friend and teammate.

"Right. That's why for the past few weeks, we've been coming here, to this outta-the-fuckin'-way diner to eat, instead of going somewhere in the same time zone as home."

Trevor rolled his eyes. Derek could be so dramatic. "I like the food here."

D laughed so loudly, several of the diner's patrons turned their direction. "What the fuck ever, man. You've had a hard-on for that tiny, little blond thing ever since we stumbled across this place."

Trevor's eyes inadvertently slid to where the petite, blond waitress stood. She was taking an elderly couple's order. When she smiled at something the older man said, Trevor suddenly found it hard to breathe.

"I don't get it, man," Derek's southern drawl grew thick.

"You're single. Haven't had a girl—serious, or otherwise—the entire time I've known you. What's the deal?"

When Trevor remained quiet, Derek's eyes widened. "Ah, shit. I'm sorry, Trev. I-I didn't know. It's cool, though. Really."

Thoroughly confused, Trevor asked, "Didn't know what?"

"Seriously, man. I don't judge anyone for shit like that. Your lifestyle's your own business. Even if you are battin' for the same team, that don't change the way I feel about—"

"Batting for...what in the hell are you talking about, Jones?" Trevor took a sip of tea the other waitress had brought him when they'd first arrived.

"I'm just sayin', being gay ain't nothin' to be ashamed of."

Iced tea shot out of Trevor's mouth, covering the front of Derek's t-shirt. "Jesus Christ," Trevor grumbled as he reached for the paper napkins.

"Whoa!" Derek put his hands palm up, scooting as far back in his seat as he could. "What the hell, dude?"

"You know, for a genius, you really are a dumbass."

Looking genuinely lost, D asked, "What did I say?"

Rolling his eyes again, Trevor impatiently explained, "Just because I don't go to bed with every woman who looks in my direction, that doesn't mean I'm gay."

Derek began wiping the mess from his shirt. "Well, good. I mean, if you were, that would be cool, too. I just meant—"

"Hey, guys! I haven't seen you here in while." Alexis, the petite waitress they'd been discussing came to their table. "How have you been?"

Trevor glared a silent warning to Derek before turning and giving her a smile. Praying she hadn't overheard their conversation, he said, "We're, uh...we're good. You?"

"Oh, you know," she grinned and shrugged a shoulder.

"I'm just livin' the dream."

Her sarcasm—and the adorable dimple in her left cheek—made Trevor smile even more. *God, she's pretty.*

"So," Alexis addressed Derek first. "What'll you have?"

D's expression tightened, as though he was contemplating something serious. "I think I'm in the mood to branch out. We should all do that now and then. You know, try tastin' somethin' we've wanted for a while, but have been too afraid to try." His eyes slid to Trevor's then back to hers. "Ain't that right, Lex?"

Trevor had never wanted to punch Derek, until now. And if the guy kept this shit up, that was exactly what was going to happen.

Giving his friend a cute as hell giggle, she said, "Sure. I guess so."

"See, Trev? Even this sweet, young thing agrees with me."

"Well, then, what are you going to try, Derek?" Alexis asked, still smiling.

"I think I'll go for the fish taco. Haven't tried yours yet, and I'm curious to see what it's like." Derek looked across the table at him, a giant, shit-eating grin spreading across his face.

I'm going to kill him. Trevor worked hard to school his expression, even though he wanted to reach across the table, and beat the hell out of the other man. Thankfully, Alexis seemed to have missed Derek's immature innuendo.

"One order of fish tacos. Got it. What about you, Trevor?" That sweet voice had Trevor's head turning back toward her. Round, crystal blue eyes locked onto his. "Have you made a decision about what you want, yet?"

Derek started coughing exaggeratedly, and Trevor barely squelched the urge to kick the asshole's shins beneath the booth.

"Oh, my gosh. Are you okay?" Alexis asked, genuinely concerned. She looked at his near-empty glass. "Hold on, I'll go get you some more water."

Before either man could stop her, the sweet woman was heading back to the other side of the counter and reaching for a pitcher.

Leaning on his elbows, Trevor spoke low and through his teeth. "What the hell's the matter with you? What are you twelve?"

"What?" Derek shrugged, his coughing fit suddenly over. "I had a frog in my throat,"

"Yeah? Well, you're gonna have my fist down your throat if you don't knock your shit off."

With humor in his eyes, Derek coughed loudly a couple more times, right as Alexis came back with a fresh glass of water.

"Here. Drink this."

"Thanks, darlin'," Derek took the glass from her hand.

While D sipped the water, Alexis turned back to him.

"Sorry. What did you decide? Did you see anything new that caught your eye?"

No, not new. Trevor wanted the same thing, every time he came in here. Too bad he hadn't worked up the nerve to ask for it, yet.

"Trevor?"

Shit. He hadn't answered her. "I-I'll just have my usual."

For some reason, this made the corners of Alexis's lips turn up, her dimple becoming more prominent with the movement. "One patty melt and fries, coming up." Staring a little deeper into his eyes, she added softly, "Let me know if you think of anything else you need."

Jesus. The temperature in the small diner seemed to

instantly rise. "I will. Thanks, Lexi."

Smiling a little wider, she turned and walked away, her wavy ponytail swinging as she went. Trevor's eyes couldn't help but follow.

"Just here for the food, huh?"

He blinked and looked across the table at Derek. He had that, I-know-you're-full-of-shit, look on his face.

Resigned, Trevor sighed. "Fine. I think she's cute. Whatever."

"She *is* cute. And she likes you."

Shaking his head, Trevor started to argue, "She doesn't—"

"Dude. She was practically eye-fuckin' you while you were giving her your order. And then there was the whole," Derek switched to his best phone-sex operator impression, making his voice low and husky, "Let me know if you think of anything else you need."

Despite his irritation, Trevor couldn't help but smirk. "She was talking about what I wanted to eat, you idiot."

"Oh, I know what you want to eat. Not that I can blame you. Lex is a hot little number. She's got that whole, blond-hair, blue-eyed, America's Sweetheart thing goin' for her. In fact, if you really don't plan on makin' a move there, I think I might just have to—"

Trevor did kick Derek then. Hard.

"Ow!" Derek leaned down, rubbing his shin beneath the table. "What the fuck?"

Leaning forward, and making sure she wasn't anywhere in earshot, Trevor growled, "Don't."

"What's your problem?"

"My problem is, Lexi isn't like all those other women you screw around with. She's not a one-and-done kind of girl, and I don't want to see her get hurt by some jackass like you

277

who's just looking for his next piece of ass. *That's* my problem."

"You got all that, just from her serving you a few meals?"

Trevor chose not to respond.

The corners of Derek's mouth turned up slowly. "I'll be damned."

Trevor knew better than to ask, but he did it anyway. "What?"

"You like her. I mean, you *really* like her."

When Trevor looked back over at the blond angel again, his heart thumped a bit harder than before. Derek might be a dumbass, but he was right. Trevor liked Alexis. A lot.

Now, he just had to figure out what the hell he was going to do about it.

About the Author

Author Anna Blakely brings you stories of love, action, and edge-of-your-seat suspense. As an avid reader of romantic suspense herself, Anna's dream is to create stories her readers will enjoy, and characters they'll fall in love with. She believes in true love and happily ever-afters, and that's what she will bring to you.

Anna lives in rural Missouri with her husband, children, and several rescued animals. When she's not writing, Anna enjoys reading, watching action and horror movies (the scarier the better), and spending time with her family.

Want to connect with Anna Blakely?

Website: AnnaBlakely.com

Email: anna@annablakely.com

Facebook Author Page: facebook.com/annablakely.author.7

Twitter: @ablakelyauthor

67518555R00157

Made in the USA
Columbia, SC
28 July 2019